A Hood Nigga's Blues

A Hood Nigga's Blues

A Novel by *Tranay Adams*

First Edition August 2017

Printed in the United States of America

Email: trnayadams@gmail.com

Facebook: Tranay Adams

IG: Tranay Adams

Cover design and layout by: Sunny Giovanni

Edited by: The Ghost

CHAPTER ONE

2005

It was a beautiful day in the hood. The sun was shining brightly, the birds were chirping, and squirrels were running up trees. Two big speakers, which were sitting just outside the picnic tables, pumped Montel Jordan's *This Is How We Do It*. There was a domino game going on, kids were running back and forth, and people were walking around with beverages of their choice. The alcohol at the function was plentiful, and the air was thick with weed and nicotine smoke. Folks were laughing and chopping it up, having themselves a good old time. It was safe to say that St. Andrews Park was alive with activity.

Marquan manned the grill. He was wearing a backwards Hoyas fitted cap and an apron, which read *Tip The Cook*. Occasionally, homie would take a casual swig of a Corona and hold it down at his side. He'd turn the cooking meat over on the grill. He had ribs, hot dogs, chicken, steaks and hamburgers simmering. The meat looked juicy and delicious. Every now and then one of his homeboys would try to steal a piece of meat, but he'd smack their hand away. Some of the women there would try to sweet talk him into giving them a burger or a hotdog, but he wasn't falling for their weak ass game either.

Seeing someone at the corner of his eye as he barbequed meat, Marquan looked up to see his comrade and best friend, Apocalypse, treading across the park. Apocalypse was a dark skinned cat that stood a solid six feet. He weighed all of two-hundred and thirty pounds. He had a face that always appeared to be fixed with a frown and a body covered in muscles. He was a ruthless killa that was about his money, and anyone standing in front of that would find themselves staring down the barrel of his gun.

Marquan cracked a smirk seeing his homeboy approaching, and he returned the gesture. Once Apocalypse reached Marquan, he sat his Corona down on the small end table of the barbeque pit and turned around to him.

"What's cracking, cuz?" Marquan gave Apocalypse a gangsta hug.

Marquan was a brown skinned nigga that stood a full six feet, two inches. He had an athletic body of lean muscle and it was covered in tattoos. He rocked a close fade that swirled with waves and a goatee. Homie was menacing in appearance and his aura screamed gangsta. When it came to looks he mirrored the Compton rapper, Game. The only difference was while the Hub City rhyme spitter was a Blood, that nigga Marquan was a Crip.

"Ain't shit, I see they got chu onna grill and shit." he said, watching his homeboy turn over the meat on the grill.

"Yeah, you know my get down. Ain't too many that can fuck with me on the grill."

"Yeah, I know that if I don't know nothin' else about my nigga." He continued to watch his man work the grill.

Marquan finished flipping the meat and shut the grill. He sat the fork he was using to flip the meat down on the small end table of the barbeque pit. He then picked his Corona up. Turning back around, he was about to take another swig of his beer until he noticed the glassy look in Apocalypse's eyes and the dry tears on his cheeks.

"Yo', you good?" Marquan's face wrinkled with concern for his right-hand man.

"Yeah, I'm straight, why'd you ask me that?" Apocalypse's forehead indented as he wondered what he was talking about.

"Cause you look like you been crying."

"Hell, naw, nigga, I just haven't been sleep. I was stretchin' and yawnin' and shit so tears came out. A nigga been up all night gettin' to that paypa. And I was freakin' off with Juanita's fine ass last night, too." He smiled and pretended to be fucking someone doggy style and smacking their ass.

"Oh, I was about to say, boy, nigga make my right-hand shed tears and I'ma shed blood. You know a nigga don't play that shit about mine. Come sit with me over here, come on," he motioned for Apocalypse to follow him over to a vacant table and bench. They walked side by side talking to one another. "You wanna beer or something?"

"Nah, I'm straight, cuz." he sat down on the bench and Marquan was right behind him. "When that meat finishes cookin', you can hook me up with a plate though."

"Don't wet it, I got chu."

"G lookin', cuz."

"Don't mention it. You know how we do."

"Sho' you right."

"Yo', man, I gotta go holla at my plug tonight. Niggaz knocked off all of that shit, that last re-up is gone."

"For real?" his forehead crinkled.

"Yeah."

"That's the fastest we ever finished off the work."

"I know, right? I ain't complainin' though. Shiiit, I'd be a mothafuckin' fool to be sittin' up here complainin' about gettin' money," He spat on the ground and looked around the park, spotting some children running, laughing and playing like they didn't have a care in the world.

"You need me to strap up and roll out witchu when you go see this fool, man?"

"Naw, I got it handled, shitta be quick."

"You sho'? This will be like the first time I don't roll witchu, cuz. You know when you switch shit up that's when things go left. The last thing we need now is for something to go wrong, especially with us being on top now and getting to these bags."

"I'm sho', I can't always have you comin' with me to baby sit. Besides, I been doin' business with Popeye for a minute now. Cuz all about his paypa, he ain't on no funny shit."

"You sho' you wanna go solo?"

"Positive. Trust me, loc, I got this shit. I'll hit chu just as soon as I'm done with homeboy."

"I don't know, man," he placed his elbows on his knees and leaned forth, letting his Corona dangle between his legs. "I feel realllll funny about this one. I'd feel better if you let me accompany you."

"Naw, I'll be fine. I'm bringin' my thang-thang with me," he patted the bulge on his hip which was where his gun resided on his waistline.

"Alright, since you insist, I'ma let it be." He took a swig of his Corona.

"Good. 'Cause I was gettin' tired of yo' worrisome black ass." he chuckled and patted his homeboy on his back.

"Come on now, you know you my man, eighty-three grand. Nigga fuck witchu, it's gone be a lotta slow singing and flower bringing. That's on everything I love, you my brotha, cuz." He lifted up his sleeve and showed off the ink on his forearm. It read *My Brother From Another, Apocalypse; From The Womb 'Til The Tomb.* The inscription was over a very lifelike looking tombstone.

"All day," Apocalypse replied as he lifted the sleeve of his shirt and showed off the same ink on his forearm as his right-hand man. The only difference was he had Marquan in place of his own name. The two best friends turned to each other and dapped one another up before hugging. "That's true love for a homeboy, cuz."

"On some real shit, you ever get tired of the game, Poc?" Marquan asked his main man as he looked him in the eyes. A serious look was written across his face.

"Hell, naw, man," he shook his head. "This all a nigga know, Quan, the day I'ma stop hustlin' is the day I'ma be doin' life or layin' face up in a coffin'. I ain't even finna front fa you, bruh, I'ma street nigga through and through."

Marquan looked away from his homeboy and across the park at nothing particular, taking a swig of his Corona. "I ain't mad at chu, homie. It's a whole 'notha thing witcha boy, though. I'm telling you, soon as I reach my million dolla goal, I'm taking my family and I'm getting the fuck outta the hood. I know if my black ass stays here, I'ma either end up murdered, or locked up for the rest of my life. I sho' don't want Antonio growing up here. The last thing I want for my boy is for him to be gangbanging tryna be just like his goddamn daddy. That would kill me, I mean really fucking destroy me. You know what I mean, cuz?"

"Yeah, I know what chu mean. For me, there ain't no place like home, I'ma live and die in L.A. Ain't no shame in my game, loc. Ain't no shame at all. I been hustlin' in these streets since I was knee high to a caterpillar. Shit, you rememba how I was gettin' it."

It was a 72 degree day in South Central Los Angeles. People were coming and going, kids were laughing and playing, and stray dogs were wandering throughout the streets.

A young Apocalypse was posted up underneath a telephone pole serving the occasional fiend that shuffled past him. He'd give a cautious look around for the police before making the exchange and sending the crackhead on about his business. Afterwards, he'd go back to watching the streets until another crackhead would come ambling up for some rocks.

Apocalypse head moved on a swivel watching the traffic. He was none the wiser to the pigeons above his head on the phone line moving about. It wasn't until some pasty white shit splattered on his shoulder that he looked up and discovered the birds there.

"Fuck, cuz!" Apocalypse scowled as he looked to the shit stain on his shoulder and then back up at the birds on the line. He looked around for something to throw at their asses, and when he found a couple of rocks, he quickly picked them up. Heatedly, he launched the rocks up at the pigeons; hitting one and making the others flap away hastily.

"Damn, cuz, they got chu good." A young Marquan, with a blue bandana around his neck, came waltzing out of the liquor store with a lemon Snapple in one hand and a couple of paper towels he'd gotten from the cashier in the other. He rocked a George Town Hoyas cap backwards. "Here you go," he passed the paper towels to Apocalypse. He drank from his Snapple as he watched him clean off the shoulder of his shirt.

"Thanks, man," Apocalypse said after balling up the paper towels and letting them fall from his hand.

"Don't mention it, homie. Well, check it, cuz, I know you out here doing yo' thang, so I'ma let chu do you. We'll get up later, I'm sho' of it."

"Cool." They dapped one another up and Marquan went on about his business.

As soon as Apocalypse turned around from talking to Marquan a police car pulled up in front of him. He started to run, but the mothafucka had the drop on him. Whomever the cop was behind the wheel was too close up on him for him to try to make a mad dash for it. Not only that, the cops around that way were known for shooting niggaz in their backs when they tried to run, armed or not, them mothafuckaz didn't give a fuck.

Seeing the cop hop out of his car and approaching, Apocalypse decided to play it cool. He folded his arms across his chest and pretended to be watching the traffic. You know, acting as if he was waiting for someone to pick him up or something. He thought by doing this he could possibly throw the cop off, and make him think otherwise of his presence, but that shit didn't work at all.

"Do me a favor. Turn around, place your hands on the wall and spread your legs." The cop ordered.

"What?" Apocalypse frowned up and looked him up and down like he wasn't shit, "Man, gone somewhere with that bullshit. I ain't doin' nothin' out here, but waitin' on my cab, I'm straight, officer!"

"I'm not in the habit of repeating myself. I'll advise you to do like I said." The cop's face tinted red and a vein bulged at his temple as he placed his hand on his holstered handgun in a threatening manner.

Apocalypse looked the law enforcer up and down with a disgusted look on his face. "Mannn, fuck you," he spat on the cop's black pattern leather boot and saw his face in it.

"Alright. That's it, you little shit!" Seething mad, the cop grabbed Apocalypse by his arm and twisted it around his back, causing him to howl in pain. The cop walked him to his police car and slammed the side of his face down on the hood of his vehicle. The impact of his face hitting the hood caused him to wince and grit his teeth. A vein bulged at his temple as the cop talked shit to him and bent his other arm around his back, snapping the handcuffs around his wrists violently.

"Don't move, don't chu fucking budge!" he punched Apocalypse in the back of his head repeatedly. Breathing hard, he looked around and saw that the streets were scarcely crowded. The people that were around were watching from a

far and didn't pose any threat to him. Seeing that he didn't have anything to worry about, he kicked Apocalypse legs apart roughly and gripped the chain of the handcuffs tightly, as he patted down the young man's waistline. His forehead creased when he felt something hard. Curiosity came across the cop's face as he pulled out whatever it was on the youth's waist and discovered that it was a gun that he had on him. "Well, look here, let's see what else you're hiding," he smacked the handgun down on the hood of his vehicle. He then patted down both of Apocalypse's pockets, feeling small lumps on his left pocket. Sticking his tongue out of the side of his mouth busily, the cop fished around inside of the youth's pocket until he'd gotten what he'd felt earlier. Pulling his clenched fist out of the young man's pocket, he held it before his eyes and revealed eight off white crack rocks. He smacked the crack rocks down beside the firearm he'd taken off of Apocalypse. "That right there, my friend, is the illegal possession of a controlled substance with intent to distribute.

The firearm and the crack guarantees your black ass a trip to lockup."

"Man, fuck you, cuz, that shit ain't mine, nigga! You planted that shit on me!" Apocalypse struggled to get loose from his captor, but he wasn't going anywhere.

Angry, the cop started punching him in the back of his head and back violently. It appeared as if the cop's face tinted redder and the vein at the center of his forehead bulged the more he punched on Apocalypse. When the cop drew his fist back to punch him again, he had white shit at the corners of his mouth and he was breathing huskily. His nostrils were flaring and his hair looked wild from assaulting his suspect.

"Shut up, shut your goddamn mouth!" He punched Apocalypse in the back of the head and back, then kicked him.

Apocalypse hollered out in pain and tried to break free, but he was under the restraint of the handcuffs and the cop wasn't letting him get away.

"Freeze, cuz!" a youthful voice bellowed from the left side of the cop, which froze his fist in mid swing. Hair wild, eyes stretched wide open and nostrils swelling, he slowly looked to his left. It was there that he found Marquan. He had a blue bandana over the lower half of his face and his eyes threatened murder. So did the gun he had pointed at the cop's face.

"You must have lost your goddamn mind pointing that gun at me, boy." He mad dogged Marquan as he slowly inched his hand toward his holstered weapon.

"You bring yo' hand any closer to that banga on yo' waist and you gone be the one losing you mind out here...pig!" Marquan warned as he stepped off the curb and picked up the gun that the cop had taken off of Apocalypse. Now that he had two bangas, Marquan pointed them both at the cop. "Take out cho handcuff key and set my nigga free."

"You got me fucked up, I ain't doing shit!" the cop said, still inching his hand towards the holstered gun on his waistline. When he said this, Apocalypse rose from off the hood of the police car and walked over to Marquan, standing beside him, hands still cuffed behind his back.

"Is that right?" Marquan glared at him and squared his jaws, as a vein pulsated at his temple.

"That's right...boy!" the cop shot back and stared Marquan down as his hand moved closer to the gun on his hip. He licked his thin, pink lips and never broke his glare on

Marquan. He was challenging the young man, trying to call his bluff.

"I told yo' ass to keep yo' hand away from that banga, don't be hardheaded now." He tilted his head to the side as he warned him.

Apocalypse looked from Marquan with his gun pointed at the cop and the expression on the cop's face. He then looked over his shoulder and saw all of the people that were outside watching them. Although there weren't many of them, one person was enough to finger them in a line up.

"Be easy, loc," Apocalypse warned him. "It's a couple of eyes out here; you'll never beat this case."

"Fuck them eyes..." Marquan stated without even taking his eyes off of the cop. As soon as he saw the cop about to draw his gun, he pulled the trigger of his gun. The gun jerked violently as it fired off a shot. The bullet skinned the cop's cheeks and he dropped his gun. The gun hit the sidewalk as soon as he grabbed the area of his face where the bullet had skinned him. When he did this, Marquan walked over to him and let off another shot by his ear. The sound of the gunshot ranging out caused the cop's eyes to stretch wide open and he smacked his hand over his ear. The shot being let off near his ear set off an eerie siren that stung his eardrum like a hot safety pin. The cop dropped to his knees as he held his ringing ear, squeezing his eyelids shut and gritting his teeth. His face was even redder now, and veins were bulging all over his face.

Swiftly, Marquan turned to Apocalypse and tucked one of the guns at the front of his Dickie's. He then held the handcuff chain away from his homeboy's back and pressed the barrel of his gun against it, pulling the trigger. A third shot rang out and a spark flew, as the chain snapped loose. Apocalypse brought his wrists back around to him and studied the area on the chain that the bullet had severed.

"Come on; let's get the fuck outta here!" Marquan took off running. Once Apocalypse snatched the crack rocks off the hood of the car, he hauled ass behind his homeboy.

"Haa! Haa! Haa!Haa! Haa! Haa!"Marquan ran as fast as he could, hearing police cars heading in their direction. He glanced over his shoulder and saw Apocalypse on his heels. "Come on, cuz, catch up!" he motioned to him with the gun he held in his hand.

"Haa! Haa! Haa! Haa! Haa! Haa!" Apocalypse ran as fast and as hard as he could. He glanced over his shoulder and saw the cop still on his knees, holding his ear.

Marquan and Apocalypse ran into someone's yard with their eyes set on a gate that led into the backyard. Marquan tucked his gun and leaped upon the gate along with his comrade. Together, they climbed over the gate and ran across the yards of three more houses before eventually taking refuge inside of a garage. They sat at the corner of the garage breathing heavily, with their chest rising and falling rapidly. Their faces were hot and sticky with sweat but they were smiling from the adrenaline rush, happy that they weren't captured.

"Here you go, cuz." Marquan passed Apocalypse his gun back. Apocalypse thanked him and dapped him up.

"G lookin' out, but, man, that was some wild cowboy type of shit. I neva expected that to happen."

"Man, these niggaz quick to get at niggaz from the other side out here, but nobody got the balls to bring it to Johnny. See what I'm saying? The way I see it, them mothafuckaz should be able to get served for coming at the homies too. You feel me, cuz?"

"Hell yeah. But look, them mothafuckaz gone be hot 'bout that stunt you pulled, we oughta just lay low here to nightfall then move out."

"Good idea."

Apocalypse placed his back against the wall beside Marquan. They chopped it up about hood politics and the mutual people that they knew. Although they were from the same gang they never kicked it like that. They only said 'What up?' to one another in passing. But after that day things would change. They would become the best of friends, and it would be rare to see one without the other.

It wasn't long before a partnership was formed between Marquan and Apocalypse. They took the steps to build their own empire. Things really took off for them once Apocalypse came across a Mexican plug that fronted him a few extra bricks on consignment. Instead of Marquan helping him move the shit, he became his enforcer in the streets. He went to pick up the bags when it was time to break bread and he was going to see niggaz that weren't trying to pay them. Rarely did the young nigga have to get his hands dirty though. Mothafuckaz in the streets knew about his reputation as a wig splitter and they didn't want any problems. It was clear why his big home, 187, had made him his little homie, Lil' 187. He was about his murder game, and anybody that violated, or didn't bow down to his gangsta was getting a cold case of lead poisoning. Straight up!

"Daddyyyyy!" a child's voice rung from Marquan's and Apocalypse's left. When they looked they found a five year old, Antonio, running in their direction excitedly. Bringing up his rear was a dark caramel, complexioned young woman. She was thick in all of the right places, and had long, wavy hair that she had braided into a ponytail. She was wearing doorknockers, a camouflage tank top and Daisy Dukes that showed off plenty of her meaty thighs. She had a Rolex chain around her neck and a matching watch on her wrist. The diamond engagement ring on her finger reflected a small rainbow from the sunlight. The tattoos on her breast and ankle gave her crazy ghetto sex appeal. The tattoo on her left breast read, *Marquan,* while the one on her ankle was of her son with him, *Antonio.*

"Heyyyy, baby boy," Marquan rose to his feet and scooped up his son. The little dude's long hair was styled into box braids that hung around his face. "I see you and yo' momma finally made it."

"Yep. We were in traffic. You shoulda seen it, daddy. Momma was screaming and cursing this man out for almost hittin' us. When the man got outta his car, momma pulled out her lil' gun and…"

"Ant, you talk too much, yo' daddy don't wanna be hearin' that mess." Adele interjected.

"Yes, I do. Come here," Marquan pulled her close and rested his muscular arm at her back while her hands held on to both of his biceps. "Now, you know better than to be pulling guns out on fools in front of our son. Whatever happened out there couldn't have been that serious for you to draw heat." He scolded her like a father. He wasn't harsh in his delivery though, his tone was more so of *I'm disappointed in your behavior* if anything.

"The fuck it wasn't, mothafucka callin' me all kinds of hoes and bitches in front of my prince. Nunh unh, I ain't 'bout to let that shit ride." Adele caught a bad ass attitude thinking about the driver that had cut her off and damn near made her crash.

"I feel you, boo, but next time handle that shit with a lil' bit mo' finesse than that. For real, Adele, we tryna raise our prince better than that. You feel what I'm saying, ma?"

Adele listened to him talk while she traced his muscular arm with her French tip nail, admiring all of that sexiness his thug ass possessed. If it wasn't for them being at the park, she'd jump his bones that minute, right there in front of everybody. She didn't give a fuck, but she was sure he did.

See, Marquan wouldn't want to get it cracking in front of all of those people. The last thing he wanted to do was to play his son's mother out by making her look like some sort of jump-off in front of an audience. This was because he looked at her as much more than a piece of ass. To him, the woman that had bared his child was his queen, and should be treated as such, regardless of her past.

The moment Adele had told him that she was carrying his seed changed the way he looked at her forever.

"Marquan's eyebrows arched as he felt that Adele wasn't paying him any mind, he gave her a quick shake at her waist as he stared into her eyes.

"Aye, you hear me talking to you?" He waited on her response.

"Yes, baby, I heard you. I promise it won't happen again, okay?" she stared into his eyes as she traced his full lips with her fingernail, wearing a smirk on her lips.

"Okay, baby, gemme kiss." He asked in a soft, masculine voice.

"K." she responded and kissed him slow and sensually. Not long after, they were kissing deep and passionately, as they held the sides of one another's faces.

"Aaaaggaggggh!"

"Aaaaggaggggh!"

Marquan and Adele's head whipped around in the direction that they heard the gagging. They found Apocalypse and Antonio poking their fingers in and out of their mouths, suggesting that their making-out made them want to vomit. Seeing this, the loved birds laughed and smiled.

"Say, bruh, you tryna turn my lil' one into a hater like yo' ass?" Marquan stated jovially as he threw the oven mitts at Apocalypse. Apocalypse moved aside as he smacked the oven mitts down to the ground.

"Hahahahaha, nah, I'm not. I'm just tryna keep my lil' nigga from travelin' down the road of a simp." Apocalypse laughed as he threw his arm around his godson's shoulders and hugged him up against the side of him.

Whatever, fool, let's see how you act once you done cuffed you a real one." he replied as Adele rested the side of her face against his chest and hugged him around his waist lovingly.

"Nevaaaa, I'm too quick on my toes to get caught up with these hoes." Apocalypse said in the same melody as Snoop Dogg as he done a little dance on his feet. His actions caused Marquan and Adele to bust up laughing. "'Sup, nephew? Lemme see if you rememba what I showed you what to do with them hands." He turned to Antonio and threw up his dukes. The little dude threw up his dukes too, and they playfully fought one another while the boy's parents looked on.

"Get 'em, baby, whip his ass!" Adele called out to her son, who seemed to be getting the best of his godfather.

That's right, son, stay on 'em!" Marquan threw punches the way his son was throwing them. It appeared as if he was controlling the boy. You know, like a puppet master?

Antonio threw a punch that laid Apocalypse flat out on the grass. He lay there pretending to be knocked out cold as Marquan stood over him counting down along with Adele

"Eight, nine, ten…It's over. Antonio 'Quick Hands' Ludlow is now the reigning heavy weight champion of the world," Adele and Marquan held up either arms of their son. The boy smiled from ear to ear and showcased his missing front tooth.

CHAPTER TWO

Marquan, Apocalypse, and Adele spent the remainder of the day eating and mingling among family and friends. By the time the sun had set, everyone had left except Marquan, Apocalypse and a few stragglers. The best friends found themselves standing in between their respective cars chopping it up and holding plates of food wrapped in foil.

"Hahahahahahaha!" Apocalypse doubled over laughing while holding the plate of food.

"Hahahahahahaha, nigga, that shit had me rolling on the mothafucking floor. For real for real," Marquan wiped his tears of laughter with his curled finger.

Apocalypse came down from his laughter and looked at his Rolex watch, seeing that he had to run. "Yo', man, I gotta get up outta here to go see this fool Popeye. I'ma get up witchu later on, cuz."

"Fa sho'." He dapped up his main man and hugged him. He then stood by his car watching him walk around his own vehicle to get inside. "I love you , cuz."

"I love you too, my nigga, from the womb 'til the tomb." Apocalypse tapped his fist to his chest and his homeboy returned the gesture. He then hopped in behind the wheel of his whip and pulled out. His car was waxed so shiny that Marquan could see his reflection on it as he backed out of his parking space.

Marquan watched the back of Apocalypse's ride as he drove away. He threw up his hood and Apocalypse responded by throwing it back up outside the driver side window.

Afterwards, Marquan turned back around to his Chevy and sat his plate of food on the roof of it. He then fished his keys out of his pocket and stuck the key inside of the slot of the driver's door. He was about to turn the key to open the door when he saw someone in the reflection of the driver's window. His eyelids stretched wide open and his heart thudded. Swiftly, he pulled his gun and turned around fast. He held his gun sideways as he mad dogged whom he believed was trying to creep up on him. His jaws were throbbing and the vein at his temple was bulging.

"Oh shit!" the formally dressed woman was startled by the appearance of the gun in the man's hand. She threw up her hands and stood frozen in her tracks.

"Yo', cuz, who the fuck is you?" Marquan spat at her.

"It's me, nigga, goddamn!"

"Who the fuck is me?"

"Jah!"

"Jah, as in Jahleysa?" his face soften as he matched a face to the name inside of his mental rolodex.

"Yeah."

"Oh, my fault," He tucked his banga at the front of his sagging 501 jeans. He then approached Jahleysa and gave her a loving hug. When he pulled back, he looked her over since he hadn't seen her in a while. "Long time no see, stranger. I haven't seen you in a while. I got a hold of yo' moms and sent out an invite and shit."

"Yeah, I know. I had some shit I had to do back at the office, which is why I'm here so late. I'm sorry about that. I was really looking forward to catching up witchu and getting me a plate, too."

"Today is yo' lucky day, big head, 'cause I still got one on deck," he turned around and picked his plate up from off the roof of his Chevrolet and passed it to her. She looked to be surprised when she saw it. Right after receiving it, she held the plate up to her nose and shut her eyelids as she inhaled the delicious aroma.

"Mmmmm, this smells bomb, you sure you want me to have it?" she asked as she hoped he'd say yes. She was a social worker and she'd been working long hours lately. She'd been so engrossed in her work that she'd lost track of time and forgetten to eat. So, it was needless to say that little momma was as hungry as a hostage.

Although Jahleysa was from the hood, she hadn't gotten quoted on to the gang like Marquan and Adele had. She also wasn't out in the streets as much as them either. She had strict parents and a curfew. She had to sneak out of the house to go to parties that the rest of the kids in the hood would attend. Her old man and old lady made a vow to raise her. They weren't about to let the streets parent their child.

Jahleysa's mother and father stayed on her ass about her studies because they wanted her to become something more in life than some hood nigga'z baby momma or a stripper. They were determined to make sure that she became something that they both could be proud of, and she had.

"Yeah, I've been eating barbeque all day long up here. That plate is just what was left over after everyone else took plates home. You know how niggaz do, niggaz gotta take a plate home for the night and the day after that, too."

"Shiiiit, you ain't never lied. Thanks, Quan."

"Don't wet it; you know we go back, so I hadda look out."

There was a long, awkward silence between them and then she broke the ice.

"Soooooo, how's little man and the misses?"

"They, uh, they straight, junior is getting big and looking more and more like me every day, I swear to God my baby boy is the spitting image of me."

"Last time I saw 'em he was a baby. How old is he now?"

"Hold up," he opened his car door and ducked down inside of his vehicle, plucking something that was wedged in the display that housed the speedometer. When he came back out he was holding a picture in his hand, which he handed to her. He watched her observe the picture with a small smile etched upon her face.

"He's cute, real cute. Looks just like his daddy," she smiled broader and tried to hand him the picture back. He wouldn't accept it though. He held up his hand and shook his head no.

"Nah, you gone and keep that. That's all you."

"You sure?" she raised an eyebrow trying to make sure.

"Yeah, keep it."

"Thank you," she said, dropping the picture inside of her purse.

"You welcome, slim."

There was another moment of awkward silence between the ex lovers. Jahleysa looked around aimlessly and whistled while Marquan rubbed the back of his neck and looked at something he imagined was on the ground.

"Well, listen, I better get going. I gotta few errands I have to run before I go back inside of the house." She claimed as she pulled her car keys from out of her purse.

"Lemme get cho number so I won't have to harass ya mom's the next time I'm tryna get a hold of you."

"Cool. You gotta cell?"

"Yeah," he pulled out his cellular and it was dead. "Fuck, my shit dead."

"What a coincidence," she stated looking at the screen of her cellular. "My phone is dead, too." She raised her eyebrows in surprise and showed him her cell phone's screen. "You gotta ink pen and a piece of paper?" she inquired as she dropped the cellular back inside of her purse.

"Nah, I probably gotta napkin or something you can write it on, though."

"Bet. Get that. I should have an ink pen or something inside of my briefcase."

"Alright," he dipped inside of his car and opened the glove box. He found the napkins he had in mind and came back out of the car, outstretching them towards her. She'd just closed the door of her Honda when she'd turned around to him. She took the napkins and jotted her name and number down on one end of it. Once she was done, she wrote down his information at the opposite end as it was relayed to her. Finishing, she tore off the end that had her info on it and gave it to him. Afterwards, she folded up the rest of the napkins and stashed it inside of her pocket.

"Alright, lemme gone and get up outta here," she kissed him sweetly on the cheek and gave him a hug that lasted just a tad bit too long for it to be friendly. When she pulled back she found herself staring deep into his soft brown eyes. At that moment, the love they'd shared was rekindled and they found themselves being slowly drawn to one another, like a moth to a flame.

Realizing that he was about to kiss Jahleysa and totally disrespect what he and his Adele shared, Marquan turned his head away and rubbed the back of his neck. Jahleysa looked saddened by his refusal to kiss her and cleared her throat, acting as if something didn't just almost occur between the two of them.

"Heyyy, well, uh, I got cho number. Maybe I'll hit chu up sometime and we can get lunch together or something." Jahleysa said as she slowly stepped back towards her car, twiddling her car keys in her hands.

"Fa sho', I'm looking forward to it."

"Okay, bye," she waved at him timidly.

"Bye." He waved back at her, and then stashed his hands inside of his jeans. He watched as she jumped back behind the wheel of her whip and backed out of the parking space. She waved to him one last time and took off, with him waving to her as she drove off.

Once the back brake lights had disappeared into Los Angeles traffic, Marquan looked down at the number that Jahleysa had written down. He smiled as he looked at her beautiful, girlish handwriting. It had been several years since he'd seen her handwriting on anything. Seeing it now brought back memories. He recalled all of the love letters and poems she used to write him back in the day when they were together.

Marquan didn't know what it was that told him to turn over the piece of napkin, but he went ahead and turned it over. What he saw made his eyes light up and a smile spread across his lips.

I *Still Love You…* was what was on the back of the torn piece of napkin that Jahleysa had jotted her number on. When Marquan seen this, he found himself looking back and forth between the torn napkin and the area that Jahleysa's car disappeared in.

Marquan kissed the napkin and shoved it inside of his pocket. He jumped in behind the wheel of his car and pulled out of his parking space. Afterwards, he threw his ride into *drive* and peeled out of the parking lot.

Although he had every intention of linking back up with Jahleysa and catching up over a hot meal, there wasn't any way in hell that he was going to rekindle the old flame that they'd once shared.

Although he chose Adele over Jahleysa he never stopped loving her…never. He always wished that it was her he laid up with that night and created Antonio with. Truthfully, if he could do it all over again, he would have chosen her and co-parented Antonio with Adele. He knew within his heart that she was the perfect woman for him, but wanting his son to be brought up in the same household as him derailed their love affair.

Marquan and Jahleysa were one another's first loves. They used to kick it real tough. In fact, you rarely saw one without the other. The love they shared was hood knowledge. There wasn't a soul that didn't know about the couple in the ghetto. They were a match made in heaven and their romance was the stuff fairy tales were made of. It seemed too good to be true, and it was…Marquan's infidelity proved that.

Jahleysa lay on the couch with her silk scarf wrapped head propped up against her French manicured hand. The blue illumination from the television screen shined on her face as she flipped through the channels with the remote control.

Knock! Knock! Knock!

The rapping at the door drew her attention. She looked to the door with a wrinkled forehead and then she looked at the clock on the wall. It was 11 o'clock at night and she wasn't expecting anyone, so she wondered who it could be at that hour. Curious, she sat the remote control down on the coffee table and got up from the couch. She was in a tank top and boy shorts that her buttocks peeked out of every step that she took.

"Who is it?" Jahleysa called out as she advanced to the door.

"It's me, baby," Marquan answered.

A smile graced Jahleysa's face hearing that her man was at the door. She had been so caught up in her studies that she barely had time to speak with him over the phone, so she was really happy to see that he'd showed up at her house.

Jahleysa was about to unchain and unlock the door until a thought went across her mind. Bitch, what are you thinking? You can't let cho man see yo' ass looking tore up from the floor up.

Jahleysa touched her head and felt the silk scarf that her hair was wrapped up in. She then held her palm to the lower half of her face and blew her hot breath into it, sniffing it thereafter. Smelling her funky breath, she frowned up and turned her head away, cringing.

Goddamn, a bitch needa Listerine Popsicle out this mothafucka.

"Babe, gimmie a sec', okay?" Jahleysa called out to her man with her hands pressed against the front door

"Alright, boo, hurry up." Marquan told her.

"Okay." She sped walked toward the bathroom pulling the scarf free from her head. As soon as she removed the scarf her long hair fell over her shoulders and back. Her hair was jet black and shiny. It looked like it was spun out of black silk.

Jahleysa stepped before the medicine cabinet's mirror in the bathroom and picked up her big black brush from off the sink. Hurriedly, she brushed her hair. Once she was done she turned her head from left to right, looking herself over. Her rich, dark chocolate complexion and super straight hair made her look very exotic, especially with her slanted eyes. She had dimples in her cheeks and one in her chin. Her unique physical attributes were courtesy of her Haitian heritage.

Having finished brushing her hair, Jahleysa brushed her teeth and sprayed on the expensive designer perfume that her mother had bought her for her birthday. Sitting the bottle of perfume down, she looked over her reflection and blew a kiss at it. Afterwards, she darted into her bedroom and opened her jewelry box, removing the gold and diamond Rolex chain her boo had gotten custom made at The Slauson Swap meet. The flawless gold necklace held to his name, Marquan, and was littered with authentic diamonds. She snapped the necklace around her neck and darted back into the living room, stopping at the front door.

Taking the time to calm herself before opening the door, Jahleysa then went on to unchain and unlock it. She pulled open the door and stepped aside to allow her man inside of her home. He crossed the threshold wearing a worried expression across his face. She was so excited to see him that she hadn't even notice the look on his face. She shut and locked the door before stepping to him. Little momma threw her arms around his neck and kissed him. Noticing that he hadn't attempted to kiss her back, she pulled back and looked at his face, seeing the worried expression there. Instantly, she became concerned. This was because she hadn't seen him looking like this before.

"Baby, what's the matter?" she asked him, caressing his cheek with her delicate hand, staring up into his eyes.

He took her hand from off his face and lifted his head, looking her in her eyes. "I fucked up, babe. I mean, I really, really fucked up big time."

Concerned, Jahleysa looked through the blinds covering the window cautiously. Seeing her do this, Marquan's forehead crinkled wondering what was going through her head. She walked back over to him looking like she had something on her mind.

"You're in trouble, huh? Gimme yo' gun, I'ma wrap it up in aluminum foil and stash it at the back of the freezer. We can make it look like some frozen meat or something." Jahleysa told him. "If The Ones are looking for you, then you're gonna needa alibi. Now, momma's been at work for the past couple of hours now. So, if they come around asking I'll say you been here all night with me. We cooked tacos, watched TV, had sex and slept. All you gotta do is remember our stor..." her words died in her mouth seeing Marquan massage the bridge of his nose and shake his head. "What? What is it? You don't like the plan?"

Marquan looked up at his lady and said, "Jah, I didn't pop nobody. I got some heavy shit I gotta lay on you..." his eyes turned glassy almost instantly. He was afraid that what he was about to reveal would break her in the worse way.

"Quan, tell me something, I'm really worried here. You're driving me nuts." She searched his eyes again, hoping that he'd tell her what was wrong.

Looking away, Marquan took a deep breath and looked back to her. "I got Adele pregnant..."

Smack!

Jahleysa's hand came across his face viciously. Before he could recover, he was hit by another one of her open palms, then another, and another and another.Jahleysa'seyes instantly pooled with tears that spilled down her cheeks. She whimpered as she held her hands to her face, shoulders shuddering. She couldn't believe that the love of her life would hurt her like this. She felt like withering up and dying right there in the living room. The emotional pain was torture. She wanted it to stop so badly, but it wouldn't come to an end any time soon.

Marquan looked back to Jahleysa. His mouth was bloody, so when he swallowed he tasted metal. His teeth were stained crimson, so he licked the blood from off them with his tongue. He looked Jahleysa square in her eyes, feeling like a piece of shit for cheating on her with some hoodrat bitch from around the way. This is the reason why he allowed her to smack him in his face and shit. Not only did he believe that he deserve it, he hoped that him enduring the pain that she inflicted made her feel better.

"Why, Quan? Why? Why you do me like this, huh? Wasn't I what chu wanted? I cooked, I cleaned, I made sure I looked worthy enough to be seen on your arm. I wasn't fucking with no other niggaz, but chu. Shit, I gave myself to you. I gave you my virginity. Your name is tattooed on me," she pulled down the collar of her tank top and showcased the ink that was his name. It was in beautiful lettering. "I devoted myself to you. I was yours, all yours. I was yo' rider...yo' mothafucking soldier out here!" spit flew from off her lips as she jabbed the air with her finger. "All the shit I been through

with you! The court cases, jail time, your financial struggles...nigga, I stayed down with cho ass when you didn't have shit! Notta pot to piss in or a window to throw it out of!" she buried her face into her hands and sobbed aloud. Her entire form rocked back and forth. She was racked with emotions. She was hurting...she was hurting really bad. She couldn't understand for the life of her why her man would step out on her. This was because she had done any and everything that he could possibly want. Whatever her shortcomings were she made sure that she made up for them. She wanted to be perfect for him. Now, to find out that she wasn't everything that he wanted in a woman destroyed her. "Oh, my God, I can't believe you done this to me, Quan! I thought chu loved me!" she took her hands away from her face and he saw her wet, red webbed eyes. Her cheeks were soaked and slick.

Seeing his lady like this brought tears to Marquan's eyes. He blinked the tears back and sniffled, wiping his eyes with the back of his fist.

"I do love you, Jah! You the best thing that's ever happened to me," He embraced her in a loving hug, allowing her to sob into his chest. He could feel her tears soaking through his shirt but he ignored them. See, he didn't want to do anything at that moment besides comfort her. Homie wanted that pain that he had caused her to rise out of her body like vapors and disappear into the air. "I love you, Jah. I love you more than I love myself, girl. Why can't chu see that, boo? I fucked up bad, I know. But there isn't anything that I can do to fix it. I made my bed and now a nigga gotta lay in it."

Jahleysa took two deep breaths while her face was pressed against Marquan's shirt. She pulled back from him with wet cheeks and a red nose from sobbing. She wiped her eyes with the back of her hands and licked her lips, trying to gather herself. The news she was delivered shocked and hurt her, and rightfully so. No one looks forward to the day that the love of their life breaks their heart. They know that they may face it one day, but no one looks forward to it...ever.

"Okay, alright," Jahleysa shut her eyelids and bowed her head to her interlocks fingers. Taking another breath, she looked back up into the eyes of the man that she loved dearly. "I can get through this. I can grow to love your son or daughter as if he or she is my own. We can still make this work...we can still be together."

Hearing her say this, Marquan bowed his head and stuck his hands inside of his Levi's 501 jeans, which were hanging halfway off his ass. Seeing this, Jahleysa's eyes took on a bleak look. She was scared of what he may have to say next, which was why she swallowed the lump of nervousness that had formed inside of her throat.

"What's the matter now?" Jahleysa asked, concern written across her face.

"We can't be together." He told her, straight up. Her eyes pooled with tears and her lips trembled. It was so quiet inside of the unit that she could have sworn that she heard her own heart breaking into a trillion pieces.

"Wh...why not?"

Marquan shut his eyelids briefly and swallowed the lump of fear inside of his throat. He hated to tell her exactly why because he knew it would only hurt her more, but he couldn't bring himself to lie to her either.

"Me and Adele have decided to be together. She and I believe that it's best that our child has both of his or her parents, especially since she and I grew up without a mother and father." Seeing all of the damage that he'd caused to Jahleysa's psych, he tried to reason with her, hoping that he could make her feel just a little better. "Trust and believe me when I say that I love you, Jah. Please do. But I want my lil' one to have a family...one with a mother and a father in the same home. You know what that's like, to have both parents. Hell, it did you good. I'm sure your parents are proud of the

woman you have become. Without them, you could have ended up a hoodrat like…"

"Like Adele," she said, staring ahead at nothing, looking like she had been put under hypnosis. Finally, her eyes shifted to his eyes. "A hoodrat like Adele, well, so much for us good girls, 'cause it seems to me that all the ain't shit bitches get the men that they want while us good girls have to settle." Tears slid down her face slow and unevenly. "You cut me, Quan, you cut me deep. So deep that I don't know if this wound of mine will ever heal. I swear to God that I just wanna curl up on this floor right her and just die…die right here and right now." Tears cascaded down her cheeks and her body shuddered, snot threatening to drip from out of her nose. Suddenly, she broke towards the bathroom causing him to frown up and wonder what she was doing. That's when he saw her cross the threshold into the bathroom and slam the door shut behind her. Next, he heard the faucet water running inside of the bathroom sink. He lifted an eyebrow as he realized that she may be trying to kill herself over him.

Marquan took off running towards the bathroom. Reaching it, he called out Jahleysa's name over and over again, but she didn't answer. That's when he heard the medicine cabinet slam shut and the sound of pills rattling inside of a medicine bottle.

"Jah, what the fuck you doing in there? Open up; open up this goddamn door now, 'fore I kick this bitch down!" he pounded on the door with his fist. The brute force he rained down upon it caused it to rattle. "Jah, open this fucking door!" Boom! Boom! Boom! Boom! He continued to pound on the door with his fist causing it to rattle even more. "Jaaaahhhhh!" Boom! Boom! Boom! Ba-Boom! The bathroom door went flying open from Marquan throwing his shoulder into it. Upon the final impact, a piece of the door's wooden frame went flying across the bathroom. He found Jahleysa standing at the medicine cabinet's mirror with an

Excedrin pill bottle in her hand. The faucet water was running and swirling down the drain. She was just standing there taking in her appearance, looking a hot mess having cried long and hard over her man.

Marquan stood where he was looking at Jahleysa with his mouth wide open, chest rising and falling as he breathed huskily. He watched as a calm Jahleysa turned off the faucet water and put the cap back on the Excedrin pill bottle. She then set the bottle back inside of the medicine cabinet and shut its door. Turning back around to Marquan, she removed her chain and took his palm. She opened his palm and placed her chain into it, shutting his palm closed.

"I almost did it…but then I realized that you're not even worth it. I'ma find me a good man. A man that's gone love me to life and treat me like I came from a royal bloodline. And when you see me out with him, and see how happy we are together, you gone hate cho self. You gone hate cho self 'cause it will be then that it hits you that you fucked up the day that you lost a real one. Especially when you waking up every morning with some skank hoe that's not gone ride as hard as I have for you. Trust and believe that, boo boo."

"Look, Jah, I…" Marquan's words died in his throat as Jahleysa placed her finger against his lips.

"Shhhhhh! Save it! What's done is done and there isn't any way that you or I can fix it. It's best now that we both move on and live our lives however we see fit."Marquan looked down at the chain with his name on it that she put in his palm. He then stashed it inside of his pocket. As soon as he placed the chain inside of his pocket, she nudged him for him to follow her. He obliged. They stopped at the door where he asked for a hug. She gave him one while she looked over his shoulder. Afterwards, she let him out of the house and shut the door behind him.

As soon as Jahleysa let Marquan out of her house, she slid down to the floor and wrapped her arms around her knees. Bowing her head to her knees, she wept long and hard, big teardrops dripping from her eyes.

Their love affair had come and gone, and he was going to leave it that way. The only thing he was focused on now was making money and taking care of his family. Anything else he didn't have time for.

****

Apocalypse pulled up at the back of the warehouse that he was supposed to meet his plug. Homeboy hadn't arrived yet, so he glanced at his watch. He still had a few more minutes so he decided to hop out, but not before checking the magazine of his Glock. Once he saw that the clip was fully loaded, he smacked it back into the bottom of his gun. He then threw the door open and jumped out. Having tucked his banga into his waistline, he made his way to the rear of the car where he leaned up against it. He folded his arms across his chest and waited for his plug to arrive. About twenty minutes had gone by with him tapping his foot impatiently. Just when he was about to hop back into his whip and head to a payphone to hit homeboy up, he saw headlights of an approaching vehicle shining on the wall he was facing. Right then, he stood up straight and adjusted his gun on him. A '00 Ford Explorer sport stopped before him. Its headlights shined so brightly, that he narrowed his eyelids and held his hand above his brows. Suddenly, the SUV's headlights died and so did its engine. The black shape sitting behind the wheel opened the door, stepping out one foot at a time. It slammed the door shut and made its way in his direction. "'Bout mothafuckin' time, nigga. Damn, I thought chu probably got popped or some shit."

"My bad, baby. I'm sorry."

"Don't wet it."

In a flash, homeboy he was talking to pulled out and shot him. Fire ripped through his shoulder as he was thrown backwards from the impact of the bullet, which went right through him. He fell up against the back of his ride and slid down wincing. He clenched his jaws and looked up at old boy through narrowed eyelids. The nigga stopped before him and moved to finish him off.

"That's it, just take the shit and go. Gone!" Apocalypse urged him, throwing up his arm to shield himself from another bullet. Old boy lowered his gun at his side and walked to the driver's door, opening it. He popped the trunk open and walked back around to the rear of the vehicle. Having opened the trunk, he grabbed the black Nike duffle bag and slammed it back closed. He then casually strolled over to his truck, tossed the bag into the backseat and hopped in. Slamming the door shut behind him, he cranked up the behemoth and pulled out. Throwing the car into *drive*, he then mashed the gas pedal and sped off.

****

Urrrrrk!

Craaaash!

Apocalypse slammed into an old red Saab that was parked at the end of the block when he bent the corner. He was woozy from blood lost and having a hard to focusing to drive, but that didn't stop him. Apocalypse continued down the residential block, crashing into other parked vehicles and making a nigga on a bike get out of the way of his reckless driving.

Finally, Apocalypse's vehicle bumped the curb and rolled up into Marquan's yard. It stopped once it bumped into the porch. Apocalypse threw the driver's door opened and fell out onto the lawn on his hands and knees. Pulling himself up by the rear of his automobile, he staggered towards the porch, wincing, and holding his bleeding shoulder.

"Marquuuaaaan! Marquuuaaan!" He called out to his right-hand man and gritted his teeth. Taking his hand away from his wound, he looked to his hand and saw that it was masked with blood.

Abruptly, the front door flung open and Marquan came running out of the house, with his banga out at his side. You could tell by his eyes that he'd been sleeping before the noise outside disturbed his slumber. His face was twisted up and his eyes glinted with murder, he was ready to lie something down. After laying eyes on Apocalypse, he looked around and didn't see any posing threat, so he tucked his gun on him and approached his man. "What the fuck happened?" He asked as he examined Apocalypse, one hand on his waist and the other on his good shoulder. "Nigga popped me and took the loot, cuz. Ssssss, ah, fuck!" Apocalypse removed his hand and looked at his palm again. Now his hand looked like he was wearing a bright red glove.

"Lemme see," Marquan looked at the darkened wound in his homeboy's shoulder and then to his dripping hand, with his brows furrowed up. "Damn, it looks like it went in and out. I don't think it hit an artery either, so you should be straight. We gotta get chu to a hospital though, fast. Fuck around and bleed to death. Come on," he threw Apocalypse's arm around his shoulders and grabbed him by the waist. "This mothafucka still mobile, bruh?" he asked as he walked him over to the back passenger side door of the vehicle. Apocalypse nodded and he opened the passenger door, helping him slide back inside of the car.

"Baby, what happened?" A worried Adele called out from the front porch. She was in one of Marquan's white T-shirts, with her thick legs on display.

"Poc's been shot." He informed her as he slammed the door behind his comrade and ran around to the other side of the vehicle.

"Oh my God!" she smacked her hands over the lower half of her face. She then slid her hands down her face. "Is he, okay?" she inquired with tears peeking out the corners of her eyes.

"I think he's gonna be okay, long as I get 'em to the hospital. Go inside. I'll let chu know what's up once I get back." Marquan slammed the door shut behind him and threw the automobile in reverse, backing out into the street. He then threw the car into *drive* and drove off down the block. He fled down the residential block, looking back and forth between his main man and the windshield. Seeing the constant wincing of his right-hand man gave him cause for concern. Especially when he saw that he was sweating and his complexion was growing paler.

"Hold on, cuz, I'ma get chu there, just hold on for me, my nigga." He reached into the backseat and grabbed his bloody hand, gripping it firmly. By him doing this he stained his own hand red considerably.

"Aahhhh, fuck, cuz, this shit hurt!" Apocalypse threw his head back hollering as he squirmed in the front passenger seat.

Woop! Woop! Woop! Woop!

The vehicle made the cars aligning either side of the street look like flashes as Marquan flew past them. Marquan made a sharp ass right at the end of the street and caused oncoming cars to blow their horns irately. He ignored them as he floored the gas pedal en route to county hospital.

Honk! Honkk! Honnnkkk!

"Fuck you, fuck y'all mothafuckaz!"Marquan roared out of his window and used the hand he was steering with to blow the car's horn hostilely.

"I'm tryna get my brotha to a goddamn hospital." His head snapped to Apocalypse and he saw that he was in even more pain than he was before. "Hold on, cuz, I got chu faded. You just gotta hold on a while longer, my nigga!"

"Alright, alright, alright, but shit, hurry up." Apocalypse gritted his teeth and squeezed his eyelids shut, creating wrinkles at the corners of his eyes and around his nose.

Marquan floored the gas pedal and flew past stop signs and red lights. He nearly crashed into other vehicles twice. In return he got insults hurled his way and blaring car horns from the drivers he pissed off. He didn't give a fuck about how they felt though. He was trying to get his homeboy to the hospital before he bled to death.

"Hold on, cuz, we almost there," Marquan adjusted the rearview mirror so that he could see Apocalypse. He saw him stretched across the backseat wincing and holding his wound, with his bloody hand.

Vroooooom!

Honk! Honkk! Honnnkkk!

Marquan dipped in and out of lanes and narrowly missed crashing into oncoming traffic. Once he'd gotten past all of the traffic, he ripped up the street, hurrying towards his destination. Every now and then he'd glance into the backseat at Apocalypse and see how he was doing. He didn't have to ask him how he was feeling because the expression on his face told it all. His wound had him at its mercy and he was in excruciating pain.

"Grrrrrrr!" Apocalypse growled as he squeezed his eyelids tighter and squared his jaws so tight that veins bulged from everywhere on him. His pain caused him to grip Marquan's hand that much tighter.

"Hold on, cuz, we almost there!" Marquan glanced over his shoulder once again, and squeezed his comrade's hand that much tighter.

Vroooom!

He flew past the red stop light that resided over the intersection. An old Buick Riviera's horn blared as it was almost hit by Marquan crossing the light at the intersection which was green.

****

Urrrrrk!

Marquan stopped his car outside the double doors of the emergency entrance. Throwing open the driver's door, he jumped out and ran to the back door. Pulling the back door open, he reached inside and helped Apocalypse out. Once he had him on his wobbly legs, he threw his arm across the back of his shoulders and placed his hand around his waist. The blood from the wound in his shoulder had expanded, so he knew that Apocalypse had lost more blood. He didn't dare mention this discovery to him for fear that he'd worry and panic.

"Yo' plug did this shit, cuz?" Marquan inquired from his main man.

"Yeah, he did, nigga tried to kill me, cuz. Ran off with the money and the work," He grimaced from the wound in his shoulder.

"You know where this nigga lay his head at? Or any place that he frequents? Gemme anything you have on 'em that'll lead me to his bitch ass, loc! I'ma serve this nigga up lovely for you. Show this nigga what time it is when you fucking with one of mine."

"Okay, grrrrrrr," he squeezed his eyelids shut and gritted his teeth to combat the pain in his shoulder. "There's this brothel that he goes to pretty often. He's a regular there. I went with him a few times…." Apocalypse gave him the address to the whore house. He then told him to pull his wallet from out of his back pocket and take the picture out of him and a dark skinned Mexican dude. "That's him, right there. That's Popeye. He got that name on the account of his bugged eyes; he always looks like he's on some shit." He gave him the rundown as he looked at the picture. "As many years as I've been doin' business with this nigga, I woulda neva expected for him to pop and rob me. I considered that connivin' ass snake a fuckin' friend of mine. How silly of me to eva think that there's friends in this game."

"Don't even worry about it, loc, in a minute you gone be reading this mothafucka'z eulogy. That's on everything." Marquan swore with a hard face and clenched jaws. He was gone give that nigga Popeye the business, ASAP.

"Aarrrrr, shiiiit!" Apocalypse threw his head back and squeezed his eyelids tighter. He gritted his teeth further and veins bulged on his forehead and neck.

"Ah, shiiit!" Marquan spat seeing the kind of pain his homeboy was in as he crossed the threshold of the emergency ward with him. His eyes looked around the emergency ward's lobby and took in all of the faces present. Everyone was watching TV or minding their own business, so they didn't notice him and Apocalypse when they came inside. "I needa doctor, I needa doctor now!" he called out, and stole everyone's attention.

"Aaaahhhhh, fuck, this shit hurt, cuz!" Apocalypse called out in pain. His shoulder was giving him hell to pay.

At that moment, some of the hospital staff came running in Marquan and Apocalypse's direction to help.

****

Boom!

The double doors of the emergency ward flew open. The hospital staff rushed Apocalypse along on a gurney, tearing open his shirt and exposing the black bleeding hole in his shoulder. His eyes were hooded, and his pupils moved around lazily. He spoke to his main man in a low raspy voice.

"Get 'em for me, cuz, get that nigga for me…"

"Don't worry about nothing, my nigga, I got chu faded, onna gang!" a vengeful Marquan promised Apocalypse, running alongside the gurney, clutching his bloody hand. The blood on Apocalypse's hand was drying. Tears danced at the corner of Marquan's eyes as he stared down at his wounded comrade, thinking about what life would have been like if he'd lost him tonight. They'd been through a lot together, and he couldn't imagine a life without him.

"Sir, I'm gonna need you to step back. We've got it from here," one of the doctors told Marquan.

"Okay," Marquan nodded and released Apocalypse's hand.

Standing where he was inside of the hallway, Marquan cupped his hands around his mouth and called out to Apocalypse.

"I love you, cuz, stay strong!"

Marquan's words echoed throughout the hallway as he stood where he was, watching the hospital staff rush Apocalypse to emergency surgery. Marquan watched as Apocalypse threw up their hood with one hand up in the air while he was being whisked away on the gurney. In response, Marquan threw up their hood with both hands. He looked on, watching the gurney and the staff grow smaller and smaller until they disappeared. Marquan lingered inside of the corridor for a moment, looking down at the picture of Apocalypse and his plug, Popeye. The sunlight was shining on the men as they chilled on a yacht in swimming trunks with a quartet of beautiful bikini clad women around them. Popeye, who had his hair slicked back, was wearing sunglasses and had a big ass cigar in his mouth. His arms were hung around the shoulders of two of the women. Apocalypse stood with two of the women. He held up a bottle of expensive champagne while one of the women hugged him from the back and the other hugged him from the front.

"I'm getting ready to wipe that smile clean off yo' face, cuz. That's on everything I love." Marquan slipped the picture back inside of Apocalypse's wallet and slid it into his back pocket. He looked down the hallway one last time and tapped his fist to chest before walking back in the other direction.

CHAPTER THREE

Marquan, blood stains covering his clothing, hustled up the steps of his house and let himself inside. Crossing the threshold, he shut the door behind him and locked it. When he turned around he found Adele sitting on the couch. She rose to her feet when she saw him; a concerned expression was across her face.

"Is Poc okay?" she asked.

Marquan slowly nodded and said, "He's gonna be fine."

"Oh, thank God." She ran over to him and hugged him affectionately. Holding her to him, he rubbed her back soothingly and kissed her on the side of her head. "I'm glad he's gonna be alright. I was worried."

"My nigga gone live, but the fool that popped 'em is going belly up tonight; you can take that shit to the bank and cash it."

At that moment, she slowly broke her embrace and looked up at him. A suspecting expression was written across her face and tears were in her eyes.

"Wait a minute, Quan, you not talkin' about goin' out there to kill the nigga that shot Poc, are you?"

"You goddamn right," he removed her arms from around him and headed down the hall. "Where's Ant?"

"He's asleep," she answered as she followed behind him. "Now, back to what we were talkin' about, you can't seriously be thinkin' about going after Poc's shoota, are you?"

"Ya damn skippy, I am," he peeled off his bloody clothing and left it in a pile in the middle of the bathroom floor, where they were standing now.

"What?" Adele shouted like she couldn't believe her ears. Her eyes were hot and she could feel the heat sizzling in them. She was on the verge of crying. She was afraid that if he went out that night he'd wouldn't make it back home. For some reason she believed that he'd wind up getting murdered or locked up for a body.

"If you can *what* me, then you heard what the fuck I said, Adele." He replied as he stood before the spray of the hot shower water, lathering himself up with soap. "You can say all you want to say, but nothing's gonna stop me from getting out there on that black top and bringing my brotha's shoota to street justice. I don't give a shit if Christ rung that doorbell right now and told me not to go through with it. I'd still have my black ass out there with my banga."

"Are you forgetting you have our son to raise? A family to look after? Should somethin' happen to you then you'll be leavin' me and the streets to raise 'em. And if that happens…if that happens…"

At that moment, he snatched back the curtains of the shower and stepped his wet, dripping body from out of the tub, one foot at a time.

"If that happens then he'll come out like me," he finished what he thought she was trying to say. "You don't think I know that? It's death before dishonor with me. And if that's something that I gotta risk then that's just what it's gotta be." He snatched the towel off the rack and began drying himself off.

Adele bowed her head and big teardrops fell from hereyes. She felt like there wasn't anything within her power she could do to stop him from going through with his plans to hit the nigga that had shot Apocalypse. Although she was attracted to street niggaz, she didn't understand what it was about the streets that made them more loyal to them than they were their families. She believed that it should have been the other way around.

Adele lifted her head up and exposed her tear streaked face. Sniffling, she wiped her dripping eyes with the back of her hand, seeing Marquan heading for the door. She placed her knees to her breasts, bowed her head and wrapped her arms around her legs. Sitting on the floor inside of the bathroom, she cried her eyes out.

****

Marquan stood before his dresser's mirror strapping on a Kevlar bulletproof vest. Once he was done, he slipped a white T-shirt on over it and, then finally, a black sweatshirt. He was about to grab his wave cap but he stopped himself short. He leaned closer to his reflection in the mirror, studying the old scars in his face from being cut going through glass. Although the cuts in his face were barely visible since he'd gotten them so long ago, they'd always serve as a reminder to him. He'd never forget the night he'd gotten them. He'd received them on the same faithful night he'd lost his parents.

On their way home from his father's friend's party, Marquan's drunken father had a car accident that led to two fatalities.

"Herald, watch ooooouuuuut!"Mira blared at the top of her lungs as she clenched the arm of her drunken husband. The bright florenscent headlights of a Mac truck shined through their windshield blinding them. The illumination was so intense that it was like the clouds parted and the heaven's shined on them.

Bunk! Bunnnk! Bunnnnnk!

The horn of the enormous truck blared aloud as it approached. Its driver slammed on the brake pedal and the transporting vehicle skidded. The truck tried to stop but it kept on sliding forward.

"Oh, shiiiit!" Herald sharply turned the steering wheel to the right. The vehicle fishtailed out of control and went off the side of the road. Herald fought for control of the vehicle, but ended up colliding with a tree. The impact was so great that it ejected an eight year old Marquan through the windshield. He hit the ground tumbling forward until he eventually stopped, lying slumped against another tree. His head was bowed and his palms were turned upwards.

"Uhhhhhh," Marquan brought his bobbling head up and peered through narrowed eyelids. His left eyelid was squeezed shut from blood running into it. Infact, his entire face was covered in small cuts from imploding through the windshield. "Mommy…daddy…" he called out to his parents seeing the wrecked vehicle pressed up against the tree. His vision was blurry and he was seeing double. After a while his vision came back into place, but he had a migraine.

Marquan went to move and a pain shot through his left arm. Wincing, he looked to it and saw that the bone was broken. As a matter of fact, the bone was poking out through the side of his arm. "Aahhhh, sssssss," he attempted to touch it, but it hurt too badly so he left it alone. Biting down on his bottom lip, Marquan slowly got upon his feet and shuffled over to the wrecked car. When he made it to his parents' car he found them dead. Their eyes were stretched wide open and their mouths were twisted in a grotesque manner. Horror was etched across their faces.

Instantly, Marquan's eyes filled with tears and his lips trembled. He opened the front passenger door and crawled inside of the car. He laid his head up against his mother's bosom and pulled her arm around him. He then shut his eyelids and cried until he finally fell asleep.

Marquan and his parents weren't found until dawn. The police tried to take him into custody but he managed to evade capture. He found himself back in the hood where he met his big homie, 187. The gangsta hit-man took the boy under his wing and raised him for a time. The little dude eventually joined up with the crips and took his surrogate father's moniker, adding Lil' to it. He became Lil' 187 and made a name for himself through murder, just like the man that had a hand in raising him did.

Having come back from recalling the tragic incident that changed his life forever, Marquan grabbed his wave cap and pulled it down over his ears. He then tucked a pair of gloves inside of his back pocket and picked up the Beretta on the dresser. He checked the weapon's magazine then smacked it back into the bottom of it. After he finished cocking one into the banga's head, he tucked it at the front of his jeans and laid his sweatshirt over it.

Marquan looked up at the mirror at a wallet size photo of his deceased mother and father. Kissing two of his fingers, he touched them to the photo, which was tucked snuggly at the corner of the dresser's mirror. Next, he took his gold chain from off dresser's mirror where it was hanging and looped it around his neck. The chain held onto a crucifix that had an action figure sized Jesus on it.

Marquan looked over his shoulder from where he was standing before the mirror and found Adele fast asleep. All the crying she'd done had given her a headache, so he brought her a glass of water and two Excedrin migraine. The Excedrin made her sleepy and she was calling hogs in no time. A slight smirk formed on Marquan's lips seeing his lady sleeping so peacefully. He walked over to her and kissed her tenderly on her forehead. Next, he grabbed his keys and headed down the corridor. He entered his son's bedroom where he was sleeping as well. He caressed the side of his head and kissed him affectionately on his temple.

Once he'd bid his family a farewell, Marquan made his way towards the front door. Coming outside, he pulled the door shut behind him and hustled down the steps. Coming into the front yard and looking to his left, he saw someone on a Beach Cruiser wearing a hood over their head. He was just about to pull out his gun, in case it was an enemy, but the nigga on the Beach Cruiser pulled the hood off his head and brought his bike to a skidding stop

"Sup, cuz?" JaQuel asked, throwing his head back. He had a royal blue bandana tied around his head and the Champion hoodie he had on was the same color.

JaQuel was a brown skinned lad who wore his hair in a baby afro. He had the face of a twelve-year-old and the eyes of a street veteran, three times his age. He had the mentally of a grown man and a sort of deep, raspy voice. Some of the hood niggaz argued that a street nigga died long ago and came back to walk the hood, using the child's body as his vessel. This was because the youngsta carried himself like someone far older. Not only that, he wasn't into playing games around the hood like most other youths. Nah, the little homie was about a dollar, and any way he could get it. He sold coke, dope, weed, hash, and jacked any niggaz he felt was handling some paper. It was safe to say that little JaQuel was a product of his environment.

"'Sup with it, my young nigga?" Marquan stepped out of the yard and dapped up his little homie.

"Ain't shit, you know me. I'm out here tryna buy me a mansion and a Lambo before my eighteenth birthday." He patted his Dickie's pocket, which had seven packets of heroin in it. He'd been out prowling the streets selling dope all night. The little nigga had almost gotten off everything he'd come outside with, so he was in high spirits when he ran into his big homie.

"Stay on it, kingpin, you'll get it. While yo' homies out here playing," he looked across the street at JaQuel's homeboys who were playing around in the hood with a couple of young girls, he was sure going to grow up to be hood rats like their mothers. Their attitudes and style of dress told him all this and he was usually a pretty good judge of character. "Stack yo' paypa to the sky so you can ball hard thena mothafucka, when its yo' time. You feel me?"

"Fa sho." He nodded in agreement. "Where you off to, my nigga? You look like you onna mission." He looked him over and made note of his all black attire, as well as the bulge underneath his sweatshirt, he was sure he was packing heat.

"Nah, ain't nothing like that, youngsta. I'm finna pick my peoples up from the hospital is all. Matter of fact," he pulled back the sleeve of his sweatshirt and looked at his watch. "I needa be getting outta here, so I'ma holla at chu once I touch the turf again." He dapped the youngsta up and stepped off the curb to his parked car. Opening the door, he slid inside behind the wheel and slammed the door shut. After firing the Regal up, he looked to the side view mirror to see if the coast was clear before pulling out. When he did this, he saw JaQuel ride off down the street where he was flagged down by a dope fiend. He watched as the youngsta hopped off his bike and motioned for the fiend to follow him. They entered a cut where no one could see them, and he was sure that his little homie served him.

"That's right, lil' cuz, get cho paypa," Marquan smirked.

Marquan made his way through Los Angeles traffic on a Thursday night, taking the occasional pull of a half smoked Black & Mild. Having sucked on the end of the thin cigar, he blew out a cloud of smoke and left it wafting around inside the confines of the hood classic. When the smoke became too much for him to bear, he cracked the driver's window and allowed the fog that inhabited his car out into the world.

Now, usually Marquan would have been blazing up that sticky icky, but he found that he wasn't any good under the influence, when it came time to putting in work. He needed a clear head before he got down on a hit. If he went in for the kill half cocked, then chances were he wouldn't make it back home. And he couldn't allow that to happen. *Fuck that!* He loved his life way too much.

Marquan made a left turn on 84th and Figueroa. Coasting down the block, he looked from left to right as he tried to find a G-ride for the night's mission. Finding one, he was satisfied with, he took the Black & Mild from his lips and a smile stretched across his face. The vehicle he had in mind, a white '99 Pontiac GT, reflected on the driver's window.

Marquan parked his car across the street and down the block from the car he had in mind to steal. Grabbing what he'd need to pop the locks on that bitch, he hopped out of his ride and slammed the door shut. Hunching over, he hastily made his way across the street, looking around for anyone that may be watching him break the law. Once he didn't see anyone, he continued towards the vehicle, reaching its driver's door. Using his tool, he popped the locks on the Pontiac and hotwired it. The vehicle roared to live and Mack 10's *Foe Life* pulsated from its speakers. After throwing the car into *drive*, he looked into the side view mirror to see if any automobiles were coming. Having not seen any, he pulled out of the parking space and drove off.

It wasn't long before Marquan found himself in East L.A. This particular part of the city was predominately inhabited by Latin Americans. There were Spanish mom and pop stores lined up and down nearly every block. There was a subway station, apartment buildings and homes that fit perfectly in the ghetto. There was also graffiti on the walls that warned outsiders whose turf they were trespassing on.

Boy, it's lil' Mexico down out here, Marquan couldn't help thinking as he saw all of the brown faces, walking the streets of East Los Angeles. A left, a right and another left a block later, he found himself on the residential street he needed to be on. Looking ahead, he narrowed his eyelids and brought his face closer to the windshield. He'd identified the address of the house he was looking for. To be sure, he pulled the small piece of paper from out of the small pocket of his jeans and looked at it. Sure enough, he'd located the exact address written across the paper. Holding the paper just above the steering wheel, he used his lighter to set the evidence, which was the paper with the address on it on fire, before throwing its remains out of the window. The paper hit the street, still burning, turning black as it curled up at its ends.

Marquan drove passed the brothel just in time to see Popeye's ass coming out of the house, placing his fedora hat on his crown and buttoning the last button on his shirt. The dark skinned Mexican had the biggest smile on his face, so Marquan knew that the whores there had shown him a good time.

Yeah, smile now die later. You put cho hands on my nigga, now you getting touched. Straight up, Marquan thought to himself, scowling and mashing what was left of his Black out inside of the ashtray. He then busted a U-turn at the end of the block and came back around. Looking ahead, he saw Popeye making his way across the street to his car. When he peeped this, he popped the glove-box open and grabbed his Glock. That bitch was cocked, locked and ready to go, so he didn't have to chamber a round into its head. With the hand he held the gun with; he smacked the glove-box shut, while keeping an eye on Popeye. He observed him about to slide behind the wheel of his whip.

Marquan smiled wickedly and bit down on his bottom lip, as he rolled down the front passenger window. He intended on waiting until Popeye was seated behind the wheel of his car before he emptied the magazine into his dome piece. That plan quickly dissolved once he saw Popeye tuck his keys back inside his pocket and walk towards the opposite end of the block.

Damn! Fuck this nigga going, cuz? Wait, he headed over there to that lil' Mexican food stand at the corner, where they slanging them tacos. Go 'head and eat cuz, this gone be yo' last supper.

Marquan parked at the center of the residential street and pulled on his gloves, flexing his fingers in them. He then picked up his gun and watched Popeye carefully. Popeye waited in line behind three other Mexican cats that were waiting to buy tacos. He toyed with the dollar bills he had in his hands as he watched the street vender hack off pieces from the hunk of juicy meat, which was slowly rotating on a steel rod. Once the vender was done taking down the meat, he'd pass the plate it was on to his female partner and she'd make the tacos up as requested. Afterwards, she'd pass the plate on to the awaiting patron.

When it was Popeye's turn to order, he stepped to the vender and held up four fingers. "Quatro tacos, senor."

"Coming right up, mi amigo," the street vender went about his business of hacking off the pieces of meat and passing the plate off to his partner.

Popeye paid for his food and received his tacos. He dropped the change he'd gotten back from his purchase into the big clear tip jar, which was sitting on the white table, where all of the condiments for the tacos were.

"Gracias," the street vender thanked Popeye, who in turn smiled and tilted his hat.

Popeye went about his business as he headed back to his car, eating his tacos. Feeling something hit his shirt, he looked down to find a salsa stain.

"Shiiiit, this a three-hundred dolla fuckin' shirt, man." He cussed and complained, but kept right along eating, heading toward his vehicle.

Seeing Popeye heading in his direction, Marquan tied a blue bandana over the lower half of his face and opened the door. He grabbed his gun and quietly stepped out of the car, stooped down low. Shutting the door back gently, he hurriedly made his way across the street, looking both ways. Reaching the driver's door of Popeye's ride, he eased his head up in the window and saw him approaching through the windshield. He was going on as if he didn't have a care in the world, sucking the salsa from off his fingers.

Popeye switched hands with his plate of tacos. Stepping off the curb, he used his freehand to fish his keys out of his pocket. He'd just reached the grill of his vehicle when Marquan sprung up from where he was stooped.

"Oh, shit!" Popeye's eyes bulged and his jaw slacked. He dropped his plate of tacos at his feet when he saw Marquan's terrifying eyes over the bandana that was covering the lower half of his face. He tried to make a run for it but his legs wouldn't cooperate, so he was left to deal with the hand that fate dealt him.

Marquan, holding his gun sideways, as he pointed it at him, said, "This for Apocalypse, nigga!"

Bloc! Bloc! Bloc! Bloc!

Popeye's brows furrowed and his mouth twisted in a grotesque manner. He fell to the ground and Marquan came up on him to finish the execution.

Bloc! Bloc! Bloc! Bloc!

Marquan shot that mothafucka all in his face and then he kicked him in his side, although he was already dead. Looking up the block, he saw the man and the woman that tended to the taco stand, looking down in his direction.

Marquan took off running across the street from where he had come and hopped in behind the wheel of his G-ride. He tossed his banga into the front passenger seat and cranked the stolen car up. He threw it in *drive* and peeled off. Right as he reached the end of the block, two police cars skidded to a halt before his eyes. His eyebrows rose wondering where the fuck they had come from. It was like they had magically appeared.

"What the fuck?" Marquan's forehead wrinkled with confusion. With no time to lose, he put the G-ride into *reverse* and threw his arm over the headrest of the passenger seat. Looking over his shoulder, he mashed the gas pedal and slammed into another police car. "Damn!" he cussed and put the car in *drive,* flooring it; he slammed into the police cars that had blocked his path at the end of the residential street. "Fuck that! I ain't going to jail!

Marquan grabbed his Glock and hopped out of the G-ride. Seeing the cop of the police car ahead of him about to get out of his vehicle, he sent some heat his way and shattered the driver's window. The broken glass rained down into the street as the cop ducked down, covering his head.

A nigga vowed to hold court in the streets before I went back to the cage, but fuck, cuz! I gotta prince to look after. If I let these crackas take me, he'll grow up a bastard, like I did. I ain't having that!

Gun still in hand, Marquan ducked low and took off running, with bullets flying over his head. Five-owe had hopped out of their vehicles and started popping at his ass as he ran towards a copper brown house. Marquan tossed the murder weapon and grabbed hold of the gate before him, leaping over it with one hand. As he ran up the driveway of the house whose yard he'd invaded, hearing the ghetto bird high in the sky. He knew it wouldn't be long before its light was shining on him.

"Haa! Haa! Haa! Haa! Haa!" Beads of sweat collected on Marquan's forehead as he ran up the driveway. He hopped the fence into the backyard and landed on his bending knees.

Looking to his right, he spotted a Doberman pinscher headed his way growling angrily. Shit, he thought to himself as he ran up a line of cars before him, descended the roof tops of them. He jumped onto a gate and had almost pulled himself over, when his foot slipped. He went to fall to the ground of the yard he was fleeing, when a loose wire of the gate snagged his jeans leg. He hung upside down twisting and turning as he tried to free himself. Hearing growling, he looked up to the Doberman about to bite into the side of his neck, so he threw up his arm. The dog grabbed the sleeve of his sweatshirt and pulled on it, whipping its head from side to side, with all of its might.

At that moment, the ghetto bird came flying up. The sound of its spinning propeller filled the air, as its light shined down upon Marquan and the hostile animal. Its illumination was so bright that it made him narrow his eyelids into slits.

"Grrrrrrrgrrrrrrr!" the beast growled, with its nub of a tail wagging back and forth.

"Ahhhh, fuck, man, get this dog!" Marquan jerked around violently as the dog threw its head around, growling.

"Grrrrrrrgrrrrrrr!"

"Ahhhh, shit, cuz! Get this mothafucking dog!"

As soon as Marquan entered the holding cell he picked up the jack and hit up Adele. As he listened to the telephone ring, he turned around and placed his back against the wall. He did this so that he could be aware of all of his surroundings and everything going on around him. The few niggaz that were inside of the cell seemed to be consumed with their own thoughts and not paying him any mind.

"Marquan," Marquan stated his name once the automated voice left him room to. His baby momma picked up the telephone. He heard the button being pushed, and then his son's mother coming on the line.

"I knew it; I knew it, oh God, why didn't you listen to me, Quan?" Adele brokedown sobbing and crying, she sniffled and blew her nose, but she continued to sob.

"I know, baby, I know," Marquan's eyes filled with tears and he turned his back to the men occupying the cell. He didn't want them to see him crying. As soon as he shut his eyelids, tears jetted down his cheeks and dripped from off his chin. He sniffled as quietly as he could and then wiped his eyes with the back of his hand. "I'm sorry, baby. I'm so, so sorry."

Adele didn't say anything, she kept right along crying. In fact, she cried the entire time she was on the telephone, never uttering so much as a word. Eventually, he hung up since they weren't conversating. Marquan felt like a world class piece of shit having gotten knocked for murder. He knew he'd be gone on an iron vacation for a long time, leaving his family outside in the cruel, cold world. Without him in his son's life, he feared what would become of him. The last thing he wanted was for him to turn out like he did. He was sure he could handle the sentence he'd get, but his son being turned out to the streets was something he couldn't stomach.

God, please, cover my son in yo' blood and keep 'em safe. I ask that chu keep my seed out of my lifestyle, Lord, and should he be led astray, guide him back onto the path of the righteous. In Jesus' name I pray, amen, Marquan silently prayed with his eyelids shut and his hands together. He was down on his knees in the corner of the holding cell with his back to everyone. Fuck what the rest of them niggaz thought about what he was doing. If his prayer was going to save his son, then he'd get down on his knees every day for the rest of his life.

CHAPTER FOUR

One week later

The sun shined through the clouds and blessed those below with its warm rays. The electric double doors of the hospital slid apart and an orderly came pushing Apocalypse out in a wheel chair. His eyelids narrowed into slits under the intense rays of the sun, and he raised his hand above his brows, looking up at the sapphire in the sky. His full lips peeled apart in a smile to reveal the golden glint of his grill. He'd been laid up inside of the hospital for a few days due to his gunshot wound, so he'd grown a five o'clock shadow over that time, and his hair beaded up into naps. None the less, he was happy to believe alive. With all the blood that he had lost, he thought that he was a goner for sure, but the Lord had other plans instore for his life and spared him.

The orderly stopped at the curb, just as the taxi cab that Apocalypse had ordered pulled to a stop before him. The orderly tried to come around and assist Apocalypse, but he refused his help. "Good lookin' out, my nigga," he said once he'd gotten upon his feet with his RX bag. He opened the back door of the taxi and jumped into the backseat. As soon as he slammed the door shut, the driver, a short Indian man, tried to have small talk with him.

"Check this out, cuz," Apocalypse began with a real serious look and tone, "I'm payin' yo' ass to get me where I needa be, not talk. So shut the fuck up and push this bitch to my requested destination. You got that?"

"Yes, I got it, buddy," The driver nodded.

"Good." Apocalypse spent the rest of the ride staring out of the back window of the passenger seat. A fixed frown was on his face as he had several thoughts running through his mind at the time. Occassionally, he'd ball his fist and hook his arm, swinging it back and forth, wincing. He could feel the pain killers wearing off that he was given before he left the hospital, so he knew that it was about time he'd popped another pill. He didn't have any water, so he used the saliva inside of his mouth as a form of liquid to swallow the pill down. It wasn't long before he found himself outside of Marquan's house, and staring at his car, which was parked inside of the driveway. The image of the car inside of the driveway reflected on the back passenger window.

Apocalypse reached inside of his pocket and pulled out a small wad of money. He peeled off a few bills to pay for the ride over and the tip. Once he passed the driver the mula, he received a 'thank you' and then he hopped out of the car. Thirsty, Apocalypse made his way over to the hose which was hidden in between the buses somewhere on the ground. He picked up the hose and turned the dial, causing it to squeak as he twisted it. The water poured from out of the green hose, and he held it to his mouth, drinking from it. He then cupped his hand below the water and splashed some on his face. Afterwards, he ran his hand down his face, and took a deep breath, sending droplets flying.

Apocalypse turned off the water and made his way upon the porch. He lifted up the welcome mat and grabbed the two sets of keys that were hidden underneath it. After pocketing one set of keys, he made his way off the porch and over to his vehicle, where he opened the trunk. Once he lifted the trunk's lid, he dropped his RX bag inside of the trunk. He looked around to make sure no one was watching him, which there wasn't. With that in mind, he slipped on a hoodie and grabbed the gun case that he found inside. He took another look around before he opened the case. Inside he found a .32, a silencer and a couple of extra magazines. He stashed the gun and the silencer on him, then slammed the trunk shut and made his way over to the driver's door. He hopped in behind the wheel of his ride and cranked that mothafucka up. He then threw it in *reverse* and backed out of the driveway. Throwing the vehicle into *drive*, he mashed the gas pedal and took off down the residential street.

****

Apocalypse climbed out of his car and slammed the door shut behind him. After looking both ways for any oncoming cars, he jogged across the street. Making his way upon the sidewalk, he pushed open the short rusting gate of a two-story white house with a dirt patched lawn. As he trekked through the yard, he looked for any witnesses as he screwed a silencer on the barrel of a .32 handgun. He then reached inside of his pocket and pulled out a wad of dead presidents, secured by a rubber band. Once he reached the porch of the two-story house, he brought the butt of his .32 around and used it to knock on the side of the door.

He looked over his shoulder to make sure no one had followed him, and then he turned back around. He was just in time to hear the deadbolt and several other locks coming undone. Once the last lock had clicked open, the thick wood door slowly came open and he found a young nigga standing before him. His hair was done in box braids and he was wearing a brown Dickie suit. The shirt of it was opened to show off the wife beater he was wearing underneath it. His eyes were glassy and red webbed from smoking. He took a pull of his roach blunt and blew out a cloud of smoke.

Apocalypse held up the money and he snatched it. He eyed the money and looked at Apocalypse, tucking the mula into the pocket of his shirt. He then moved aside and waved Apocalypse inside of the shooting gallery with his Tec-9. Next, he stuck his head outside of the door and looked up and down the block for anyone that may have seen him let homeboy inside. When he didn't see anyone, he shut the door and locked all the locks that kept the place secure.

As soon as Apocalypse crossed the threshold inside of the house, he was greeted with the overwhelming smell of shit, piss, sex and vomit. He felt like he was walking on egg shells as his sneakers crushed the drug paraphernalia that littered ever square inch of the hardwood floors. His head was on a swivel as he looked at each and every room he moved passed, with the young nigga at his side. In the rooms he saw walls sprawled with graffiti. He also saw dope fiends shooting up, tying a belt around someone's arm to inject them with heroin or sexing someone for drugs.

If there's a hell on earth, this fuckin' place is definitely it, Apocalypse crossed himself in the sign of the crucifix as he kept on walking. They crossed a foyer and found themselves at the bottom of a staircase. The steps appeared as if they'd collapse under the slightest weight, but Apocalypse was willing to travel up them if it meant he'd get to who he was looking for. This was exactly what he thought as he looked up the long flight of steps.

"Up the stairs, inside the bathroom, on the right hand side, my nigga, you can't miss it."

"G' lookin'," Apocalypse dapped him up. He moved to go up the steps but something on the floor stole his interest. His brows furrowed as he looked down and picked them up.

He smiled evilly and tucked his gun at the small of his back, making his way up the raggedy staircase.

****

Avery sat on the edge of the tub as he prepared himself a shot of dope. After sticking his needle into the small cotton swab that lie soaked in the spoon, he pulled back on the small plunger that was at the back of the syringe. As he did so, the shaft of his syringe filled with the liquid poison. Bringing the syringe before his eyes, he thumped it twice with his thumb and index finger. He then pushed in the plunger a little and some of the dope squirted out of the head of the needle. Once he'd done this, he bit down on the syringe and stood up. He pulled his worn leather belt from out of the loops of his jeans. Next, he sat back down on the edge of the tub.

Avery's eyes filled with water that obscurbed his vision, causing it to look like he was looking through crystal. Teardrops fell from his eyes as he looped the belt around his forearm and pulled it tight, causing the meat of his scrawny arm to bulge around it. The pressure the belt was applying to his limb caused what looked like green veins to form up and down the inside of his arm. There were several scabs on the inside of his arm from him shooting dope over the years, but he didn't pay them any mind as he searched his arm for a vein ripe for the plucking. Coming across one, he smacked it a couple of times to make it become more pronounced. Once he could see it clearly, he took the syringe from out of his mouth and brought it towards his arm. His eyes focused on his arm as he brought the tip of the needle towards the bulging vein.

Avery licked his lips in anticipation as the needle broke through the surface of his flesh. As soon as it did the blood rushed inside of the syringe and changed the color of the dope to a dirty yellow. He then pushed the plunger into the back of the syringe and forced its contents into his vein. As soon as the drug entered his system he felt at ease. He shut his eyelids and he licked his lips as a smile spread across them. The dope had him feeling lovely. All day long he'd been fiending for a fix and he'd finally gotten it. He needed it badly too, especially with how guilty he'd been feeling recently. See, Avery's wife had been infected with AIDS and she'd died a week ago. The tragic news struck him like a fist to his gut, knocking the wind out of him. This was because he was pretty sure he'd passed the disease on to her.

See, Avery wasn't only sharing needles. Nah, he was freaking off with niggaz unprotected for money for his habit. It was from this that he was pretty sure he'd contracted the disease and passed it on to his woman. His lady didn't sell pussy to get high and she only shared needles with him. He was positive of all of this. So there was without a shadow of a doubt that he was responsible for her death. The revelation fucked him up royally. His pockets had lint so he didn't have any paper to get high. He had to do what he had to do in order to get the dead presidents he needed to get high with.

There wasn't any way that Avery could fuck anyone for the paper he needed to get his drugs. The nigga looked like a walking cadaver thanks to the Monster eating away at him. Since he couldn't make money by selling dick, he snatched this old lady's purse as she was coming out of the Food 4 Less supermarket. He'd nearly gotten caught because a security guard wanted to play hero. Homeboy had tackled him to the ground and had almost subdued him, but he jabbed him in his neck with his knife.

"Arghhhhh!"

The security guard's face wrinkled as he winced and gritted his teeth, smacking his hand over the blood squirting wound in his neck. The squirting hole slicked his hand wet and stained the collar of his uniform as he fell over on the asphalt.

Avery scrambled to his feet and grabbed the purse, which contents had spilled once he was tackled to the ground. He looked back at the security guard. He was lying on the ground and flapping around like a fish, bleeding everywhere. People had begun emerging from out of the supermarket behind the woman Avery had stolen the purse from. As soon as he and the security guard started scuffling, she'd run inside to get help

As Avery was hauling ass across the parking lot with the purse tucked under his arm, he looked back again at the scene behind him, which was growing smaller and smaller the further he got away. Police cars and an ambulance had just pulled up. By this time, the security guard's movements had ceased. It was from this that Avery knew he was dead and he was looking at a murder charge should he be caught. The police officer walked up on the scene, and appeared to be talking with the bystanders. Most of them pointed towards Avery as he was fleeing across the parking lot. He'd just turned the corner out of the parking lot, out of sight.

Avery ran under the freeway underpass and across the train tracks into the borderline that separated Watts and Compton. His adrenaline was pumping madly and his heart was jacked. He was sweating hard as hell and found his brow dripping sweat. Huskily breathing, still in motion, he wiped his forehead with the back of his hand. He could hear the police sirens heading his way as well as a helicopter. When he looked up, across the sky, he could see a helicopter hastily approaching.

"Shit!" Avery saw the helicopter. He knew once those police helicopters got on you that you were as good as

nabbed. "Haa! Haa! Haa! Haa! Haa! Haa! Haa! Haa! Haa!" he continued to run as hard as he could. Darkened spots around the collar of his shirt and under his arms had formed on account of him sweating. He turned down a residential block and kept on running, occasionally glancing over his shoulder. He heard dogs barking as he sprinted up the sidewalk, with his legs looking like blurs. He was moving so fast that the heels of his raggedy sneakers were hitting him in his behind. He grabbed a short gate and hopped over into a yard. As soon as he landed on his bending knees, he took off running down a driveway. He turned the corner at the end of the driveway and made it into the backyard. Placing his back up against the house, he slid down to the ground and sat down on his ass. Breathing heavily, he pinched the collar of his shirt and wiped his sweaty face off.

Having calmed himself some, he peeked around the corner of the house to see if any police were coming. He saw a police car creeping up the street slowly as it shined its light on everything. Hearing the helicopter above, he looked up to see it in the sky, flashing its bright light everywhere except for the area that he was in. He pressed his head against the house and shut his eyelids. He then said a silent prayer and licked his lips. Before he knew it the helicopter was flying off into the night and he could hear the police car speeding off down the street.

"Thank you, thank you, Lord," he breathed huskily and crossed himself in the sign of the crucifix. He then rummaged through the purse and pulled out the few dollars that was inside. Afterwards, he sifted through the purse again until he discovered a small change purse. He opened it and dumped the copper and silver coins into his palm. Tossing the change purse aside, he sifted through the coins, counting what he had in his possession. "Thirty dollas and sixty seven

cents..."Avery stuffed all the money from his strong arm robbery into his jeans and stood up. Having forgotten the change purse, he picked it up and shoved it inside of the purse. Next, he walked it over to the black trash can and dumped it inside. Turning around, he straightened himself out and took a deep breath before casually strolling out of the backyard.

CHAPTER FIVE

Avery wanted to escape the hardships of his reality, which was the reason why he went to the shooting gallery and scored himself a couple of packets of what some dope fiends claimed was the best heroin on the black market, *Pandemonium*. Until tonight, he hadn't indulge in the streets poison of choice, but as soon as he had he understood what all the fuss was about.

Avery had just began to fall into his dope fiend lean, when the doorknob of the bathroom door rattled as it was twisted and turned crazily. There was a bump up against the door that woke Avery up out of his nod. When his bobbling head lifted up and he looked at the door, it was assaulted by pounding. The pounding against the door startled him. He figured he should get up and answered it so he did.

Avery grabbed hold of the dirty porcelain sink which was broken in half and pulled himself upon his feet. He was wobbly from the *Pandemonium*, but he tried his best to hold himself together. After taking a deep breath, he set out in the direction of the bathroom door, hearing it pounded against along the way.

Once Avery unlocked the door, he tugged on its knob three times before it eventually popped open. He was startled when he found a man standing before him wearing a hoodie, with his hands behind his back. Inside of his hood was pitch-black, so he couldn't make out his face. For a second, he thought he'd died from an overdose and was meeting the Grim Reaper, but then the man in the hood spoke.

"Virgie wanted you to have these!" the man in the hood said and swung his hands out from behind his back, revealing the syringes in his hands. The faint lighting of the bathroom shined on the syringes and caused the tips of their needles to twinkle. With a grunt, the unidentified man slammed the syringes into Avery's eyeballs with all of his might.

"Aaaahhhhhhhhhhhh!" Avery threw his head back and screamed bloody murder, causing the uvula to shake at the back of his throat. Blood seeped out of his wounded eyes and ran down his cheeks. He grasped the syringes and stumbled backwards in a hurry. He bumped into the filthy tub and fell over into it, lying slumped there. Avery continued to scream as he pulled the syringes out of his eyes and threw them aside. "My eyes, my eyyyyeees," he whimpered and brought his palms to his wounded eyes.

Apocalypse casually strolled in Avery's direction. He lifted up the lower end of his hoodie and pulled out his silenced .32. His shadow loomed over Avery as he stood before him, pulling off his hood and exposing his scowling face.

"Your eyes are the least of your concerns, homeboy, rest in shit!"He pointed the small handgun down at Avery and shot him in his chest repeatedly. He took the time to study his handiwork before tucking the murder weapon. Apocalypse picked up the items that Avery used to shoot heroin with and stashed them inside of his hoodie. Next, he fished through his pockets and found two packets of dope which he shoved inside of his pocket. After throwing his hood back over his head, he put his hands inside of his pockets and strolled out of the bathroom like he just didn't catch a body.

****

Apocalypse opened the front door of the house and walked inside, shutting the door behind him. He could hear the television inside of the bedroom from where he was inside of the living room. The volume was so loud that he knew that the next door neighbors could hear it.

Apocalypse stashed his keys inside the pocket of his hoodie and made his way down the hallway. He peeked inside of the bedroom and saw the ruffled covers in the bed, but there wasn't anyone lying in it. His brows furrowed because he was expecting her to be there, but she was gone. He journeyed back down the hallway and heard the faint sound of splashing water. Placing his ear near the door, he knocked just loud enough for whoever was on the opposite side to hear him.

"Y…yeah?" A feminine voice responded.

"You alright in there?" he asked.

"Y…yeah."

"No you not, I'm finna come in," Apocalypse opened the bathroom door and stepped inside. He found the woman that he was looking for inside of the tub, taking a drag from a withering cigarette. Her eyes were so swollen from sobbing that they looked like she'd been punched in them. She had white sprawls on her cheeks from the tears that had dried there and her nose was red.

When Adele saw Apocalpse she turned her head because she didn't want him seeing her face. He kneeled down to her and turned her to face him, looking into her eyes. Iinside of her eyes he saw great sadness and hurt. He knew that without a doubt that he was in part to blame for her current emotional state. Afterall, he was the one that had recruited her to setup Marquan. But he didn't give a fuck though. That nigga had to suffer just like he had.

"You fucked up behind the shit that went down behind Marquan, huh?" Apocalypse asked her and she agreed. "I'm not surprised. In fact, I suspected this. I mean, you got history with the nigga. He's practically yo' husband and ya'll have Antonio together. Shit is expected, so I ain't even on no jelly shit. You feel me?" she nodded. "Look, I got somethin' that'll ease that achin' heart of yours, lil' momma. Now you probably not gone feel what it is 'cause it has a bad stigma and all, but let me be the first to tell you, don't knock it 'til you try it."

"What is it?" Adele looked up at him with glassy, hopeful eyes. She sincerely hoped that Apocalypse had something that would be her salvation from her world of grief and turmoil.

Without saying a word, Apocalypse pulled out something inside of his fist. He outstretched his fist before her eyes and opened his hand, revealing one of the packets of *Pandemonium* he'd stolen from off Avery's dead body. Adele looked at the packet and then back up at Apocalypse's face. She looked in decisive of what she should do, but her first mind was telling her to leave that shit alone.

"Oh, baby, I don't…I don't wanna get strung out on that stuff." She told him timidly, staring up into his eyes.

"You won't get strung out, momma." Apocalypse let the lie roll off his tongue easily, as he combed his fingers through her hair and looked at her like she was the most attractive woman he'd ever laid eyes on. Adele shut her eyelids and licked her lips as she enjoyed the feeling of him combing his fingers through her hair. Leaning forward, he kissed her on the forehead and continued playing in her hair. "I won't let that happen, trust me. I'ma take good care of you. You mine now, fuck Marquan!" He kissed her tenderly on her neck. "Now, you want me to go ahead and fix this up for you so you can feel better?" Adele nodded as she wiped the tear that dripped from her eye with her curled finger. "Okay."

With that understood, Apocalypse pulled out the items from his hoodie that Avery had used to shoot heroin with and lined them up on the edge of the tub. He then unbuckled his belt and pulled it loose from the loops of his jeans. Still holding his belt, he sat down on the tub alongside the items.

Adele watched Apocalypse attentively as he prepared a shot of dope for her. Now, she'd never seen heroin prepared before, but she had seen coke cooked to crack cocaine. Her brother, Bumpy, used to whip powder into crack. He worked as a clerk at a Shells gas station full time, and he sold crack on the side to make ends meet. When Adele saw what crack did to people in her neighborhood, she vowed to never fuck with it, no matter how hard she'd hit rock bottom. And she never did, she never fucked with the shit. She fucked with weed and alcohol, but she'd never put her lips on the end of a glass pipe to smoke 'ready rock', what niggaz called crack in Los Angeles when it first popped off back in the 80's.

Once Apocalypse finished drawing up the syringe of dope, he held it up before his eyes and admired it. He smiled wickedly and licked his top lip, squirting the heroin from out of the tip of the needle.

"I feel horrible, babe. I feel really, really horrible. My guilt is eatin' me from the inside out," Adele told him as tear cascaded down her cheeks. She watched as he gently placed the syringe on the edge of the tub and repositioned himself where he was sitting.

Well, the heroin is goin' to wash away all of your hurt and guilt. It's goin' to make things a whollllle lot betta than they are for you now." He told her as he held her chin up and stared into her eyes convincingly.

"You promise?" she wept and sniffled.

"I promise," he nodded confidently. "Happy will whisk you away from all of the heartache of this world to a euphoria all your own." He referred to the heroin needle.

Thinking of how much her heart ached at that moment, Adele wanted to visit this place that would cleanse her of her worries and pain. If the place that Apocalypse was talking about would really take her from the ills of her reality, then she couldn't wait until she got there.

"Okay. Alright," Adele nodded her head rapidly.

"That a girl. Now, sit back. Relax. And prepare to enter the doors of enchantment." When Apocalypse told her this, she laid her head back against the tub and shut her eyelids as she licked her lips. Next, he picked up his belt and buckled it around her arm. He pulled it so tight that the meat of her arm bulged around it. Looking down, he felt around her arm until he found a vein ripe for penetration.

"Okay, baby," she rasped and braced herself for what was to come.

After tightening his belt around Adele's arm, Apocalypse smacked her forearm until a vein appeared, then picked up the syringe. Bringing the syringe towards the vein, he looked up into her eyes and a smile stretched across his face, giving him the appearance of The Grinch that stole Christmas. Apocalypse kissed Adele's lips before injecting her with the dope. Once he was done, he released the belt from her arm and capped the needle, sitting it on the edge of the tub. He watched as she was granted entrance to the euphoria he'd told her about.

"Mmmm." her eyelids fluttered as she moaned and licked her lips. Her reaction to the dope was kindred to that of an orgasm. Apocalypse groped her beasts and pinched her nipples. He then stuck his hand inside of the water and rubbed her thigh, allowing his hand to travel near her pussy.

"Shit feel good to you, momma?" he asked in a low, deep voice as he gently fingered her twat.

"Yes, baby," she uttered, experiencing the ecstasy that the drug brought her.

Apocalypse took his hand out of the water and smelled his fingers. He smiled when he inhaled her sweet scent; he then flicked the water off his fingers. He leaned close to Adele's ear and said, "From this day forth, you my slave, I'm yo' master and this here," he held up the empty packet of dope, "is my whip." Sitting the packet of dope back down on the edge of the tub, he kissed her on her temple and rose from where he was sitting on the tub. Afterwards, he walked to the door and pulled it open. He was about to walk out of the door, but he held it open and looked back at her. He smiled sinisterly before proceeding through the door.

Apocalypse left out of the bathroom pulling the door shut behind him quietly. He then made his way down the hallway inside of the master bedroom and picked up the pillow from off the bed. Next, he walked out of the bedroom and made a beeline towards Antonio's bedroom. He turned the knob gently and pushed his way inside of the bedroom. The light coming from the master bedroom's television set shined down the corridor and outlined Apocalypse as he stood in the doorway. Apocalypse stood where he was watching Antonio sleep peacefully.

Apocalypse had it in mind to destroy everything that Marquan loved and then him. He had already set Adele down the road to addiction, now he was going to suffocate his son. He knew doing this was sure to fuck Marquan up royally once he found out, which was why he was going to do it.

Apocalypse smiled evilly as he slowly walked towards the boy's bed, holding his pillow up by both ends. Before he knew it he was standing over Antonio's bed. He went to smother the innocent child when something Marquan had said that day at the cookout came to mind.

Man, soon as I reach my million dolla goal, I'm taking my family and I'm getting the fuck outta the hood. I know if my black ass stays here, I'ma either end up murdered, or locked up for the rest of my life. I sho' don't want Antonio growing up here. The last thing I want for my boy is for him to be gangbanging tryna be just like his goddamn daddy. That would kill me, I mean really fucking destroy me. You know what I mean, cuz?

Apocalypse smiled fiendishly and nodded. Right then, Antonio was stirring awake from his sleep. He rose up in bed and twisted his knuckle at the corner of his eye, wincing.

"Uncle…Uncle Poc? What're you doing here?"

"I just came through to check on you and ya moms." He lied. "Here, I brought you a pillow." He tucked the pillow he'd come into the boy's bedroom with behind his other pillow. Antonio laid his head against the pillows and Apocalypse draped the covers back over him. "Goodnight, nephew," He kissed him on the side of his head and touched his shoulder affectionately.

Standing over Antonio, he thought to himself, *When I get finished witchu, lil' cuz, you gone be one of the coldest gangstas to have ever walked the streets of South Central, Los Angeles, that's onna gang!*

Apocalypse made his way to the door and pulled it open. He gave Antonio one last look before continuing out of the door and pulling it shut behind him.

~A few days later~

Apocalypse was smiling like a mothafucka as he nodded his head to WC's *The Shadiest One*, which was pumping from his vehicle's speakers. He'd just left a meeting with his new plug on the other side of the city. He'd just closed a fifty brick deal for a lovely price per kilo. Needless to say, he was happier than a pig in shit. With this amount of cocaine in his possession, he was about to change the weather in California in the middle of the summer. He was about to make it snow forever out of that bitch.

"Yeahhhh, boy," Apocalypse glanced back and forth between the windshield and the ashtray, which his half smoked blunt was residing inside of. Sticking the blunt in his mouth, he picked up the lighter and fired it up. After sucking on the end of the blunt, he blew out smoke and tossed his lighter aside. His head was on a swivel as he took in all of his surroundings, smiling. When he looked to his right again, the jovial expression dropped from his face when he saw some fools hustling on his corner.

Instantly, Apocalypse dabbed out the blunt he'd just lit up. He parked around the corner from the store that he saw the niggaz hustling out in front of. Reaching underneath the driver seat, he pulled out his gun and cocked that bitch. Opening the driver's door, he hopped out and stuck his banga in front of his jeans. Afterwards, he slammed the door shut and made his way around the corner. En route, he looked around to see if there was anybody watching him. The few people that were around were going about their everyday life and minding their business.

As Apocalypse neared the fools that were hustling on his corner, he could hear the conversation between two of them.

"Yo', DeTay, this mothafuckin' corna jumpin', cuz. We done founda gold mine out this bitch, for real, for real." A tall, long neck nigga wearing an L.A Dodgers fitted cap and matching jersey said to a light skinned dude.

DeTay, who was the light skinned dude, rocked a thin mustache and a mole above his upper lip. He wore an untied doo-rag over his head, white T-shirt and sagging jeans. At the moment, he was eating a bag of Sunflower seeds and spitting their shells out on the sidewalk.

"I told you, cuz, stick with me, and you'll neva grow broke again." DeTay dapped up his homeboy.

"Yo', you holdin'?" Apocalypse asked the nigga in the L.A fitted cap.

The nigga in the L.A fitted cap frowned, looking him up and down, "Cuz, who the fuck is you?"

"Come on now, man, you know me..." he looked at him like he was waiting for recognition to come to him.

"Cuz, you know this nigga?" L.A fitted cap looked to DeTay.

"Hell naw, I don't know this fool!" DeTay scowled as he spit out more shells from his Sunflower seeds.

"You should, 'cause this my mothafuckin' corna y'all hustlin' on!" Apocalypse's face twisted into a mask of hatred and he pulled out his gun. Pointing it at fitted cap's sneaker, he pulled the trigger and his lanky ass dropped to the ground. He hollered out in excruciation and held his bleeding foot with both hands, blood oozing between his fingers.

When homie got shot in the foot, two of his homeboys took off running and left DeTay behind. DeTay had dropped his bag of Sunflower seeds and went to draw his gun, but he was too slow on the draw. That nigga Apocalypse pointed his smoking gun at his face as he mad dogged him.

"Move a fuckin' muscle and that's yo' ass!" Apocalypse glared at him. Still pointing his gun at him, he removed the banga from his waistline and ejected the magazine. Having kicked the magazine off the curb, he flung the gun aside and addressed DeTay. "What's yo' name?"

"DeTay," DeTay answered. His hands were up and his palms were showing now. He looked like he was afraid of being shot.

Apocalypse took the money out of DeTay's pocket and the drugs out of L.A fitted cap's pocket. He stuffed the money inside of pocket and looked at his fist. When he unfolded it, there were eight off white crack rocks in his palm, which he dropped to the sidewalk. He then stomped the narcotics and scraped his foot back against them. When he did this, the crack rocks were left mashed against the sidewalk like gum, with the imprint of his sneaker embedded on them.

"Alright, DeTay," Apocalypse finally got back to addressing the young man after completing his actions. "I don't wanna see you or yo' punk ass homeboys on my corna again. 'Cause if I do," he pressed his gun against the side of his big ass nose, causing his eyes to bulge with terror. "I'ma lay every last one of you bitches down, is that undastood, bitch-boy?"

"Yeah, yeah, it's understood, I got chu!"

"Good. Now, pick this bleedin' ass nigga up and kick rocks." Apocalypse pointed his gun at L.A fitted cap. He watched as DeTay got his homeboy to his feet and threw his arm around his shoulders. He then helped him limp away from out of the front of the store, dripping blood along the way. Once Apocalypse watched them for a minute, he tucked his gun back on him and made his way back around the corner. A moment later, he was jumping behind the wheel of his car and peeling away.

Police car sirens filled the air as he ripped up the residential block.

CHAPTER SIX

A few months later

A blunt dangled from Apocalypse's lips as he sat on the living room couch. He was hunched over playing Madden, thumbs jabbing on the buttons of the controller, causing it to teeter from left to right. All of his tattoos were on display being that he only had on his boxer briefs. Apocalypse's tongue hung out the corner of his mouth. He was really into the game he was playing, it was his sole focus. So much so that his hunger pains didn't bother him as much as they were earlier. You see, a few hours ago he'd sent Adele out to get him some Mexican food, but she hadn't returned yet. He'd tried to hit her up on her cell phone, but then he remembered she'd sold it for heroin. Being that she'd fucked it off, he refused to buy her ass a new one because she'd wind up doing the same shit again.

Fuck is this broad at, man? I'm starvin' like a mothafuckin' hostage, Apocalypse thought to himself when he heard his stomach growling. He was about to call up Pizza Hut, but then he remembered that he lived out of their range of delivery. *Fuck,* he shook his head and took a deep breath. *I shoulda never sent her ol' dope head ass out to get me somethin' to eat, cuz.*

Hearing someone coming through the door, Apocalypse paused his video game and dabbed his blunt out inside of the ashtray. When he looked up he saw Adele coming through the door. His forehead wrinkled when he saw that she didn't have any bags of food in her hands.

"Yo', I know you just didn't walk up in this mothafucka without the food I sent cho ass out for! I just know you didn't!" Apocalypse said, he already knew the answer to his question and he was pissed the fuck off.

Adele stopped where she was, looking stuck for a response. She didn't know what she was going to say to him because she for damn sure forgot the food he'd sent her out for.

"My…my bad, I forgot." Adele scratched up her arm and avoided eye contact with him.

"You forgot?" he rose to his feet and threw the controller down to the floor. "Bitch, you been gone three hours in my mothafuckin' ride, and you ain't come back here with so much as a goddamn honey bun! Ain't shit in the 'frig, butta box of baking soda! You left me and Ant in here starvin'!"

"I said, 'I forgot', what chu want me to do? Damn!" she made her way towards the hallway, en route to the bedroom.

Angry, Apocalypse ran up on her and grabbed her by her arm. "What I want chu to do is get me somethin' to eat, now!" he squeezed her arm so tight that she grimaced. It felt like if he applied more pressure that the veins in her arm were going to explode.

"Alright, alright, alright, you hurtin' me," Adele grabbed him by the wrist and tried to pry his hand from off her arm.

"I don't give a fuck, go get me somethin' to eat, shit!" he shook her violently by her arm and made her frizzy individual braids bounce a little. She almost fell from his brute force.

"Okay. I am, fuck!"

"Yo', stupid ass, man, you get on my fuckin' nerves with that shit!" Still holding her arm, he shoved her and let her arm go. She stumbled a little bit, but recovered before she could fall. Standing where she was, she rubbed her hand up and down her aching arm, wincing.

Still rubbing her arm, Adele watched as Apocalypse walked back over to the couch and sat down, picking the controller back up. He was about to start back playing Madden until he looked over at Adele and she looked like she was waiting for something.

"Fuck you still doin' here, bitch? Breeze," he picked up his half smoken blunt from the ashtray and stuck it between his lips. He then picked up the lighter from off the coffee table. He was just about to re-light the end of his blunt when she said something that stopped the flame of his lighter at the withered end of his blunt. Hearing this, he tossed his lighter back down and snatched the blunt from out of his mouth. He then turned his angry eyes on her. The look in his eyes could have turn hell into an ice berg. "Fuck you mean you need money for the food?"

"I need some mo' money, I spent what chu gave me earlier." She said timidly, as she continued to rub her arm, eyes cast down at the floor. She was too afraid to look the nigga in the eyes. How could she tell him that she'd spent the money he'd given her for food on dope? She knew that he'd flip his mothafucking wig as soon as she broke the news to him.

"I gave you the money for the fuckin' food, so what the hell did you do with it? And I swear 'fore God if you lie to me I'ma beat the brakes offa yo' ass, on my momma, cuz! That's on alla my dead homies rest in peace." He tossed the half smoken blunt onto the coffee table alongside the lighter he'd been trying to light it with earlier. She now had his undivided attention.

Gathering the courage to look him in the eyes, she lifted her head and looked him in his face, saying, "I used it to get high."

With that said, Apocalypse rose from off the couch and walked halfway across the room. Stopping, he cupped his hand at his ear and leaned towards her, saying, "I'm sorry, I think I heard you wrong. I thought chu said you spent the money I gave you to buy food with on dope. Now I know I couldn't have heard you say no shit like that, so do me a favor and run that by me one mo' time, boss." He waited for her response, still holding his cupped hand at his ear.

Adele swallowed the lump of fear that had formed in her throat and looked to the floor. She took a deep breath trying to calm her nerves. She was afraid of what was going to happen once she repeated herself. Adele wasn't any one's fool; she knew Apocalypse heard what she said. The moment she opened her mouth again, she was sure that he was going to go upside her head like he'd done so many times before, but what choice did she have in the matter? If she didn't tell him again then he was going to beat her ass, and if she did, he was still going to beat her ass. She was in a *damned if I do, damned if I don't* situation.

Fuck it. It is what it is. I shot up his money so now I gotta deal with the consequences, Adele thought to herself.

She then took a deep breath and answered him. "I used yo' money to cop…"

Brack!

Apocalypse punched her dead in her mouth and her head launched backwards. The impact from the punch caused her eyelids to squeeze shut and her teeth to clench, showcasing her bloody mouth. She bumped the back of her head against the wall and slid down to the floor. The bitch saw stars, half moons and chirping birds circling her head.

"That's what the fuck I thought chu said!" Apocalypse spat heatedly. Afterwards, he went to work stomping her ass out like she was a fucking man. Once he got exhausted with stomping her out, he started punching her in her face and the rest of her exposed body. "Bitch, you must think I'm some fuck-nigga that's for play! You think you gone spend up my paypa on yo' get-high? I'm insulted, bitch, you got me so fucked up! You know what I'ma do, hoe? Of course you don't, but I'ma tell you, though. I'ma 'bouta burn yo' mothafuckin' ass up. Come here, hoe!" He grabbed her by her ankle and dragged her towards the kitchen. She kicked and screamed trying to get free, but her efforts were useless. Whatever he wanted to do to her was going to happen whether she wanted it to or not.

"Noooooooooo! Noooooo, lemme go, Apocalypse! I'm sorry, I'm sorrryyyyy! I swear to God, I won't do it again! Please, don't do this to me, I'm beggin' you!" Adele begged for mercy, but homeboy wasn't having it.

"Bitch, fuck what chu talkin' 'bout, yo' ass gone learn to…" his words died in his throat. He tried to pull her over the threshold inside of the kitchen, but something stopped him in his tracks. He looked over his shoulder and saw that she'd grabbed hold of the corner of the kitchen counter. "Let it go, bitch! I said, 'let it go!'." Seeing that she wasn't going to listen to him, he took a frustrated breath and started stomping her hands. She howled out in pain, but held fast to the corner of the counter. Realizng this, he kicked her in the face twice. The second kick busted her nose and had blood squirting from out of it. As soon as she smacked her hands over her squirting nose, he pulled her ass inside of the kitchen with no hassle. Holding onto her ankle with one hand, he turned on the burners of the stove. *Frooosh!* The blushish flames burst free and licked at the air.

"There we go," Apocalypse smiled vindictively as he feasted his eyes on the flames of the burner. "Now bring yo' thick ass here, bitch!" He grabbed a handful of her individual braids and began pulling her towards the stove. Adele screamed in horror and grabbed him by his wrist, trying her damndest to break free of his stranglehold. She kicked and screamed constantly as she was dragged along. All she could think about was having her face being burned off, and how excruciating it must be.

"Please, no, stop! I won't do it no mo', I won't do it no mo'!" Adele pleaded over and over again. Tears burst through her eyes and slid down her cheeks. Her mouth stretched wide open feeling the braids in her scalp being pulled so hard that beads of blood oozed out of her head.

"Oh, I know you won't, especially not after this." Apocalypse put her in a headlock that made her eyes water and caused her face to turn red; a vein at her temple threatened to burst under so much pressure from his bicep. She clawed at his flesh but it didn't do any good. He scowled and clenched his teeth, applying more pressure to her throat through his bicep. Hearing her gag and feeling her struggle, he decided to loosen his grip around her neck. This was only because he really wanted to set her black ass on fire while she was conscious. "Yeah, hoe, you gone respect my gangsta once it's all said and done." Still holding her in a headlock, he grabbed a handful of her braids again and brought them near the burner. Her braids were nearly in the fire when a battle cry ripped through the air.

"Get off my mommy!"

Snikkkt!

"Aaahhhhhhhhhh!" Apocalypse screamed out in bloody murder as he felt fire rip through his back. His eyes bulged and his mouth stretched so far open that every cavity was shown inside of his grill. Instantly, he dropped Adele's ass to the floor. She gagged and coughed rubbing her neck, staring up at him accusingly, "You lil' fucka!" Apocalypse called Antonio out of his name once he'd turned around to find him pointing a butcher's knife at him, which was dripping blood on the floor.

"Leave my mommy alone!" Antonio shouted at him. His eyebrows were arched and his lips were twisted. He was ready to cut a nigga a hundred different ways for fucking with his momma.

"You lil' bitch ass nigga, you got the nerve to cut me, after all the toys and shit I done bought cho lil' ass? Gemme that fuckin' knife for I fuck you with it…" Apocalypse went to grab the butcher's knife and Antonio sliced his palm open. "Ah, fuck!" he drew his hand back and cradled it. When he made his wounded hand into a fist and saw blood seeping between his fingers, he became angrier than he was before. "Alright, I ain't playin' witcho lil' ass no mo'! Now gemme the knife, gemme the goddamn knife now!" He reached out for the knife and Antonio tried to cut his ass again.

Snikt! Snikt! Snikt!

The butcher's knife cut through the air several times. It nearly opened up another wound on Apocalypse, but he snatched his hand back in time to avoid another injury.

While this was going on Adele was still trying to recover from being beat down and choked out.

"Get out, leave us alone!" Antonio hollered out, still holding the dripping knife. His face was balled up tighter, his nostrils were flaring, and his chest was jumping with every breath.

He was afraid, but he'd die protecting his mother if need be. His biogical father had always told him that he was the man of the house once he was gone, and it was his duty to love and protect his mother. That's what he was doing now.

Apocalypse snatched the damp towel from off the kitchen sink and twisted it up tight. By doing this, he created a handmade whip, but he had other uses in mind for it. When Antonio swung the butcher's knife at him again, he whipped the towel out at him. The towel wrapped around the bottom of the knife where the handle began. Tugging with all of his might, Apocalypse snatched the bucther's knife clean from out of the boy's hand. The knife flew across the kitchen and deflected off the wall, landing on the floor.

Terror filled Antonio's eyes and he gasped. Apocalypse smiled wickedly before he'd back hand slapped the boy, dropping him to the linoleum. On his hands and knees, Antonio rubbed his throbbing cheek. He looked up just in time to see his surrogate father kicking him in the stomach and knocking the wind out of him. The impact from the kick lifted him up and dropped him back down on the side of his face. He lay there breathing in pain and unable to get back up.

Standing over him, Apocalypse wrapped the towel around his wounded hand and tied it tight with his teeth. "Lil' mothafucka tryna box with the God, fuck is wrong witchu, cuz?"

"My baby, my baby," Adele scrambled over to Antonio and pulled him to her. He looked to be dazed as he scared at her, with the side of his face swelling from the backhand slap. "Are you, okay, baby boy?" she asked as teardrops fell from her eyes.

"I'm…I'm sorry, mommy, I tried to save you, but he was just too strong." Antonio said wincing and holding his stomach.

"It's okay, it's alright." She hugged and kissed her son.

While Adele was tending to Antonio, Apocalypse went to clean his wounds inside of the bathroom. Afterwards, he got dressed and came back inside of the kitchen, where he dropped an outfit for Antonio to put on. Instead of a towel tied around his wounded hand, he now had a blue bandana around it.

"Put cho clothes on, cuz, we gone go for a lil' ride." Apocalypse told Antonio with a serious expression and voice.

"Wait a minute, where are you takin' 'em?" Adele panicked, getting in front of her son to stop her man from taking him to do only God knew what to him.

Apocalypse frowned up and glared at her evilly. His jaws throbbed with hostility. "Like I said, 'we goin' on a lil' ride.' Now, let the lil' nigga get dressed so we can roll."

"No, no," Adele shook her head. "I'm not lettin' him go witchu unless you promise me you not goin' to hurt 'em."

"Fine," he said like she was getting on his fucking nerves. He then raised his hand up in the air and said, "Scouts honor, I won't puff that lil' nigga'z wig out. Now move the fuck outta the way so he can get dressed and we can roll."

With that said, Adele stood aside and watched her son as he got dressed. Once he was done, she hugged and kissed him, assuring him that everything was going to be alright.

****

Apocalypse gangsta leaned in his car, nodding his head to 2pac's *Me Against The World.* Occasionally, he'd glance back and forth between the windshield and Antonio. The boy wasn't paying any attention to him; his eyes were focused out of the window, watching the happenings in the streets. He had a scowl fixed on his face, but Apocalypse could tell that he was a little nervous. Seeing this, he turned down the volume on the stereo and addressed the youngsta.

"You scared, cuz?" Apocalypse asked as he looked back and forth between the windshield and Antonio.

"Who scared?" Antonio scowled further and looked at his father's best friend like he was crazy.

"Who scared?" he mocked his voice and laughed, "Yo' ass, nigga, who else in this mothafucka besides me and you?"

"Nah," he shook his head. "I ain't scared."

"Bullshit!" Apocalypse took on a serious expression. He then reached over and placed his hand on the boy's chest. Eyes focused through the windshield, he waited until he felt his heart beating. "Yeah, just like I thought. Yo' ass scared, ain't nothin' to be ashamed of. You don't know where I'm takin' you or what I'ma 'bouta do to you. You don't have a clue. As a matter of fact," he reached underneath the seat and pulled out his gun. "I could pull this mothafuckin' car ova, nod you, and leave yo' lil' ass on the side of the road," Seeing the gun in Apocalypse's hand caused Antonio's eyes to bulge and his heart to race. "See how yo' eyes lit up just then? You don't know what I'ma 'bouta do with this strap, so who could blame you for bein' scared, you feel me?" Antonio nodded. "I thought that chu would, but don't wet it though, cuz. I ain't finna pop you," he slid the gun back underneath the seat. He then went back to gangsta leaning in his car, "You hungry, young nigga?"

"Yeah. I'm starvin'," he admitted.

"Me too."

Apocalypse rolled up to McDonald's. He ordered his self something and got Antonio whatever he wanted. Shortly, he was driving off and they were both eating Big Macs, occasionally taking sips of their strawberry shakes. Once Apocalypse finished off his French fries, he balled up the wrapper of his burger and let down the window, throwing the balled up wrapper out into the street. The rest of the ride he listened to his music, and occasionally glanced at Antonio, who was devouring his Big Mac hungrily.

Before Antonio knew it they were driving up to the emergency ward at the hospital. They hopped out and made their way inside. The medical facility was scarcely filled so they didn't have to wait long. About an hour later, Apocalypse was being called to the back. He went through all of the shit hospital staff puts you through before your medical emergency is taken care of. You know? Your blood pressure, weight, height and a series of other questions. Once that was out of the way, Apocalypse wounds were being stitched up by a pretty nurse who he openly flirted with. He hollered at her like Antonio wasn't even there. For a moment the boy thought he was invisible, but that wasn't the case. Apocalypse just didn't give a fuck.

"Alright, lil' momma, I'ma holla at chu, take care of yo' self," he finished writing her number down and slid it inside of his pocket. He then took her by her hand and kissed her tenderly on it as he held her gaze. Afterwards, he patted her hand and assured her that they were going to go out on a date before he motioned for Antonio to follow him towards the exit.

****

Apocalypse drove through the city streets seeing the back brake lights of vehicles driving ahead of him. He took casual pulls from a withering blunt as he took in his surroundings, blowing smoke into the air. His eyelids were narrowed and his eyes were red webbed. He slowly nodded his head to Westside Connection's *Gangstas Make The World Go 'Round*, which was playing softly from the speakers.

He looked over at Antonio with his weed slanted eyes and held the blunt pinched between his fingers out to him, but he declined.

"Suit yo' self, lil' nigga, mo' fa me," Apocalypse continued to indulged in his poison of choice. Once he'd gotten the blunt down to the size of a thumb nail, he snuffed out its ember inside of the ashtray. This left a black smear behind and a little smoke rose into the air. He then fanned the air with his hand to extinguish any smoke that may still be lingering. "Cuz, how long I been fuckin' witcho momma now?" he asked Antonio, glancing back and forth between him and the windshield.

"A minute now," Antonio said with his arms folded across his chest. He looked to be pretty angry with what had gone down between him and Apocalypse.

"Four months to be exact…Four mothafuckin' months. Now, you'd think since yo' old punk ass daddy didn't want anything to do with you, and I took you on as my own, you'd have the utmost respect fa a nigga, but, nahhhhh, you don't respect me. I offer you a helpin' hand and you tell me to go fuck myself. Now, what kind of disrespectful shit is that, huh?" Antonio didn't say anything. He sat there staring out of the passenger side mirror, acting like the nigga wasn't even talking to him. "Huh?" When the boy didn't answer, he continued to say *Huh* and smack him upside his head. The impact of his palm caused the little nigga's head to jump forward. The youth scowled and his face flushed with redness. He was pissed off and wanted to throw hands with Apocalypse, but he was smart for his age and realized that he'd never win in a head up fade with him.

When Antonio still didn't answer, Apocalypse was hotter than he was earlier with his anger. He wanted to grab the youth up and toss his little ass out of the moving car, but he knew better than to do that. He knew exactly what he had to do in order for the little nigga to fear and respect him.

For a minute Apocalypse looked back and forth between the windshield and Antonio. His eyebrows were sloped and his nose was scrunched up, nostrils flaring. "Okay, alright," he nodded his head with an evil grin etched across his face. "Check this out; I got somethin' I wanna show you."

Apocalypse bent a few corners and he ended up on a dimly lit block. He killed the engine and slumped low in his seat, motioning for Antonio to do the same. Looking just over the dashboard, the two of them watched a few Mexican teenagers play soccer in the front yard of a white house with a dirt patched lawn.

"What are we doing here?" Antonio asked in a hushed tone. He checked his surroundings, and then focused back on the teenage kids playing soccer on the block.

"You see that Spanish kid right there, with the Mohawk and the yellow and green soccer jersey?" Apocalypse nodded in the direction of the kid he was observing closely. At the moment, the Mexican kid was bouncing the soccer ball from knee to knee with expertise.

"Yeah, I see 'em, what are you 'bout a do?" Antonio's forehead wrinkled. He looked from Apocalypse to the kid playing with the soccer ball.

A smiling Apocalypse sat quietly observing the scenery before him. Insanity twinkled in his eyes as a smirk graced his lips. He'd just saw the soccer ball being smacked from out of the kid wearing the Mohawk's possession, flying toward the street. The ball bounced out of the yard and rolled out into the middle of the street. The kid with the Mohawk threw playful punches at the kid that had smacked the ball away from him. They laughed and talked shit before the kid with the Mohawk made a beeline out of the yard towards the soccer ball that had rolled out into the street.

"You 'bouta see right now, lil' nigga," Apocalypse sat up in his seat excitedly. He then cranked up his vehicle and pulled away from the curb. After cutting off his headlights, he mashed the gas pedal and sent his ride flying down the block. His whip blew past the other cars lined up on the block, leaving debris and loose trash in the air. From the look on Apocalypse's face Antonio could tell that he was in anticipation for something…he just didn't know what. But he was damn sure about to find out.

"What? Wait…What're you talking about?" Antonio looked back and forth between Apocalypse and the windshield at the boy wearing the Mohawk.

"Pay close attention," Apocalypse said, looking like he was in a trance. All of his attention was focused on the youngsta wearing the Mohawk. The man's heart thudded and his chest rose and fell, as he tightened his grip on the steering wheel. He mashed the gas pedal further and the hand on the speedometer spun around past the numbers hastily. The Regal was speeding so fast down the residential street that the cars lined up on the block looked like flashes of colors.

The kid wearing the Mohawk had just bent down to pick up the soccer ball. At that moment, Apocalypse activated the headlights. They popped on brightly and blinded the young man, making him narrow his eyelids and place his hand over his brows. He was trying to see exactly who or what it was speeding toward him.

Antonio's head whipped back and forth between Apocalypse and the youth standing in the middle of the residential street. He was fearful of what was about to be done to the innocent young man.

"Wait a minute, you're not gonna...you are!" Antonio finally realized what Apocalypse intended to do to the Mexican kid that had just picked up the soccer ball. "Noooooo!"

Antonio tried to grab the steering wheel away from Apocalypse, but he punched him in the chest. The impact caused him to fall up against the passenger door. The boy tried to grab the steering wheel again, but this time he was punched in the side of the head. The assault made the boy slightly dizzy. By the time he shook the fog off his brain and looked ahead, it was far too late.

"Nooooooo!" Antonio outstretched his hand towards the Mexican kid in the street like he could help him from where he was inside of the car.

The kid wearing the Mohawk eyes stretched wide open in fear and his mouth formed an O. He went to run back inside of the yard, but he wasn't quick enough on his feet.

Ba-dunk!

The kid went up into the air and the soccer ball went even higher, deflecting off the roof of a nearby parked car. The kid landed on the side of his head and his body came behind him, falling last. His face was bloody and three of his limbs were broken. He lay where he was in the street breathing funny and struggling to get upon his feet.

Seeing the horrible incident, the young man's family came running out of the yard to attend to him. At that moment, the Regal came to a screeching halt, lurching forward. Apocalypse had just mashed on the brake pedal and looked over his shoulder out of the back window. Through it, he saw the kid he'd ran over family spilling out of the yard. The kid was struggling to get upon his feet, but his broken limbs left him immobile.

"Lil' Spic bastard still kickin', time to change that," Apocalypse threw his vehicle in *reverse* and mashed the gas pedal. The car sped towards its intended victim. Again, Antonio tried to grab hold of the steering wheel but Apocalypse fought him off.

"Mommaaaaaa!" the kid wearing the Mohawk screamed bloody murder, the back brake lights illuminating his form.

"Miguellllll!" the boy's mother called out to him, tears spilling down his cheeks. She was a head of the pack of the youngsta's family, her hand outstretched in an attempt to reach her son in time.

Bunk! Bunk!

The Regal rocked from left to right as it ran over the Mexican youth, killing him off violently. The young man's family screamed out in horror seeing their loved one horrifically murdered in cold blood.

Apocalypse brought the Regal to a halt and looked at the roadkill he'd created himself. The Mexican teenager looked like a pile of bloody flesh. Apocalypse smiled in satisfaction, but he wasn't done yet. Not by a long shot. Seeing the young man's family at the curb screaming and sobbing, he threw the car into *drive* and mashed the gas pedal. The automobile took off like it had the first time he ran over Miguel.

Antonio, tears streaming down his cheeks, sat there helplessly watching what was to unfold next.

Bunk! Dunk!

The Regal's tires ran over Miguel's head and burst it like a pimple. Blood and brain fragments oozed out of the poor kid's skull into the street. The vehicle rolled along with the victim's Mohawk and brain fragments plastered on its tires. The slain youth's family dropped down to their knees hollering aloud. Seeing what had happened to their loved one brought the family great grief. They all ran out into the street to see the bloody mess that was once Miguel Rodriguez Jr.

The Regal sped off down the street until its back brake lights disappeared into the night.

****

Apocalypse pulled up inside of a neighborhood self carwash and killed the engine of his Regal. Looking over at Antonio, he saw him crying his eyes out and looking at his hands, which were visibly shaking

"That was fucked up what I did to lil' Felipe back there, huh?" Apocalypse asked calmly as he reached underneath his seat and pulled out his banga. "Yeah, I know, lil' cuz, you ain't even gotta say so. I mowed someone's innocent child down like a fuckin' dog in the streets. The crazy part about it is neither him nor his family had done anything to me to deserve that. So, imagine what I'm goin' to do to a lil' punk mothafucka like you that raised his hand to me," he said, pressing his Glock against the side of Antonio's head and causing it to bend to the side. The boy's eyes bulged and his mouth quivered uncontrollably. "The next time yo' lil' ass call yo' self puttin' yo' goddamn hands on me, I'ma blow yo' stinkin' head off. You understand me?"

"Y…Yes," Antonio stammered with his eyes staring out of their corners at the black compact gun pressed against his temple. His hands were up in surrender and his bladder had grown hot, piss threatening to burst from his penis.

"Another thing," Apocalypse continued. "Yo' momma is my bitch, that's my pussy. So, she does what I say when I say it, or I'ma discipline her ass however I see fit. You understand me?"

Antonio nodded rapidly. "Let me hear you say it." The boy obliged him. "Good. Now here," he smacked a few dollars into his lap. "Get cho ass out this car and wash it…hurry the fuck up too, so we can get rid of this mothafucka." Antonio snatched up the wrinkled bills and hurriedly hopped out of the car. He paid the fee he needed to get the car washing system going. Once it started up, he scrubbed the car down, getting it soapy. He then went about the task of rinsing the car off. Once he was done, he hopped back into the front passenger seat and Apocalypse pulled off.

Apocalypse took the Regal to a chop shop that he knew of that one of his homeboy's ran. He got a couple hundred dollars for the car, and watched for a moment as it was dismantled. Afterwards, he caught a cab home. The next day, he would have one of the homies take him to a used car lot to find himself another vehicle, identical to his last one.

CHAPTER SEVEN

The next day

Marquan stood in line impatiently waiting for his turn to use the pay phone. As soon as it was his turn, he snatched up the telephone and proceeded to make his call. Once the time came, he stated his name and waited for the chance to talk to whoever had accepted his phone call.

"Well, goddamn. It's been months, it's 'bout time someone answered." Maquan waited for a response but he didn't receive one. He did, however, hear the television in the background which was playing cartoons. His brows furrowed and he said, "Hello?"

"'Sup, my nigga?" a familiar voice asked.

Marquan's brows furrowed further as he wondered why Apocalypse was answering the phone at his house. "'Sup, cuz? What chu doing at the house?"

"Oh, you ain't know, cuz? I'm the new nigga that's dickin' yo' baby momma down," he took a sip from the straw in his Hi-C juice box. He was laid across the couch in blue Dickies, socks pulled up near his knees, and corduroy house shoes. He was wearing a wife beater, and the gunshot wound on his shoulder was fully healed.

There were toys scattered throughout the living room, and at the moment, little Antonio was playing with his Tonka truck.

"Yo' , cuz, now ain't even the time to be playing, I need you to see about getting me a lawyer before I go to trial."

"Nigga, I ain't gettin' you shit! You gone rot up in that mothafucka! Fuck I look like helpin' yo' bitch ass?" he frowned up. Hearing the suction sound coming from the Hi-C juice box, Apocalypse shook it to confirm that it was empty. Once he found that it was, he burped and tossed it aside.

"Yo', Poc, is you high or something, my nigga? 'Cause you tripping right now, for real for real."

"I'm speakin' with a real soba tongue, my head is clear, homeboy. So, I hope you undastand me when I say that I ain't got no holla fa you. That bullshit you tangled and twisted in, you gone have to face on yo' own."

Marquan's nostrils flared and a vein at his temple twitched violently. He shut his eyelids and clenched his jaws. He then took a deep breath to calm himself down before speaking again.

"Alright, cuz," he began. "You don't wanna help a nigga out? Cool, just lemme holla at Adele so she can see about getting my paypa and getting me a lawyer."

"You mean that two-hunnit racks you had saved up? All that's mine now, homie."

"My nigga, if you spent my money you betta get ready to…" Marquan stopped himself short, he wasn't trying to threaten this nigga over the jack, and have the cops all up in his shit. Besides, if he did manage to get somebody to pop his ass, he didn't want the heat coming back at him over this phone call.

While this was going on, Adele had came walking out of the kitchen with a small red T-shirt on that left her ass cheeks peeking out of the bottom of it. She had just warmed up some left overs from the other night. Seeing her meaty buttocks jiggling as she walked past him, Apocalypse smiled thirstily and smacked her on her ass.

"Awww, mothafucka," She reached over and smacked him on his arm. "That shit hurt!"

"Adele? Adele?" Marquan called out his baby momma over and over again, having heard her voice.

"That bitch gone back into the room, man. She 'bouta get ready for me to blow her back out once I'm done shootin' the shit witcho bitch ass."

"Loc, put my baby momma onna phone 'fore I…"

"'Fore you what, nigga?" Apocalypse scowled as he cut him short. He then sat up on the couch and gave him his undivided attention. "You can't do shit, cuz, notta mothafuckin' thang! Yo' hoe ass is in jail! I'm yo' bitch's new nigga and yo' son's new daddy! So, sit tight and get used to it! You may not like it, but chu gone have to roll with it, 'cause that's how it is now. You feel me?"

Marquan pressed the telephone closer to his ear and turned his shoulder, so none of the other inmates could hear him. "Look here, you bitch ass nigga, if you don't…"

Apocalypse disconnected the call.

Marquan's eyebrows rose and he looked at the telephone, surprised. Instantly, he hung up and called back.

"On me, cuz, if I was out I'd go over there and smash this mark ass nigga!" he punched the telephone booth and listened intently as the phone rang. His eyebrows were sloped and a vein was bulging at his temple. As soon as homeboy answered the phone he was going off on his black ass. The operator came on the line once the phone was picked up on the other end. The operator announced that the answerer had a collect call and allowed him to say his name. "Marquan!" The operator went on to ask if the answerer would accept the call. They did. "Hello?" he listened for a moment as the phone was passed. "Hello?" Marquan said into the phone again, he was about ready to bang on dude, but the voice that came on the line took him off guard.

"Hey, daddy," Antonio spoke into the receiver.

"Hey…Hey, lil' man, how you doin'?" The hostility drained from off Marquan's face and voice. The last thing he expected was his baby boy answering the telephone.

"Fine," Antonio replied as he sat on Apocalypse's lap. Old boy was tying a blue bandana around his head while he played with his Tonka truck. Once he had done this, he looped his gold Cuban link chain around the little nigga'z neck. The boy listened to what Apocalypse was whispering in his ear attentively. He then repeated it to his father. "Daddy, my new daddy said he's my daddy now, and he's the one running shit from now on. And if you don't like it, suck his dick, this crip!"

"Antonio, don't talk like that! I'm yo' father, don't listen to what Apocalypse is telling you, son. He ain't no man, he's a coward! Real men don't talk shit over the phone! They line it up; they get it from the shoulders! Only women lip box and play lil' punk ass games like…"

"Cuz, you tellin' yo' son I'ma coward? Nigga, fuck you and yo' dead parents! You ol' punk ass, bitch ass, busta ass nigga, mark ass nigga, suck my dick!" Apocalypse spat heatedly.

"Fuck you, cuz!" Marquan fired back.

"Fuck you, too, nigga!" He roared back.

"Fuuuuck youuuuu!" Marquan banged the telephone on the hook several times, violently. The multiple impacts of the telephone against the hook caused a reoccurring clanging sound and made surrounding inmates back away from him. They all wore furrowed brows and wondered what the fuck got him so fired up. Marquan walked off mad at the world, letting the telephone dangle from its cord. If he was certain about anything in his world, it was that Apocalypse was a mark ass nigga and he was going to kill him just as soon as he got released.

Marquan was in Men's Central County Jail for several months until he finally went to trial. He had to accept a public defender to work his case since Apocalypse stole his money and he couldn't afford his own lawyer. Without a decent lawyer on his side he knew he was fucked. The fools that the courts provided to work your case wasn't worth a shit. They didn't try to give you a fighting chance. They took whatever deal that the D.A threw out on the table for them, and Marquan's situation wasn't any different. Homie winded up getting ten years flat.

~A few nights later~

Naymond pushed the wheel of the G-ride that he'd procured for the night's mission. He and Apocalypse were dressed in black from head to toe. Covering their eyes were black sunglasses while neoprene masks covered the lower half of their faces. Apocalypse was busy loading the extended magazines into the butts of his Glocks. *Clicks! Clacks!* And

Pacts! Resonated throughout the confines of the vehicle, as he put hollow tip rounds into the heads of his matching weapons.

"You sho' this the corner them fuck-niggaz be serving on, cuz?" Naymond asked him as he looked back and forth between him and the windshield.

"Yep. This most definitely it," Apocalypse said, looking out of the passenger side window. "These the only mothafuckaz that's still tryna sling on my block. Niggaz musta thought shit got sweet 'cause Quan got locked up. Dumb bitches must don't know he ain't the only nigga from the gang that's 'bout this murda shit. I ain't new to this I'm true to this. They asses gone find out tonight though."

"You hollered at these niggaz before about slinging out here?" His forehead creased.

"Yeah, I hollered at the young nigga who seemed to be runnin' the show, DeTay. Cuz acted like he undastood, but when I drove by here the otha night, he and his people were still out here like the words of the realest nigga in the streets don't mean shit. Okay, okay," he nodded as he scowled and clenched his jaws. "I'ma show alla these bitches what time it is with me!"

"We gone tighten these bitch niggaz up, cuz. Don't even worry about it, I got chu all of the way faded." Naymond gripped his .9mm automatic firmly. "I think that's them coming up right now." He nodded to a few hoodlums kicking it out on the corner. It didn't take a rocket scientist to figure out that they were out in the streets hustling.

"Yeah, that's them. I can tell that's that nigga DeTay from his mannerisms. Well, I'ma 'bouta change alla that shit." Apocalypse tucked one of his Glocks into the front of his jeans, but held the other at his shoulders. He then positioned himself at the door, his freehand on the door's handle so he could hop out as soon as the vehicle halted.

The sounds of the squealing tires halting in the streets drew the attention of the fools serving crack on the corner. As soon as the G-ride stopped, Apocalypse jumped out and drew his second Glock. Naymond came out of the car right behind him with his .9mm automatic. It was time to get busy.

All of the hoodlums' eyes lit up and they scrambled away, seeing death roll forward. For as fast as they could run, not a man among them could outrun hollow tip bullets.

Blocka! Blocka! Blocka! Blocka! Blocka!

Splocka! Splocka! Splocka! Splocka! Splocka!

"Ahhhhhhh!"

"Arrrrrr!"

"Gaaaaah!"

"Rahhhhhh!"

Niggaz screamed and hollered feeling hot shit rip through their backs, abs, and skulls. Blood and brain fragments went up in the air and came raining down to the surface, blood droplets splattering on the ground. Hearing hurried foot falls at his right, Naymond whipped around expecting to see some of the fools they'd jumped out on coming at him. Instead he saw that nigga Apocalypse chasing after one lone survivor. Not long after came the gunfire that mimicked his very own.

"What I tell you, DeTay, stay the fuck off my corners, right? Right?" Apocalypse called out to him, running after him as fast as he could, both Glocks out at his side.

"Don't kill me, man, don't kill me! I'll leave, I'll leave tonight. I promise, I swear 'fore God!" DeTay called out over his shoulder, trying to get away from Apocalypse. The brazen crip had twin guns in his hands and he was sure he'd cut his black ass in half with them.

Nah, cuz, I gave youa chance, you didn't listen, now that's yo' ass!" Apocalypse slowed to a stop, breathing hard. His chest jumped up and down as he lifted and pointed his twin Glocks. Before his eyes he saw the backs of his guns, which were aimed at a fleeing DeTay's back as he ran for his life. He pulled the triggers of his weapons and they spat fire rapidly.

Blocka! Blocka! Blocka! Blocka!

Naymond heard Apocalypse's victim hollered out in agony as he flopped to the ground like a fish out of water. Looking down, he saw the poor bastard squirming and trying to get away. He watched as Apocalypse casually strolled over to DeTay with his trusty Glocks at his sides. He whistled like murder wasn't anything, but another day at the office. As soon as he stopped before him, DeTay slowly turned over to face him. The young nigga winced as he stared up at the killa. He lifted his hand and pleaded for his life; his begging fell on deaf ears as Apocalypse leveled his Glocks at his dome. He squeezed his triggers and set DeTay free from this life.

Blocka! Blocka! Blocka! Blocka! Blocka! Blocka!

Apocalypse lowered his smoking guns at his sides. He then took the time to admire his handiwork before tucking his warm burners on his waistline and jogging back towards the G-ride. He hopped into the front passenger seat and Naymond jumped behind the wheel. The doors of the G-ride slammed shut simultaneously and the vehicle drove off. The brake lights of the automobile disappeared into the darkness, just as police sirens filled the air.

****

Antonio sat on the floor watching cartoons and playing with his toys. Hearing the locks of the front door coming undone, he looked up to see Apocalypse entering. As soon as he crossed the threshold inside of the house, he whipped out his twin Glocks. He then shut the door behind him. The first thing Antonio noticed was the speckles of blood on his jeans and sneakers.

"'Sup, lil' cuz?" Apocalypse threw his head back. "Where yo' moms at?"

"Takin' a shower."

Without saying a word, Apocalypse headed to the back porch where he peeled off all his clothes. After he'd gotten the washer ready for a wash, he tossed his blood stained clothing inside. He was just about to shut the lid on the washer when he noticed the speckles of blood on his sneakers. He picked them up and looked between them, seeing the speckles of blood on them. Shrugging, he tossed his sneakers inside of the washer, too.

Once Apocalypse got the washer going, he picked his guns up and headed back down the hallway. He was in his wife beater, boxer briefs and socks when he entered the bathroom. When he opened the door he was greeted by a warm temperature of the shower water and a thick fog.

"Yo!" Apocalypse called out to Adele.

"Yeah?"

"I'm finna hop in witchu right quick."

Antonio made his way down the corridor listening to Apocalypse and his mother's conversation. Having made it to the bathroom door, he cracked it open just in time to see Apocalypse sitting his Glocks down on the porcelain sink. He then watched as his surrogate father, peeled off his wife beater and stepped out of his boxer briefs. Apocalypse was fully nude, displaying the hairs that led down his torso to the nappy nest of public hair, which was above his flaccid veined penis.

"There's dry blood on your neck and the side of your face. What happened?" Adele questioned with concern as she rubbed the side of Apocalypse's face. He'd just stepped inside of the shower and pulled the door closed.

"Niggaz wouldn't get off my cornas…thought shit was sweet 'round here, so I hadda show 'em it was sour."

"You okay?" she inquired as she applied body wash to a loofer and began washing him up. His back was to her and his palms were flat on the tiled walls of the tub.

"I'm straight."

"Good. I'm glad you made it home to me, daddy. Is there anything I can do to help you relax?"

"When we done in here fix me some tacos and then get ready so I can beat cho back up."

"Okay."

Antonio crept inside of the bathroom and carefully picked up one of Apocalypse's Glocks. *Wow,* he thought to himself as he held the four pounds of black metal and plastic in his innocent hands. Looking to the glass shower doors, he could see the silhouettes of his mother and her boyfriend. They were so engrossed in their conversation that they hadn't noticed he'd crept inside of the bathroom and picked up one of the lethal weapons.

Antonio journeyed down the corridor toying with the gun, which was still slightly warm from the murders it was used to commit just minutes ago. The boy stopped at the center of the hall and held the gun with both hands. He shut one eyelid and took aim at an imaginary bad guy. He then made gunshot noises with his mouth and visualized the bad guy falling as a result of his gunfire.

"Bow! Bow! Bow! Bow!" his lips flickered as he made the noises. Suddenly, he grew silent and imagined that another bad guy was running from him as he aimed the gun at him. Once he had the bad guy's head set in his sights, he squeezed the trigger.

Blocka!

The blowback from the gun sent Antonio's little ass flying backwards and landing on his back, bumping his head on the carpet. The fired shot had gone wild and slammed into the side of the door, leaving a visible hole behind.

Apocalypse and Adele came running out of the bathroom with towels on them. They both wore looks of concern on their faces as they wondered what had happened.

Adele's heart thudded as she looked to her son on the floor and the hole on the side of the door. Quickly, she pulled the boy up to his feet and examined him for wounds. Seeing that he was okay, she snatched the gun from his hands and smacked him upside the head viciously.

Apocalypse snatched the gun from out of Adele's hand.

"You stupid ass mothafucka, fuck are you doin' playin' with guns?" Adele jerked her son around by his arm and spanked him on the ass as well. While she disciplined him, tears spilled down her cheeks. "What the fuck are you doing playin' with those things, huh?" she stared him in the eyes and shook him violently. Antonio stared at his mother with tears in his eyes, visible shaken by what he'd done and the spanking he'd gotten. "Get cho ass in yo' room and go to bed, and don't wake up 'til I tell you to!"

Smack!

Adele smacked Antonio to the floor and he scrambled back to his feet. He then took off running to his bedroom, crying his eyes out. He slammed the door shut behind him and dove into the bed, sliding up under the covers. He eventually cried himself to sleep.

****

Adele grabbed a duffle bag from out of the closet and started loading it with whatever guns, drugs and paraphernalia around the house. Apocalypse had ordered her to do this because he knew that the police would come knocking as a result of the gun being fired inside of their home.

Adele took a step back and placed her hands on her hips, staring at the duffle bag. Thinking, she massaged her chin as she thought about if she'd forgotten anything else.

Adele snapped her fingers and said, "Almost forgot." She ran over to the bed and lifted up the mattress. Lying toward the edge of the bed was a Tec-9. She picked it up and stuck it inside of the bag with all of the other shit she'd put in there. Afterwards, she zipped the duffle bag up and carried it up front. It was here that she found Apocalypse covering up the bullet hole in the wall with Fix All. She handed him the duffle bag and he passed her the container of Fix All, with the tool he'd used to apply it.

"Okay. I'ma drop this shit around the corner at my homeboy's house." He informed her. "Now, remember, when The Boys come, you don't know jack shit about any gun being fired. You were lying in bed asleep. You got it? You don't know shit!"

"Alright, I got chu, daddy."

"Good. Put that Fix All away, I'll be back later on." Apocalypse went out of the door and pulled it shut behind him.

****

Apocalypse came back to a dark house. The only light he saw was the blue one coming from the television in the master bedroom. Apocalypse made his way down the hallway and into the bedroom, where he found Adele lying stretched across the bed asleep. His face twisted and his nose wrinkled, seeing that she'd been shooting heroin.

Apocalypse frowned and shook his head, "Dope fiend bitch."

Not far from Adele's hand was a syringe she'd been using to shoot dope with. Apocalypse figured she must have nodded off after she'd gotten high. Realizing this, he picked up the needle and threw it into the waste basket. Afterwards, he threw a blanket over Adele and headed out of the master bedroom, pulling his gun from out of his waistline.

Apocalypse made his way down the corridor until he reached Antonio's bedroom door. He used his gun to push the bedroom door open and stepped inside, shutting the door behind him. He found Antonio in bed, under the covers, asleep. Apocalypse sat down beside him on the bed and turned on the lamp, partially illuminated the bedroom. Next, he nudged the boy with his gun until he stirred awake.

Antonio sat up in bed wiping the corner of his eye as he stared at his surrogate father with his partially opened one.

"Yeah?" Antonio spoke groggily. He was in a very deep sleep when he'd been awoken.

"Did the police come ova here?"

"Yeah."

"What cho momma tell 'em?"

"She told them that there wasn't no shooting over here, and that she didn't keep any guns inside of the house. They talked for a while and then they left."

Apocalypse nodded his approval of how Adele handled the situation. Abruptly, he grabbed Antonio by his bottom jaw tightly and his lips puckered up. The pain that shot through the lower half of the boy's face caused his eyes to bulged. His mouth was wide open now and his jaws were aching from being clenched. Scowling, Apocalypse shoved his gun inside of the youngsta's grill. His banga was so far inside of his mouth that it caused him to gag and his eyes to water.

"Lil' nigga, if you eva in yo' mothafuckin' life put cho ball scratchas on anything else that belongs to me, I'ma pop yo' mothafucka top off. Do you undastand me, cuz?"

Antonio cried and trembled with fear. He stared at his surrogate father wide eyed and afraid. He then nodded his understanding. Having put the fear of God inside of the boy's heart, Apocalypse took his gun out of his mouth and wiped its glistening end on his covers.

"Good, boy…goodnight," Apocalypse ruffled his hair and then kissed the top of his head.

Apocalypse left Antonio's bedroom, leaving the boy under his covers sobbing and trembling.

Fucking monster!

CHAPTER EIGHT

Marquan stared out of the gated window of the transporting prison bus watching the scenery pass him by as he mentally prepared himself for the hell that awaited him. He took a glance around him at the rest of the cats that were on the ride with him. They all seemed to be apprehended by their own thoughts. Turning his attention back out of the window, Marquan allowed his thoughts to take him back to a happier time and place in his life. A smile stretched across his face as he recalled the night his son had been born. As cliché as it may sound, it truly was the happiest day of his life.

Before Marquan knew it the transporting bus was pulling to a stop inside of the prison. When he looked up, he came face to face with the facility he'd be calling home for the next ten years of his life. A few minutes later, Marquan and the rest of the convicts were being hauled off of the transporting bus and escorted to the prison. Walking, his eyes took in what appeared to be the faces of one thousand convicts. All of which who stopped doing what they were doing to watch him and the niggaz that were bussed to the facility.

When Marquan looked up, he narrowed his eyelids against the blinding rays of the sun. Up in the towers, he saw the silhouettes of guards with what appeared to be assault rifles in their hands.

Damn, shit just got real, Marquan thought to himself.

~A few minutes later~

Chino was stretched across the bottom bunk wearing glasses and reading a book when his homeboy Napoleon entered their cell. He glanced up at him as soon as he crossed the threshold into their house, making sure it was the man he shared his personal space with. Once he saw who it was he went back to reading his book.

"Hey, jefe, you won't believe who just entered the yard," Napoleon said as he stood at the entrance of the cell. He was a portly man with a bald head and stubby fingers.

"Who?" Chino inquired, focusing on the pages before him. He was a man of average height with slicked back hair and a bushy mustache.

"The mayate that greased Popeye."

Instantly, Chino sat up on his bunk and shut his book. He sat the novel aside on his bed and removed his glasses, setting them aside in a safe place. "This isn't a time to be joking, homeboy.

"Nah, that fool that popped your compadre is here. I swear on The Virgin Mary," he crossed himself in the sign of the crucifix and kissed his fingers, throwing them up to the Lord Almighty, "The homies just got word from in-take, it's definitely him. He's on his way over here now."

"Bullshit."

"Come see for yourself. Come look," Napoleon motioned for the shot caller of his car to follow him out on the tier.

Chino jumped to his feet and followed his right-hand man out on the tier. They stood out on the tier alongside several other criminals looking down below at the new prisoners that were filing inside of the tenement. Niggaz was yelling and calling out all kinds of shit at the fools on the floor. The new dudes that were being ushered in moved along like the niggaz making all of the noise weren't even there.

"There he is, right there, he's ahead of the pack," Napoleon nodded below at Marquan who was holding his bed roll and being led to his designated cell.

"Find out who his celly is, I want that mothafucka hit, ASAP." Chino frowned up as he clenched the guard rail. His grip was so tight on the rail that his knuckles bulged in his hands and so did his veins.

"Alright," Napoleon patted him on his back and moved to do what he'd been ordered to do.

****

The correctional officer showed Marquan his cell. As soon as he entered he was surprised by who he saw lying stretched on the bottom bunk, reading a book.

"OG, is that chu, cuz?" A smile stretched across Marquan's face as he sat his belongings on the top bunk.

"Lil' 187?" the dude that had been reading the book set it aside on the bed and rose to his feet.

"It's me, homie." Marquan slapped hands with his big homie, 187, from his hood. Old boy stood six foot one and had a lean, ripped body of muscle. He had an almond hue and a bald head. He wore a thick salt & pepper beard. As of now, he was wearing a kufi and glasses, looking like one of them Muslim niggaz in Philly, although he wasn't religious. His uniform was crisp and clean. It looked like he'd just gotten it out of the cleaners.

187 earned his reputation through intimidation and a gun. He had more kills than anybody from his gang. As a teenager he worked at the supermarket as a stocker and cashier until he joined the color war. He caught his first body when he was sixteen, and after that, killing became as easy as lacing up his sneakers. While most homies took up selling dope and jacking for them dead presidents, he got his through murder. That's right; homie became a hit-man. He took a contract with anybody just as long as they had the loot to pay for the execution. It wasn't long before he garnered a reputation that got him a business relationship with a shot caller from a notorious organization that was feared throughout the United States.

"I see you got cho welcome home gift." 187 nodded to the old scar on Marquan's neck.

"Yeah, man, soon as I touched down in county, the Mexicans made they move on me."

"What, chu caught a beef back home?" his forehead wrinkled.

"Nah, it turns out that the fool I popped to end up in here…well, cuz was connected to some serious people, some higher ups. You feel me?"

"What's dude's name?" 187 asked curiously.

"Popeye."

"Popeye? That was you?" his eyebrows rose.

Marquan nodded.

"Shit," 187 took a deep breath and rubbed his hand down his face. He then placed his hands on his hips and paced the cell. This made Marquan's forehead wrinkle.

"What's up, loc?"

"Them wetbacks out numba us in here, their car bigga than ours."

"Yeah, I know." Marquan nodded as a serious look crossed his face. "Look, OG, I'm not 'bouta bitch and complain now. I made my bed and it's time to lay in it. If them niggaz come then they come. Fuck it! I'ma vest up and strap down and bang it out with them boys 'til I see Hell or Heaven, whichever comes first. Ain't shit for me to stand on my own, you feel me? I'm street certified, straight A's on my G report card."

187 gripped his shoulder and looked into his eyes. "I feel you, gangsta, but as long as I got breath in my body you ain't standin' alone on nothin'. You my younga homie, I'm 'pose to look out for you."

"I know how you get down, cuz. I'm just saying."

"Respect, loved one," They gave one another a G-hug and patted each other on the back.

187 went on to give Marquan the rules and regulations of the prison as well as the politics. He also schooled him on cell mate etiquette.

"Long as you stick to them fundimentals, we gone be straight, cuz."

187 patted him on his shoulder.

"Don't trip, I got chu faded, OG." Marquan told him as he made up his bunk. "How many homies we got up in here?"

"Man, our car twenty-three homies strong now that chu here, cuz. I'ma calla meetin' and introduce you to alla homies once I finish this lil' bit of weed, you care to join me?" he showed him the joint he had stashed on him.

"Nah, I'm good, cuz. I'ma kick back in here 'til you come back."

"Cool."

They slapped hands and embaced once again before 187 went on about his business. Once the OG was gone, Marquan climbed upon his bunk.

****

Marquan lay back in bed thinking about his son. Thoughts of his little boy made him have second thoughts about his decision to crush Popeye's ass. Although he'd smashed homeboy for shooting and robbing his man, his actions were exactly what had landed him behind bars. Now, he'd be away from his son for a long time.

Not being able to kiss, hold, or touch his little man was driving him crazy. He was already thinking about ways he could break out of prison and get back to him. He could bust a few moves for some loot and cross the border somewhere far away from American soil.

Although he was entertaining the idea of busting up out of The Beast, Marquan didn't want to spend the rest of his life looking over his shoulder for the law. Should he be caught, he'd have to experience the same heartache and sadness he did the first time he was torn away from his son.

Nah, cuz, that shit ain't even worth it. When a nigga come home, it's gone be to stay. I'ma go legit and live my life righteously. Stay my black ass from outta them streets. My right hand to God, I'm done with them wicked mothafuckaz!

Needing to clear his head, Marquan jumped down from off his bunk and walked over to the sink. Turning on the faucet, he cupped his hands under the water and splashed some on his face. Eyelids shuts, he threw some water on his face a couple more times. While he was doing this, a Mexican assassin wearing a prison made ski mask over his face and gripping a shank, emerged at the entrance of his cell. His scowling face shown behind the mask, his vengeful eyes were focused on Marquan. He clenched his prison fashioned blade tighter and a small gleam swept up the length of it.

The Mexican assassin crept inside of the cell and lifted his shank. He smiled evilly and swung his blade downward. Marquan's eyelids peeled open and he looked to his right. He was just in time to see the shank flying down at his face. Quickly, Marquan grabbed the Mexican's assassin's wrist with both of his hands. His actions stopped the tip of the shank at his cheek. His eyelids were stretched wide open in fear and he was gritting his teeth. He and the assassin's arms shook as they struggled against one another. Thoughts of Antonio ripped back and forth across Marquan's mind. Thinking about his boy rejuvenated his strength.

"Grrrrrrrowl," Marquan kneed the killa in his crotch. The man dropped his shank and doubled over. His eye bulged and watered as he grabbed his aching balls. Next, came a foot to the center of his face. The impact from the kick sent him flying backwards and bumping his head up against the cement wall.

Bwap! Wap! Crack!

Marquan slammed his fists into the Mexican fool's face and made him see explosions of white before his eyes. Marquan then grabbed him by the back of his neck and slammed his face into the metal sink repeatedly, slightly rearranging the bone structure in his face. When the Mexican assassin dropped, he lay face up on the floor, staring up at the ceiling, eyes rolled in the back of his head. His nose was broken and his chin was bloody, he spat his broken teeth out of his mouth, lying where he was moaning in agony.

Marquan spat on the Mexican nigga he'd dispatched and said, "Bitch ass nigga!

Just then, another Mexican assassin rushed inside of his cell. He had a hard face and shank so big that one hit from it would do some serious damage. Seeing the Mexican assassin put Marquan on alert. He jumped back a few times avoiding the jabs that the assassin tried to take at him. As he consistently avoided being poked full of holes, Marquan pulled off his shirt and twisted it up. When the Mexican cat went to jab him again, he flung the opposite end of his twisted shirt at him. The end of the shirt stung the assassin's wrist like a scorpion's tail and he dropped the shank. Before the assassin knew it, the end of Marquan's shirt was licking at his face back to back. He hollered out in pain, feeling the lashings against his face.

Whap! Whap! Whap!

Marquan licked at his attacker's left and right knees, making him grab them and leave his neck exposed. The Mexican assassin took a lashing at the neck. He howled in pain and grabbed his neck. This left his torso open, and Marquan took full advantage of it. He ran forward and kicked him in his chest. The impact from the blow sent him flying out of the cell, sliding across the floor and bumping up against the wall. He lay there slumped; head bowed and palms facing upwards. He breathed easily as he sat there barely conscious.

Breathing hard, nostrils flaring, Marquan looked between the two men he'd laid out. At that moment, two correctional officers rushed his cell. Before he could say or do anything, one of them sprayed him in the face with mace. He hollered and grabbed his face, staggering backwards. The correctional officers threw him to the floor and restrained him. He lay with the side of his face pressed against the cold floor. His eyelids narrowed into slits as he tried to keep the mace from burning his eyes any further.

"Get off me, get the fuck off me, you mothafuckaz!" Marquan hollered out over and over again, spit jumping off his lips and clinging to the floor.

Outside of his cell he could hear the prison in an uproar having seen some of his brawl with the two Mexican assassins.

Unbeknownst to Marquan, Napoleon stood amongst the few convicts that had witnessed his lethal fists.

"Damn, homeboy gave them eses that work." One inmate said.

"Dude, beat the brakes off they asses!" Another inmate commented.

Having heard this, Napoleon walked off to deliver the bad news to Chino.

****

Chino sat on the bench watching the scenery. There were convicts playing basketball, handball, and chopping it up amongst one another. Every section of the yard belonged to different cars that were run by its own shot caller. There were also niggaz playing the outside of those sections, acting as guards, strapped up and ready in case some shit jumped off. Each area of the grassy field was like its own world. Nothing could be said different from the area that Chino and his hittas were kicking. A few bad ass looking cholos surrounded him in a half circle. Most of them were of average height, but there was a few of them that were much taller. It was safe to say that most of them were in fantastic shape too. They also sported tattoos like jewelry.

Seeing someone approaching at the corner of his eye, Chino looked to his right and found Napoleon coming his way. He gave him a questioning look and he shook his head no. At that moment, Chino looked away and said 'fuck' to his self. When he looked back around, Napoleon was standing before him.

"What the fuck happened? Those were two of our best." Chino asked with furrowed brows.

"There isn't much of a story to tell," Napoleon told him. "I found both of those fools bent the fuck up. That mayate Marquan did a real number on 'em," he looked away and shook his head. The way that the hittas that Chino sent at Marquan came out after the beating he'd thrown him made him feel sorry for them.

"Where they at now?" Chino inquired with curiousity.

"The homeboys are in the infirmy and Marquan is in the hole."

"Good. We gotta get someone in there to take care of 'em."

"Who do you have in mind?"

"Lemme think on it," he massaged his chin as he stared at nothing, pondering a choice of men he could send to give Marquan that obituary. Coming to his decision, he nodded and looked to his second in command. "I got it."

Chino told Napoleon about who he had in mind to handle the hit on Marquan. Receiving the name, the shorter man looked over the men that were present until he found the hitta he was looking for.

"Pokey," Napoleon called out to the nigga he was looking for, and he came running over. Pokey was a tall cat with a dark caramel complexion and tattoos covering every inch of his body. He was one of the darkest Mexicans on the yard. In fact, he could blend in with the brothers on the yard, but his features and his deep accent would probably give him away.

"'Sup, aye?" He threw his head back as he stopped before Napoleon.

"The jefe has a mission for you, homie."

"It's time you brought cho cuchillo out of retirement. You ready to put some holes in a pinche Negro?" Chino asked him seriously as he stared directly in his eyes.

"Simon," Pokey's eyebrows sloped and wrinkles formed at the beginning of his nose. He had dedication and determination in his eyes. It was from this that Chino knew that Marquan was living on borrowed time.

Chino patted Pokey on his back and pulled out a few folded one hundred dollar bills from out of his boot. He took a cautious look around before passing them to Napoleon on the sneak tip. He then said, "Napoleon, I want chu to get this to Mack. Have 'em see to it that Pokey gets down to Solitary."

"I got chu." Napoleon nodded his understanding.

Marquan was a dead man.

****

Correctional officer, Mack, went about the task of unlocking the door to Marquan's solitary confinement cell while Pokey stood aside, waiting. While this was going on, the dark skinned Mexican lifted up his shirt and pulled out a weapon he'd fashioned himself. It looked like a small sword from the length of it. A gleam swept up the lethal weapon and it twinkled at its tip. There was the sound of metal unlocking and squealing as the correctional officer pulled open the door of the cell. As soon as there was enough room for Pokey to slide up into the small holding cell, he oozed inside and found Marquan fast asleep underneath the covers. Pokey smiled devilishly as he moved in to carry out the mission he'd been hand picked for.

Gripping his shank firmly, he reached to draw back the covers to deliver the kill-shot to the man the shot caller of his car deemed unworthy of existence. His hand had barely touched the covers when they came flying upwards in his face. Marquan came from off his mattress, eyes darkened, nose scrunched and lips peeled back in a sneer. The small razor edged shanks he clutched in each hand twinkled at their tips. He lashed out like a feral animal, slicing at specific areas of Pokey's body. His hands were moving so fast that his aggressor couldn't detect their movements.

Snikt! Snikt!

Speckles of blood clung to Marquan's face and bare chest as his miniature blades cut through the ligaments in Pokey's knuckles, causing him to drop his sword length knife. He then moved with the grace of a ball room dancer, slicing and severing all of the ligaments, tendons and fasciaes in his enemy's body.

Snikt! Snikt! Snikt! Snikt! Snikt! Snikt!

The last tendon Marquan severed dropped Pokey down to his knees. He couldn't move a muscle in his entire body. He was as helpless as a baby. He was bleeding from every where, creating small puddles of blood on the floor. All he could do was stay where he was, tears in his eyes, wincing in pain, limbs as limp as cooked noodles. Wincing, he batted the tears in his eyes away, and looked up into the unforgiving eyes of his attacker. Marquan stood over him in just his boxers, the miniature shanks in his hands dripped blood at his feet. His slightly hairy chest rose and fell as he took breaths.

"It ain't so fun when the rabit got the gun!" With a grunt, Marquan slammed the shanks into Pokey's shoulder blades and twisted them. The Mexican hitta hollered out in excruciation before he was kicked square in the face. The impact from the kick pitched his head backwards. He hit the floor hard and busted the back of his bald dome. Stepping around him, Marquan opened his cell door wide enough for him to drag Pokey's body through. Afterwards, he grabbed him by the collar of his shirt and dragged him out into the corridor, where Mack was waiting. Once Pokey was lying flat out inside of the hallway, Marquan snatched the shanks out of his shoulder blades and wiped them off on his clothing. Kneeling down, he said to him, "You tell that spic Chino, that the next nigga he sends at me is coming back to his ass in a body bag," he placed his shank to his throat. "You got that?"

“Yeah, I got it, I got it!” Pokey winced in agony.

“Good,” Marquan rose to his feet and kicked Pokey across the chin, knocking him out cold. He then turned to Mack and gave him a nod. He then returned to his cell, shutting the door behind him.

Once Marquan was back in his cell, he looked around and saw the dots of blood covering the wall beside his mattress and the floor. Hastily, he grabbed the kite that was tucked under his mattress. It had a drawing of a human body on it and showed several points on it that had been circled with a pencil. All of the points on the drawing were the same ones that Marquan had attacked on Pokey. When he turned the kite over there was a message on it written by 187.

Chino is sending one of his hittas at you. I sent you down some straps to protect yourself. Hold it down, young homie.

One love.

187 wasn’t just some gangbanga shooting niggaz in drive bys. Nah, the nigga was the real thing. He was taught by some of the best. He was skilled in two martial arts, knew how to handle several firearms and throwing knives. He had the art of murder down to a science, and he knew how to kill a nigga easily.

Mack, the correctional officer that had brought Pokey down to Maquan’s solitary confinement cell, played both sides of the fence when it came to the cars in prison. He worked for whomever payed him the most. Once Chino had lined his pockets to get Pokey down to Marquan, he told 187 what was going down since that was his man. Having gotten the news, 187 dropped some paper on Mack to deliver the kite and the knives to Marquan to protect himself. It was from this that Marquan was glad that pretty much anyone could be bought in prison, because had it not been for that, he was sure he'd be a dead man right then.

187 smoked weed inside of the rest room. He'd positioned one of his homeboys outside the door to alert him whenever a correctional officer was approaching. Occasionally, his homeboy would stick his head inside and take a few pulls of the potent weed before going back to his job as lookout.

"One Time," his homeboy called out from where he was outside the door. He'd just saw a thick bodied correctional officer approaching. Having given the warning, the homeboy walked away from the rest room door and went to find him some other business.

When the correctional officer pushed open the rest room door, 187 had just emerged from flushing the contraband down the toilet.

"Aww, shit, Mack, it's just you?" 187 said, disappointedly. Mack was one of the cooler C.O's. Had he known it was him coming then he wouldn't have flushed his shit down the toilet.

"Well, damn, don't be too excited to see me," he smiled sarcastically.

"'Sup with it, Mack?" 187 stepped before the mirror to straighten himself out and make sure he didn't look too high.

"Ya boy, the new nigga they dropped off in here, Marquan," he started off.

"What about my young homie? He good?" 187 questioned with concern.

"He's okay, but he ran into a lil' turbulence, if you know what I mean."

"How so?"

"Them eses tried to hit 'em a second ago. But don't worry; he gave 'em the business, put 'em in a real bad way." He reported. "They got shipped off to the infirmary, but they finna lock ya man up in the hole."

"Good. Fuck 'em,long as my people straight."

"I don't know how long that's gone last."

When he said this, 187 looked up at him with confusion plastered across his face. "What chu mean?"

"Hold up, OG," Mack stuck his head outside of the rest room door. He looked up and down the hallway to make sure that there wasn't anyone around to ease drop. Afterwards, he ducked back inside of the rest room to finish talking with 187. "Chino just greased my palms. He wants me to get one of his hittas down into solitary to finish yo' homeboy off."

"Shit. Them mothafuckaz really are after Quan for splittin' they homeboy's wig out on the streets. The boy's been green lighted," 187 said to no one particular as he placed his hands on one of the sinks and leaned over it, thinking to himself.

When Marquan first touched down in prison he'd told him that the eses wanted his head for murdering their homeboy in the streets. Now he knew shit was really real. The botched hit proved that to him.

If Quan is down there then nine times outta ten he ain't strapped up. I gotta get him a banga in his hands, pronto.

187 took his hands from off the sink and turned around to Mack.

"Yo', I needa getta banga into youngin's hands. If I don't, then he's dead up in here."

"I can do that...for a small fee of course," he smiled excitedly as he rubbed his hands together.

"I got chu faded, but I need you to make that move for me for you even think about takin' Chino people down there."

Mack nodded and said, "I can do that."

Marquan balled up the kite and tossed it into the toilet. He then tossed the shanks in there as well. Standing to his feet, he flushed everything down the metal toilet. Next, he wiped his cell down, and washed himself up inside of the sink. Once he was finished, he got dressed in his prison issued clothing. The only reason why he'd taken them off was because he didn't want to risk getting blood on them. He knew that had he gotten them stained with blood and the other C.O's came down, he'd surely be charged with slumping Pokey's ass. The last thing he wanted was to get any more time added on to his sentence. *Fuck that!* He was trying to go home.

CHAPTER NINE

"Yo' boy that chu sent at Ludlow, he ain't ever gone walk again. Matter of fact, the only thing that'll ever move on him again is his mouth and eyelids," Mack informed Chino as he looked out from his tier, with his back to the doorway of his cell. At the time Chino was writing a letter to his daughter back home. As soon as he heard the news he dropped his rubber pencil and looked to Mack, only seeing his back.

"What the fuck happened? That fucker was practicially gift wrapped for Pokey." His forehead crinkled with lines and he squared his jaws.

"Ludlow was ready for 'em," Mack told him. "He was all over yo' boy, to tell you the truth, I'm surprised he didn't kill 'em."

"Fuuuuck," Chino said in a hushed tone. He was on his feet now and pacing the floor, hands on his hips. Stopping, he ran his hand back down his slicked back hair. Taking a deep breath as he stared at the floor thinking, he went on to talk. "Alright, listen, Mack, you take 'em out, hit 'em for me. Name your price and I'll cash you out."

"Unh unh," he shook his head as he held on to the rail, watching everything up and down the tier. "I'm not getting caught up in this mess for any kind of money. Setting a nigga up to bust a move is one thang, but I'm sure as hell not getting my mothafucking hands dirty."

"Shiiiit," Chino sat back down on his bed. He bowed his head and rested his elbows on his knees, letting his hands dangle between his legs. "Fuck am I going to do now?"

"I don't know. But when you figure it out and you need my services, just shout me a holla, homes." With that said, Mack walked off down the tier whistling and taking in his surroundings.

****

187 was busy cleaning his cell when he felt someone's presence. He looked up from where he was wiping the floor and saw a pair of leather boots. He eyes followed the legs and landed on Mack's face. He told him to keep on cleaning while he talked, so he obliged him. Mack went on to pretend to be tying up his boots while he was relaying what he knew to 187.

"Pokey got at cho man, but the youngin' handled his. The boy sliced his ass up something awful, left 'em in bad shape, my man. Real bad shape." Once Mack finished tying up his boots, he walked off down the tier whistling, just like he'd done with Chino.

Having gotten the news, 187 went on to finish cleaning his cell, smirking. He was happy that Marquan smashed out Pokey. He was worried at first about his young homie, but he proved that he could handle his own when it came down to it.

~33 days later~

187 was doing pushups on his cell's floor, which caused the muscles of his body to bulge. Beads of sweat covered his entire form. Sweat began to accumulate on his forehead until some of it formed droplets and fell to the floor, splashing beneath him. Hearing the locks of the iron door make metallic clicks as its locks were unlocked, 187 got to his feet and grabbed his towel. He wiped himself down as he watched the door open and his young homie walk inside. It

had been over a month, so Marquan had grown a small afro and his facial hair was plentiful.

Marquan and 187 smiled at one another, as the door was shut to their cell. They gave one another a manly hug and patted each other on the back.

“Damn, cuz, it seems like I haven’t seen you in years.” 187 told Marquan as he continued to dry himself off.

“Man, who you telling?” Marquan grinned.

“On a more serious note,” 187 began. “This shit with Chino and his boys ain’t gone come to a close ‘til we come to some kind of mutual undastandin’.”

“What understanding? Far as I can tell, that mothafucka ain’t gone let up ‘til I’m dead.”

187 took a deep breath and said, “Maybe not. The nigga owes me a favor. I can probably ask him to raise up offa you, and I’ll call it even.”

“I don’t know, cuz, but it’s worth a shot.”

“Aye, I’ma throw the line out there, if he doesn’t bite, then its war. I’ll tell the homies to strap up.”

Damn, cuz, you really riding for a nigga,” Marquan placed his hand on the OG’s shoulder.

“This is bigga than crip, we family in here. I’d do the same for any of the homies.I’m the oldest outta alla y’all here, so I look at y’all like my brothas and sons. I gotta look out for my loved ones, loc.”

At that moment, Marquan's eyes turned glassy. He was on the verge of crying, but he wasn't about to let the tears manifest.

"What's wrong, homeboy?" 187's forehead creased.

"It's just that ever since I lost my pops, you been like a father to me. Thank you."

"Don't wet it, loco, you always been like a son to me."187 gave him a fatherly hug and patted him on his back.

"Alright, cuz, enough of that soft shit, I'm too G for that." Marquan joked and smiled after they broke their embrace.

187 laughed and threw playful punches at Marquan. He countered by throwing some back at him. Afterwards, they got on their bunks and indulged in their vices.

"OG, you gotta broad you bidding with?" Marquan inquired.

"Man, I gotta few broads I fuck with. Ain't none of them serious though. Hell, how could they be? I ain't neva leavin' up outta this mothafucka." He gave him the truth, raw and uncut. "How about chu, my young nigga? You got an old lady you doin' ya bid with?"

"Nah, man, I thought that was gone be my baby momma, but that ain't happening. Turns out, she's fucking the nigga I'm in here for riding for. You know that nigga Apocalypse, right?"

"From the gang?" his brows furrowed.

"Yeah, that's him."

"I know you two were as thick as thieves, I'm sorry to hear that, cuz."

"Me, too, but it is what it is."

"Now, I know you say that shit went sour witcho B.M, but what about cho side piece? I know you got mo' than one playa on ya team."

"Nah," he shook his head. "Once she got pregnant with my son, I hung my jersey up. I was done with being a playa. I wanted us to be a family. Know what I'm saying? Can't be a real family if I got all these different broads here and there, you feel me?"

"Yeah, I got chu." 187 nodded his understanding. "But I know there's gotta be an old girlfriend or somethin' you can holla at that you can do this time with."

"Yeahhh, there's somebody." A big ass smile stretched across Marquan's face when he thought of Jahleysa.

"Whoeva she is has yo' nose wide open, cuz. I can hear yo' ass smilin' up there. Gone 'head and give lil' momma a call tomorrow, see if you can put her unda yo' spell, if you know what I mean."

"I'ma do just that."

That night, Marquan fell asleep with thoughts of Jahleysa on his mind and a smile curling his lips.

~The next day~

Marquan picked up the telephone and wiped it off on his shirt. He then pressed the telephone to his ear and made his call. He smiled as he dialed the number of his teenage heart throb, Jahleysa, it had been a while since he'd seen her at the park that day, but he was confident that her telephone number was still in service. He smiled that much harder when he heard someone pick up the telephone. He stated his name when summons by the operator and waited to see if Jahleysa would accept his call. She did.

"Heyyyyyy, handsome," Jahleysa greeted him excitedly.

"'Sup, Chocolate Drop?" Marquan smiled hard.

"Same old, same old."

"Same here."

"Yeah, I noticed where you called me from."

They both laughed. For as long as Jahleysa had known Marquan, he had been in and out of jail. He'd never done more than a year until now.

"See what had happened was…."

They busted up laughing again.

Marquan and Jahleysa chopped it up until his time on the jack was up. Before the line was disconnected, Jahleysa agreed to come see him soon. With that in his mind, Marquan went waltzing back to his cell hearing the song *Walking on sunshine* by Katrina and The Waves.

I used to think maybe you loved me now baby I'm sure

And I just can't wait till the day when you knock on my door

Now every time I go for the mailbox, gotta hold myself down

'Cause I just can't wait 'til you write me you're coming around

I'm walking on sunshine (Wow!)

I'm walking on sunshine (Wow!)

I'm walking on sunshine (Wow!)

And don't it feel good

~A few days later~

Marquan poured inside of the visiting room among the crowd of inmates. Stopping at the center of the floor, he scanned the area. His eyes lit up and a smile stretched across his face when he spotted his first love. It took all he had in him not to break out in a full sprint to meet her. No matter how hard he tried not to smile, his smile couldn't be concealed. So he just let it be, right there on his face.

"Damn, Marquan," Jahleysa smiled. She'd just hugged him briefly and sat down at the table.

"What's up?" Marquan frowned, not having a clue as to what she was getting at. He then sat down at the table.

"You done got fine as a mothafucka up in here. I mean, you were always a sexy ass nigga with yo' thug ass, but goddamn, zzzaddy." She bit down hard on her curled finger. He was just that good looking to her.

"Thank you." He blushed and glanced down at the table, then looked back up into her eyes. Holding both of her hands in his own, he caressed them with his thumbs. "You got big, too." She claimed taking in his muscular build.

"Yeah, ain't much to do in here besides eat, workout and read. I do a lot of the above."

"Well, that's good." She told him. "Have you thought about what chu wanna do once you on the other side of these walls?"

He looked off to the side, wearing an expression that let her know that he was doing some thinking. He took a deep breath and looked back to her. "I know I'm not going back to the streets, no matter what." He allowed what he had just said to marinate in her brain before continuing, "I figure I gotta crawl before I walk, so I'ma get myself a job, any job. Work and stack me a lil' paypa and save enough to open up my own trucking business."

Jahleysa nodded and said, "That's a great idea. I hope you let me help you." She searched his eyes trying to read him before he could say anything. "I appreciate the offer, Jah, but I don't wanna be a burden on you. You gotta life, so I'm sure you gotta 'nough going on."

"Yeah, I gotta life, but it ain't much of one without you in it." She cracked a dimpled smile and tilted her head to the side. Little momma had a big smile and the most dazzling set of teeth that he'd ever seen. Her lips were full and succulent. He could see himself kissing them all the time…forever.

"Check, baby out, spitting that G." He smiled at her and bit down on his bottom lip, giving her that sexy ass look of his that she adored so much.

"That wasn't no G, this real life I'm getting at chu with, Marquan."

"Is that right?" He took on a serious expression as he looked in her eyes. Although he chose Adele over Jahleysa he never stopped loving her…ever. He always wished that it was her he laid up with that night and created Antonio with. Truthfully, if he could do it all over again, he would have chosen her and co-parented Antonio with Adele. He knew within his heart that she was the perfect woman for him, but wanting his son to be brought up in the same household as him derailed their relationship. The crazy part about it was that although he didn't want his son growing up without him, he would anyway being that he ended up getting locked up.

Adele sat on the couch patting her baby boy asleep as she flipped through the cable channels. Hearing a knock at the door, she turned the volume down on the television with the remote control.

"Who is it?" Adele called out, still holding the remote out towards the TV.

"A past due ass whooping, open the door, bitch! Bring that ass outside, you past due for this one." She heard whoever it was on the other side of the door.

Adele sat the remote down on the coffee table and picked up her baby, carrying him off to the bedroom. Entering the master bedroom, she found Marquan sitting down on the side of the bed, counting up them dead presidents. He had nine rows and counting of stacks of wrinkled bills. This was all the money he'd made out in the streets.

"I need you to watch my back while I handle this hoe out here, she trippin'. I'ma have to tap that ass." Adele said,

passing her baby boy off to Marquan. She then pulled her hair back in a ponytail and tangled a rubber band around it.

"Baby, who you talking about?" Marquan's forehead creased.

"Yo ex-bitch, Jah," She answered him as she stuck her socked feet inside of her sneakers.

"Jah? Who she out there with?"

"Hell if I know, but I'ma 'bouta beat the brakes off this bitch, poppin' up at my house talkin' about whippin' somebodies ass. She got me fucked up." Adele threw on a tank top.

"Nuh unh, you not 'bouta squabble with Jah."

"The hell I ain't. She wanna waltz her ass over here to fight me over some dick, well, she 'bouta get her ass whipped over some then."

Marquan grabbed Adele by the arm and said, "You not 'bouta throw hands with that girl. We gotta son, set an example for 'em." He gave her a stern look as he talked through clenched jaws.

Adele folded her arms across her breasts and twisted her lips, shifting her weight from one leg to the other. She then looked at the money he made off the streets.

Marquan looked at the dirty money that Adele was eying and turned back around to her.

"Save that shit," he told her. "I do what I do to keep a roof over our heads and food on the mothafucking table. Besides, I don't hear you squawking 'bout them grips yo'

thirsty ass be hitting me up for. And let's not forget about cho taste in designer labels and shit."

Adele rolled her eyes and blew out her frustrations. "Whatever, nigga. Look, I'ma 'bouta beat this bitch ass. Come out here to watch my back in case she tries some funny shit."

"What the fuck did I just say?" he gave her an eye that she read as Sit your ass down.

"Nuh unh," she shook her head. "I done let cho ass punk me a thousand times. I'm not finna let chu chump me on this one. Now, bring yo' ass on, and watch my back."

Marquan took a deep breath and said under his breath, "I never shoulda knocked up this hoodrat, but, nooooo, I hadda run up in this bitch, and raw at that." After lying the baby down on the bed, he picked up his Glock from off the nightstand and chambered a deadly round into its head. "Let's go, cuz." He headed for the door. Adele kissed baby Having done this, he and Adele kissed their son on his head and headed walked out of the bedroom.

Marquan opened the front door. As soon as him and Adele stepped foot out on the front porch, they were amazed by everyone they saw standing in their yard. It looked like half of the neighborhood was out there waiting for them. At the front where everyone had gathered, there was a hyped up Jahleysa. She was standing in between two girls, who were mad dogging Adele. Those two mean looking bitches looked like they were ready to put hands and feet on her ass.

Jahleysa's eyebrows were slanted and her nose was scrunched up. She was wearing a blue bandana around her forehead and a navy blue tank top.

"'Bout time you came out, I was starting to think you bitched out," Jahleysa told her.

"Bitch, thata be the day I'm scared of anybody on this planet. You betta ask somebody." Adele said calmly with a scowling face.

"Talk that shit, boo."

"I am, 'cause ain't nan' bitch 'bouta stop me."

"We gone see about dat." One of the mean looking bitches beside Jahleysa said. She and the broad on the opposite side of Jahleysa were twins. They were a couple of Precious looking bitches, who you could only tell apart from their hairstyles. One had pigtails while the other had cornrows.

"Nah, ain't nobody jumping nobody," Marquan stood in front of Adele with his Glock held down at his side. "Jah and Del gone shoot the fair one and that's it. 'Cause if anyone jump in, female or not, this thang at my side gone jump in."

Jahleysa's twin cousins glared at Marquan and talked shit under their breaths as they separated from her.

"You got it," Jahleysa told Marquan, then looked to Adele. "Now, get that ass out here and get these hands, bitch!"

"You ain't said nothin' butta word," Adele jumped from off the porch and charged towards Jahleysa's screaming, a vein twitching at her temple.

Bwop! Bwap! Wap!

Jahleysa's fists came lightning fast and whipped Adele's face from left to right, sending blood flying everywhere. Once she turned back around blood was running out of her left nostril, but she still kept her fists up. She moved in on Jahleysa and threw a couple of jabs, but she finessed them, dodging them with ease.

Bwap! Crack! Wap! Wap!

Adele dropped down to one knee with her eye beginning to swell shut and more blood running from her nose. She wiped her bleeding nose with the back of her fist and blood smeared against it. Seeing the blood enraged her. Her face twisted in a scowl and her head whipped around to Jahleysa. She found her opponent pouncing from foot to foot with her fists up, ready and waiting to tap that ass again.

"Come on, bitch, get on up, I got some more for your mothafucking ass!" She claimed, nostrils flaring and chest heaving.

"I'm gonna fuckin' kill youuuuuu!" Adele exploded with rage and charged Jahleysa. Jahleysa used her momentum against her by flipping her over her back. Adele went high into the air and slammed down hard as a mothafucka on her back. Lying where she was, she winced over and over again from the painful fall.

"Stomp her ass out! Stomp that scandalous ass bitch out!" One of Jahleysa's twin cousins called out from where she was standing beside her sibling.

"Nah, ain't gone be none of that!" Marquan spoke up with his gun at his side. He had his banga outside like he had a license to carry it. He made his way through the crowd so that he could be seen and his presence could be felt.

"Hell naw, fuck that, Quan, you ain't 'bouta save her from this ass whooping." Jahleysa told him and then whipped her head back around to Adele. "You ain't had enough, huh? You ain't even got no licks in yet!"

It came to a surprise to most present that Jahleysa had gave Adele them hands that day. What everyone didn't know was that her pops used to box while he was in the Navy. He had a pretty impressive record, too, fourty and owe to be exact. When his wife was pregnant with his child, he had his fingers crossed for a baby boy that could share his name, but he winded up getting a little girl. Still, he was happy because he had a healthy baby girl to call his own. He went on to teach Jahleysa all he knew about surviving in the world, this included fighting. He's been training her since she was eleven years old. Back then, he saw that she was born to not only be a scholar, but a fighter as well. Little momma was lethal with her hands, and he knew that when the day came that she had to get down, whomever was on the opposing end of her fists, would have hell to pay. There weren't any doubts in his mind about that.

"No..." Adele staggered to her feet and spat blood off to the side. She wiped her bleeding mouth with the back of her hand and took a deep breath, throwing up her bare knuckles ready to fight some more. "I ain't done with this bitch!"

"See," Jahleysa looked from Adele to Marquan, smiling. "She still in the fight," She then turned back around to Adele and threw up her fists. The two combatants circled one another, focusing their eyes on each other's shoulders to see what would be the other's next move. The people surrounding them cheering and egging them on looked like blurs of colors to them.

Marquan made an annoyed face and took a deep breath. He started to stop the girls from fighting but he figured that it was probably best that they got their beef off their chests.

"You know what, fuck it, cuz. Y'all handle y'all B.I." Marquan waved his freehand while he kept his other one at his side, holding his gun.

"Lights out, bitch!" Jahleysa threw a couple of jabs that Adele easily avoided. She then threw a combination that skinned the side of her opponent's head.

Adele jumped back and moved back in, looking for a flaw in her opponent's technique. She faked a left and then a right, left again, and then she launched a hard right. The blow snapped Jahleysa's head back. When she brought her head back down, a sliver of blood ran from out of her left nostril. She smiled and licked the blood from off her top lip.

"Yeahhhh, bitch, that's what I'm talking about. Bring that shit, hoe!" Jahleysa bobbed and weaved the assault that Adele brought her way next. She moved around as she studied her opponent for her next move. When Adele took two wild swings at her head, she ducked and gave her two mean ass body shots to either side of her ribcage. Coming back up, Jahleysa launched an upper cut that lifted up Adele's chin and threw her off of her feet. Her shadow cast on the lawn as she went up into the air and crashed down upon her back. She lay where she was, pupils moving around inside of her head, and moaning. A trail of blood ran from the corner of her busted mouth.

The crowd that had gathered to see the street brawl cheered on Jahleysa and chanted her name triumphantly. Jahleysa, tired and breathing hard, turned around to

Marquan. "And this the bitch chu chose over me, huh? I'm so disappointed. I'm really, really disappointed. You could have done much better than this tired ass skeeza. I mean, damn, at least let me be able to see why the bitch had one up over me. This is a fucking disgrace right here, I'm fucking embarrassed." Jahleysa's eyes followed Marquan as he approached a defeated Adele tucking his gun at the small of his back.

Reaching Adele, Marquan pulled her up to her wobbly legs and threw her arm around his shoulders. He then proceeded back towards the house, giving Jahleysa the evil eye the entire time he was en route. The crowd dispersed seeing that the fight was over and the loser had been brought back inside of her house. The only people still left outside were Jahleysa and her twin cousins.

Jahleysa stared at the backs of Marquan and Adele until they disappeared through the door of their home. As soon as the door shut, tears went pouring down her cheeks and her shoulders shuddered. Seeing that their cousin was emotionally hurt, the twins rushed over to console her aching heart. They held her from either side and kissed the top of her head.

Jahleysa thought that whooping Adele ass would make her feel better, and, truthfully, it had, but that was only for the time being. After she'd sicced them dogs on her (her fists), she went right back to feeling the confusion, hurt, and desertion Marquan's infidelity had brought her.

"Oh, my God, he really doesn't love me anymore, he doesn't want me..." Jahleysa broke down crying even harder than she was before. Her cousins wrapped their arms around her even tighter to bring her comfort and show her love.

"It's okay, Duck, it's gonna be alright," one of the twins tried to sooth her pain, calling her by her childhood nick name.

"You don't need that nigga, fuck him, girl." The other twin said with a scowl. "He's the one that lost, not chu."

"Come on. Let's raise up outta here." The sister that had spoken first ushered Jahleysa along with her other sister back to the car they'd driven over Marquan's house in.

"You know you always have had a slick tongue," Jahleysa told him. "It was that slick ass tongue that got me to give you my virginity."

"This slick tongue got chu to do more than give up yo' v-card," he smiled and licked his lips. This caused her to blush and smile hard.

"Damn." He said taking on a more serious expression.

"What's up?" a worried expression engulfed her face.

"Nothing," he looked down at the table and rubbed the back of his neck.

"Nah, seriously, Quan, what's the matter?"

"Nothing. It's just that," he looked back up at her, finally finding the courage to say what was on his mind. "It's just that you got even more beautiful than the last time I saw you." She tried not to smile, but eventually she succumbed to the inevitable. "I mean, I always wondered if I'd find heaven on earth, and it's clear that some point in my life I had. That's gotta be true, 'cause I've known an angel nearly all my life."

Jahleysa bowed her head and looked away. She surpressed her smile for as long as she could before looking back at him, saying, "See, that's what I'm talking about right there, that slick as tongue."

"It may be slick, but it speaks the truth."

"Always?" she raised an eyebrow.

"At this very moment it does."

"Good. 'Cause there's something I've gotta ask."

"Shoot." Marquan adjusted himself in his chair.

"Lord, please, forgive me for asking, but I've gotta know," Jahleysa looked up at the ceiling before focusing her attention back on the man she'd loved since she was a teenage girl. "Have you ever stopped loving me? I mean, even after you broke it off with me, and started yo' family with, you know, her?"

Marquan licked his lips and leaned over the table. He made sure to be looking her dead in her eyes as he responded. "I, Marquan Ludlow, have never stopped loving Jahleysa Thompson...even after I started a family with *her*; I still was very much in love with chu. My body was there with *her*, but my heart was always with you. I chose who I chose on the account of my son. That's it. That's the truth, the whole truth."

Marquan sat quietly watching Jahleysa. Tears pooled in her eyes and splashed on the table top. Taking her curled finger, she wiped her dripping eyes and sniffled, "For real, Quan, no bullshit?"

"Hey, if I'm lying, may I spend all of eternity in this shit-hole. These are straight facts I'm getting at chu with, Jah."

Jahleysa sniffled again and wiped her eyes with the back of her hand, saying, "The crazy thing is I never, ever, ever stopped loving you, either. It killed me when you broke up with me. I thought I was going to die, but that love, this love that's inside of me," she pressed both of her hands against her chest and more teardrops splashed on the table top. "It kept on burning like a fire. It would not die. It was that strong. And I always hoped that one day that you would come around, and see what you had in me…What you still have. 'Cause I can look you in your eyes right now and tell you, baby, I don't want anyone else. Don't another nigga in this world compare to you. I'm yours…"

"And I am yours…always." He spoke sincerely, matching her gaze.

"You serious? 'Cause I gotta tell you, bae. I can't take another heart break like I did before."

"I'm dead ass, lil' momma, if you willing to take this ride with me again, I promise you'll never regret it. That's on everything I love."

"I'm riding, then."

The biggest smiles emerged on Marquan and Jahleysa's faces.

"I would get up and give you a hug and a kiss right now, but you know these punk ass guards ain't having that shit."

"Well, I got chu faded once the visit's over."

"Cool."

Marquan and Jahleysa spent the rest of her visit smiling and reminiscing. Once it was over, they kissed for as long as they could before one of the correctional officers broke it up. Once the loved birds finally parted they both were floating like they drunk Red Bulls.

Marquan dropped $500 dollars on Mack to get him a cell phone. Every night he'd call Jahleysa and they'd chop it up until she fell asleep. They talked about any and everything that came across their minds. The time seemed to fly by any time they got on the phone with one another. There wasn't a time during their conversations where they weren't talking, laughing, smiling or joking. It seemed like good times to them, and they loved it.

"Alright, I love you, too. Peace." Marquan disconnected the call and stashed his cellular where he always did once he'd gotten off of it.

"Awww, to be young and in love," 187 stated from where he was on the bottom bunk reading a Smooth magazine. A smile was across his lips.

Marquan laughed and said, "I can't front, OG, it feels good, real good."

"Happy for you, young homie; love can be a beautiful thing. I hope everything turns out how you want it to once you released."

"I hope so, too. But if it doesn't, I'ma say fuck it and roll with the punches. You feel me?"

"I most definitely do. That's all you can do, shit. Believe me, I know how it goes."

Silence fell in the cell and the two men were left with their thoughts. 187 continued to read his magazine while Marquan's mind brought him to his son. It had been a while since he last talked to Antonio. All the letters he sent him went unanswered and his phonecalls were never answered. The thought of not speaking to his son until he was free was driving him crazy. He loved his little man to death, and to hear his voice again would bring him great joy.

Marquan grabbed his contraband cell phone and hit up his baby momma. The phone rung and rung, he was about to hang up when Apocalypse answered.

This surprised Marquan because no one would answer the last million times he'd called.

"'Sup with it, cuz? I heard you droppin' the soap on purpose up in there." Apocalypse laughed like he told the greatest joke in the world.

Marquan shut his eyelids and massaged the bridge of his nose as he took a deep breath. He knew it was important he kept his cool if he was going to get the chance to talk to his son.

"Yo', man, you think it's okay if I talk to my son?"

"Hmmm, lemme think," Apocalypse was silent for a moment before responding again. "Fuck no! Ain't shit changed, loc. It's like I told you, I'm daddy now, and I'm runnin' the show."

Marquan's brows mushed together and he bit down on his bottom lip hard. He was on fire inside. The vein at his temple twitched as if it was going to explode as he clenched his fist. His nostrils expanded and shrunk as he tried to calm himself. He took a few short, quick breaths to settle his nerves before responding to Apocalypse.

"I can't believe Adele ass done let cho punk ass play me like this! Both of y'all ain't shit, two disloyal ass bitches, cuz, on me!"

"You straight, homie?" 187 called out from the bottom bunk. There was concern dripping from his vocal cords.

"Yeah, I'm good, OG, just chopping it up with this mark ass nigga that I thought was my ace." Marquan responded to his big homeboy.

"Whateva, nigga," Apocalypse blew off what he had to say. "Anyway, here's a bit of info you may wanna know…You gettin' knocked fa that murda and gettin' alla that time…Well, me and wifey set that up," he laughed heartedly and then said, "Yeah, baby, team work makes the dream work. Goodnight, bitch-nigga!"

"Grrrrr," Marquan forced his face into the mattress, screaming and punching it. He was frustrated as a mothafucka and this was his only way of releasing it. Feeling someone grab his leg, he turned around on his bunk, fist clenched, ready to bust a nigga in his mouth. The tension eased from his body once he saw that it was just 187.

"What's up, young homie?" 187's forehead deepened with creases.

Marquan shut his eyelids briefly and took a breath before telling him what had happened. "…Yeah, so the nigga admitted that him and my baby momma set me up, cuz."

"Damn," 187 bowed his head and rubbed the back of his neck. "Boy, I tell ya, it seems like loyalty and respect no longa exist anymore. There ain't a mothafucka you can trust in here or out in them streets."

"You ain't never lied, G," Marquan sat up on his bunk, looking to be thinking about something. "This whole thing is fucking with me though. 'Cause I can't figure out why this nigga played me like this. I was ride or die for that man, loc.If he asked me to lay down and die for his ass I woulda done it with no questions asked. That's how much love I had for that mothafucka." His face twisted up and he balled his fist so tight that his knuckles bulged in his hands. He then bowed his head and ran his hands down his face, taking a deep breath. When he looked back up at 187, the OG could tell that he was stressing from the expression on his face.

"My nigga," 187 began. "I'm up in this mothafucka with you, but you know I'm plugged in with some powerful cats. My reach exceeds these walls; I can get cha man out there touched. All you gotta do is gemme the word and I'll put in the call."

Marquan looked at 187 like he was thinking it over. He then said, "Thanks but no thanks. I gotta be the one that splits this cock sucka's wig. If he gone get touched then he's gotta get touched by me, this shit is personal."

"I undastand," he claimed. "But should you change ya mind, holla at me."

"Fa sho'."

After they dapped up, 187 lay back down on his bunk and went back to reading his Smooth magazine.

Marquan lay back on his bunk with his fingers interlocked behind his head. He stared up at the ceiling, thinking. Eventually his eyelids grew so heavy he could no longer keep them open and he found himself asleep. He dreamed about a million ways he could kill Apocalypse. A smile slowly spread across his face.

****

187 reached out to Chino for a sit-down and he obliged. He was hoping to holla at him to see if they could come to some sort of mutual agreement so Marquan wouldn't have to walk the yard with a second pair of eyes in the back of his head. 187 and Chino, the shot callers, agreed to meet one on one inside of the library.

"I called for this sit-down in hopes we could come to some kind of mutual agreement." 187 began. He and Chino were standing on either side of a book shelf that stretched as long as the asile. They could partially see one anothers faces as they conversed and pretending to read books.

"I already know what you're gonna ask, and the answer is no."

"No?" 187 frowned up. The last thing he was expecting to hear was no.

"That's right, no." Chino said in a harsh whisper with his thick eyebrows slanting. There were creases at the beginning of his nose. He couldn't believe that 187 had the audacity to ask him to let that nigga Marquan breathe after he'd smoked his homeboy.

Hearing a noise coming from his left, Chino looked and saw another convict searching for a book to check out. The man appeared to be minding his own business and not paying any attention to him so he carried on with his conversation. "The Vato that your compadre wasted was my daughter's godfather, and he was like a brother to me. No way am I going to let this one slide, you'd do yourself a favor staying out of the way."

"And if I don't?" 187 shut his book and put it back in its rightful place. Using his finger, he looked through the names of the books which were located on their spines. The way he was carrying on, anyone looking would assume that he wasn't conversing with anyone. He was just a man looking for something interesting to read.

"Then it's gonna be two dead mayates, instead of one!" Chino spat sharper than he was suppose to and snapped the book shut. His nostrils were flaring and his chest was enlarging and shrinking with each breath he took. A vein bulged on his temple from his being so angry. Since he found out about Popeye's murder, he had been fucked up in the pen. The nigga was drinking pruno and getting high. This was bad. He was a shot caller among his soldiers so he always had to be ready to lead them and make calculated decisions. He knew that he couldn't do that if he was fucked up on all of the poisons at his disposal. Those two weeks he was getting shit-faced, he really let himself go, and promised himself when he stopped that he'd never fuck around with drugs and alcohol again.

187 looked up and down the aisle for anyone who may have heard Chino's hostile ass, but he didn't see anyone standing by, so he went on to address him. "Say no more, do what chu gotta do, homeboy."

"Oh, believe me, I will." Chino assured him. "Popeye's murder is not something I'm willing to over look, no matter what. I believe in death before dishonor, and I would be dishonoring my friend if I allowed his killer to live. I'm sure you understand."

"Indeed I do."

"Good. I know you have love for this Marquan character, so outta respect for you, I'll make sure my people make his death as quick and as clean as possible."

"Fuck you," 187 spat heatedly and walked off. He left Chino in the aisle, placing his book back where he'd gotten it and pulling out another one.

CHAPTER TEN

A couple of days later

Chino stood before the mirror slicking his hair back. Once he was done, he combed his hair back and looked himself over. Seeing that he had a few long strands of hair that didn't lay down, he combed his hair back some more and then patted it down. Satisfied with how he looked, he then went about the task of smacking on some aftershave and straightening out his uniform. Smiling from ear to ear, he turned around to Napoleon. He outstretched his arms and struck a pose, with his feet forming half of the number four.

"Say, Napoleon, how do I look?" Chino asked in his thick accent.

Napoleon, who was lying down on his side, looking at some naked flicks some girls had sent him, looked up at Chino.

"You look like a million bucks, homie." He told him. "Who came to see you, your old lady?"

Chino frowned up and said, "Hell naw, that hood rat left me hanging in here a couple of years ago, I told you about that shit."

"Oh yeah, you did," he recalled. "It must have slipped my mind."

"I don't exactly know who it is, but I'm banking on it being my sister. She's the only one that comes to visit me around this time of the year."

"Shit, man, I won't see my chica 'til next month, you're lucky."

"Lucky? Shiiit, if I was lucky it would be some fine piece of ass for me to run up in and not my kid sister coming to see me." Chino gave himself one last look before he headed out of his cell.

****

Chino made his way inside of the visitors' room along with all of the other convicts. One by one, the convicts located their loved ones and went to meet up with them. Chino stood where he was, looking all around for his sister, brows furrowed. Across the room he spotted a Mexican man of average height. He looked like he could be anywhere from thirty to thirty-five years old. His head was shaved on the sides and his jet black hair was slicked back. He was clean shaven and had an ugly scar on his cheek. The white T-shirt he had on was crisp with a crease down the middle of it. The man motioned Chino over, which was odd to him, because he didn't know him from a hole in the wall. Still, Chino's curiosity got the best of him, so he decided to see what the man requesting an audience with him wanted.

"What's up?" Chino threw his head back as he stood beside the table.

"Have a seat," the man motioned towards the chair sitting on the opposite side of the table.

"Do we know each other?" His forehead creased.

The man smirked and motioned towards the chair again, speaking more sternly this time around, he said, "Sit down."

Chino adjusted his glasses and took a breath before sitting down across from the man that had came to visit him.

"Okay, state your business."

"You don't know us, but we most definitely know you."

"Us?"

"Yes, my people and the organization that we are affiliated with."

At that moment, Chino searched the man's arms for tattoos. He definitely had some. In fact, he was covered in them from neck to sleeve. The ink that stood out the most to him was the one on the inside of his arm. There was a burning skull with a capital *S* behind it. There were also snakes coming out of the eye sockets of the skull and a revolver sticking out of its mouth. The number one and the number seven was on either side of the pistol. This made the complete number 187 which was police code for homicide. The ink on the inside of his arm represented the Sanchez Cartel. This was one of the most infamous and ruthless cartel's south of the border.

The Sanchez Cartel? What the fuck do they want with me? Chino tried to compose himself as best as he could. The last thing he wanted was this mothafucka sitting across from him to think that he had him shook, even though he did.

When Chino looked up, he found homeboy smiling at him devilishly. He could see all the shiny gold teeth inside of his grill. It was from his sinister smiling that he learned the man's name. As soon as Chino captured the letters spelled out across his gold grill, the man's wet tongue slid across it. Chino looked to the man's hands and noticed that his finger tips had been burned off. This was so the authorities wouldn't be able to identify him easily through fingerprinting. It was from this that Chino knew that old boy was definitely the notorious hit-man known as…

Skarfase! I remember this fool! I saw 'em on youtube hacking off the limbs and head of a rival cartel's hit-man. I mean, he was masked up so I couldn't see his face, but the tattoo and the gold grill is a dead giveaway. How in the fuck did he get over the border and inside of this prison?

"I can tell by that look on your face that you're familiar with my organization and our work. That's good, that's realll good. You know why?" Skarfase went on to answer the question he'd posed himself. "'Cause that means I don't have to tell you what will happen to your loved ones if Lavar Chiles or Marquan Ludlow are harmed."

"Oh yeah? Well, tell me, Mr. Skarfase," Chino leaned forward and interlocked his fingers on the table top. His eyebrows were sloped and his nose was scrunched up. "What will happen to my loved ones if Mr. Ludlow and Mr. Chiles' throats are slit from ear to ear?"

Skarfase looked around the room to see if anyone was eavesdropping on the conversation at hand. At that time, there wasn't anyone paying attention to them. Acknowledging this, Skarfase focused his attention back on Chino. He licked his lips as he massaged his chin before addressing him.

"Anita, Rebecca, Cynthia, Jessica, Patrick, Charlie, Emanuel, Jesus, Lisa, Teddy, Cedric, Danny…" Skarfase went on to name about thirty family members of Chino's before he eventually stopped and leaned forward so that only he could hear what was about to be said next. Jabbing his crooked finger down into the table top, he said, "I have specific orders to take out your entire bloodline should anything happen to Chiles or Ludlow behind these walls. And once those orders are carried out, I am to make sure that you meet the same fate as your relatives." With that said, he leaned back in his chair wearing that smirk he had earlier, when he first spoke to Chino. He decided to let what he had said settle in Chino's mind before he continued their conversation. "Do we understand one another here, Mr. Rodriguez?" he called him by the last name listed on his birth certificate.

Chino looked at Skarfase with a defeated look on his face and said, "Yeah, I understand."

"Good. Now, smile and wave to our buddy over there across the room," Skarfase threw his head to his left.

When Chino looked to where Skarfase had thrown his head and found 187. The OG smiled and waved from where he was sitting at the table talking to his loved one. Chino gave him a weak smile and waved at him awkwardly.

"Adios mi amigo," Skarfase rose to his feet and approached Chino. Leaning forward, he whispered into his ear. "Remember what I said, puto, nothing happens to the Negroes or else." He took his face from the side of Chino's and made his way out of the visitors' room.

Once Skarfase had left, Chino found himself still sitting at the table, watching 187 from a far. The OG, still smiling, held up two middle fingers and chuckled. He then waved Chino off and carried on with his conversation with his loved one.

****

Marquan sat up as soon as he saw 187 return to their cell after his visit. Sitting up where he was, he watched the older gangsta prepare to clean their cell up.

"Well?" Marquan stated.

"Well, what?" 187 asked as if he didn't know what he was talking about.

"Are you shitting me, man?" his forehead wrinkled.

187 chuckled and said, "I'm fuckin' witchu, my young nigga. My folks got at cuz in a real way, had 'em lookin' like he saw a ghost. I know for sho' ain't shit gone happen to you or me now. We good. In fact, Chino's gone make sure don't nobody fuck with us 'cause that'll be his brown ass. You dig?"

"You got it like that, OG?"

"Man, listen, that spic don't want no funk with them niggaz I'm plugged in with. My boys are…" he ran to the cell and looked up and down the tier to make sure that no one was listening in on his conversation. Once he saw that there wasn't anyone listening in on them, he made his way back over to Marquan, talking in a hushed tone. "My boys are in one of the most dangerous cartels that there is, The Sanchez Cartel. He'd be a suicidal mothafucka to buck against them beanas. They don't play, I'm sho' you seen their handiwork."

"Yeah, cuz, who don't know about them boys and what they do? They're about that action." He confirmed. "What I wanna know is, how the fuck you manage to get plugged in with them cartel niggaz?"

"I slumped the bastard that raped the head of the cartel's daughter."

Marquan's brows creased. "Mothafucka raped the head of the cartel's daughter?"

"Yeah, man, can you believe it? Lil' momma was just eight years old." 187 shook his head as his eyes became misty. He thought about how the little girl had been done. The word was out in the streets that the suspect had fled over into the United States to escape persecution from the Sanchez Cartel. He'd gotten drunk one night at a Mexican bar and started crying like a bitch, confessing his sins to the bartender. Word of his sick act spread throughout the streets like a wild fire, but no one sought out to make the sadistic bastard pay for his evil deed. "Anyway, I tracked that mothafucka down and dismembered him. I filmed the entire thang and made sure the head honcho got his hands on the footage. I told him that this was my gift to him. That all I wanted in return was his friendship, and that's how I gained favor with them boys, man. I knew that one day I'd find myself behind these walls for the shit I was doin' out there in them streets, so I wanted to have somebody that would look out for me. I ain't no fool. Family is family, but outta sight outta mind…mothafuckaz will forget about chu while you up in here."

Marquan nodded his head. He understood where the OG was coming from. He knew that during his bid his loved ones would forget about him too, and that was something he'd have to cope with.

"OG, I'm not tryna be all up in yours, but…"

"You wanna know what I'm caged up for, right?" 187 cut him short, already knowing what he was going to inquire about.

"Yeah. I mean, you ain't gotta say, I'm just curious. That's all."

"Alright, I'll tell you…" 187 began as he lay back on his mattress.

187 was as tired as a race horse when he pulled into the driveway of his home. He had just gotten off of his construction job, so he was dressed in a reflector vest, jeans and boots. There were also smears of dirt on his clothing and he was a little musty, but he didn't mind. His hard labor gig was better than the last job he had in prison, which was making him peanuts compared to the dough he was racking up now.

187 killed the engine of his Blazer and unbuckled his safety belt. Smiling, he grabbed the Tiffany & Co bag lying on the front passenger seat and opened it. Reaching inside, he pulled out a small burgundy velvet box and opened it. Propped up inside there was an 8k platinum and diamond engagement ring. The ring was absolutely beautiful, and had set 187 back like a mothafucka. He didn't care though. He knew that his girlfriend, Vernetta, of six years would love it.

"Boyyy, wait 'til my baby sees this," A smile stretched across 187's lips and revealed the teeth at the bottom of his mouth, which were bunched together. The sunlight shined in through the driver's window and kissed off the diamonds of the engagement ring, creating a colorful rainbow.

187 shut the velvet box and stuck it inside of his pocket. He then hopped out of his truck and slammed the door shut. Heading across the lawn, he recited to himself what he was going to say in his proposal to his girlfriend.

187 came inside of his house and shut the door behind him. He called out to his girlfriend, but she didn't respond. He went to all of the rooms down stairs calling out her name, but still, he didn't receive a response. Journeying upstairs, he heard the pleasured moans of a woman...his woman. He silently prayed to God that he was in the Twilight Zone, and that his ears were deceiving him, but he knew better.

Cracking open his bedroom door, 187 saw some nigga fucking his girlfriend like a donkey. All he could see was homeboy's muscular form. His slightly hairy buttocks slammed into her from behind as she called out in pleasure. Beads of sweat rolled down the back of his neck and disappeared between the crack of his ass.

Heartbroken, 187 closed the bedroom door halfway, and walked back inside of the hallway. He placed his back up against the wall and wiped the tears that slid down his cheeks, with the back of his fist. He tilted his head back and shut his eyelids and swallowed the ball of hurt in his throat. Bringing his head back down, he peeled his eyelids back open and frowned. Madness danced in his pupils and he squared his jaws, etching out the bone structure in them. Abruptly, he peeled himself up from off the wall and made his way down the staircase casually. As he walked downstairs and headed towards the garage, he could still hear that nigga upstairs in his bedroom donkey fucking his girlfriend.

187 opened the door that led inside of the garage and stepped down the small set of steps. He flipped on the light switch and made a beeline towards the tool box. He opened its lid and rummaged inside of it. Pulling out a hammer, he looked at it and tested its weight. All he could think about was the damage he could cause with the hammer.

187 went to turn his back to leave when his eye caught something above on the wall. Looking up, he saw an ax sitting on two hooks. Its blade was razor sharp and shined. In fact, the blade of the tool was so clean, 187 could see himself in it when he picked it up from where it was placed on the hooks.

187 set the hammer back down inside of the tool box and took the ax into both hands. Still hearing his girlfriend getting fucked upstairs, he practiced swinging the ax at different angles. Once he was done, he held the ax down by his side and headed out of the garage. He made his way back up the staircase and down the hallway, making his way towards his bedroom.

187 reached his bedroom and pushed it open gently. The door squeaked, but that didn't stop the man from lapping away at Vernetta's buttocks. Her cries of pleasure bounced off the walls as the man continued to hump her and smack her across her ass. He was hot, sticky, and sweating. He dripped his perspiration on her back and grunted as he pumped madly.

"Ah, fuck, I'ma 'bouta cum, I'm 'bouta cum!" Vernetta called out with her eyelids squeezed shut. The side of her head was mashed down against the mattress from the weight of her fuck-buddy's foot. He was banging that ass out, laying pipe like a porn star and making her make sounds that her boyfriend never had. "Don't stop, don't stop, Oooooooh my God!" her eyes rolled so far back inside of her head that only the whites of her eyes were visible. Her mouth hung wide open because she was having the sound fucked out of her ass.

187 eased inside of the bedroom and hoisted up the ax. A gleam swept up the blade of the tool and it twinkled at its sharp end. Vernetta had just had an orgasm, when he lifted his ax and swung it downward. Half of the ax was buried into the back of the skull of the man that was fucking Vernetta. His eyes stretched wide open and his mouth hung open. With the ax still buried halfway inside of his head, the man turned around and looked at 187 with accusing eyes. He outstretched his hand trying to touch him, but he stepped out of the reach of him. The man's pupils rolled up into the back of his head and he fell over the side of the bed, with the ax still sticking out of the back of his dome.

"Ahhhhh! Ahhhhh! Ahhhhh!" Vernetta screamed in horror as she stared down at her dead fuck-buddy and trembled all over. Her hands were shaking so much that they looked like blurs to a mad dogging 187. He spared her a menacing look as he grabbed the ax and pressed his boot against the dead man's back. He tugged on the ax three times before it finally came loose and sent blood splattered everywhere. 187 took the time to admire his handiwork before kicking the dead body to make sure that it had expired. Confirming the kill, he hopped upon the bed and hoisted his ax above his head. He towered over his girlfriend as she stared up at him screaming louder and louder.

With a grunt, 187 brought the ax down with all his might. The blade cut through the ligaments of Vernetta's fingers and embedded its self into the center of her face. She went cock eyed and blood poured from the opening in her face. Nostrils flaring and chest thumping hard, 187 snatched the ax out of his girlfriend's face and hacked away at her like she was lumber. 187's shadow cast on the wall as he brought the ax up and down on the carcass, fast and angrily. Blood splattered on the wall that the shadow was on and made the scene more horrific.

When 187 was done, he stood in bed and looked down at his handiwork. His nostrils flared and his chest expanded as he breathed. He wiped his sweaty forehead with the back of his hand and jumped down from off the bed. Making his way towards the door, he came across the mirror of the nightstand. When he turned around, he found that his forehead was smeared with blood where he'd wiped the sweat off. The rest of him was covered in splatters of blood from the double murder he'd committed. 187 looked the craziest in this moment, but he didn't give a shit though. For that level of disrespect, both of those mothafuckaz deserved what they'd gotten.

187 made his way out of the bedroom and down the staircase. He made a beeline inside of the kitchen, dropping the blood stained ax and continuing towards the refrigerator. He opened the refrigerator and grabbed himself a Corona from off the bottom shelf. Closing the refrigerator back, he opened the kitchen drawer and grabbed the bottle opener. He popped the lid off the beer and took it to the head. His throat rolled up and down his neck as he drunk from the golden, ice cold Corona bottle.

187 took the Corona from his lips and looked at the bottle admiringly. Hearing his stomach growling, he decided to make himself a sandwich. By the time he was done making the sandwich, he was grabbing another beer, pickles and a bag of Lays plain potato chips. With that, he headed back inside of the living room and turned on the TV. He watched the football game as he ate and drank his Corona, covered in blood, like he didn't just brutally murder two people.

"Damn, OG, like that?" Marquan asked as he lay on the top bunk.

"Yeah, young homie, I lost it."

"If you could take it back, would you?"

"Honestly," he took a deep breath. "Yeah, I regret it. I lost my cool and acted on emotions. Men don't operate on emotions, we move off logic. Just like a woman, I allowed my feelins to get the best of me. If I could turn back the hands of time, I would. Don't ever kill no man behind no woman that ain't yours. In fact, unless that woman is blood or has proven her loyalty to you, you shouldn't be raisin' gun or fists behind her. You hear me, cuz?"

"Copy that, OG."

"Shiiit."

"What's up?"

"Talkin' about that shit made me think about my daughter, man. I been down eight summas, I've been gone a chunk of her life. I went in when she was a teenager."

"Yo' daughter isn't by homegirl you hacked up, is she?

"Naw, my princess is by a broad I slapped skins with back in the day. One night stand, man, I fucked around and got her pregnant."

"Damn, OG, I didn't even know you hadda daughter. Hell, I never even thought it was a possibility. I mean, with the way you were out there in the streets ripping and tearing shit up. It never occured to me that chu had a lil' momma somewhere."

"Yeah, I said the same thang, but killin' can become addictive, especially when you add money to it."

"Or a cause…" Marquan interlocked his hands behind his head. "I done tore many heads off in the name of the set. Done laid many bustas down over bad business too."

"I can dig it, young homie."

"You gotta picture of yo' daughter, OG?" Marquan looked over the edge of his bunk.

"Sure," 187 reached underneath his pillow for the picture of his daughter, Heiress. He kept it here because he looked at the photo every night before he went to sleep. Pulling out the picture, he took a good look at it before he passed it up to Marquan.

Receiving the picture, Marquan lay back on his bunk and looked at the teenage girl in it. She had the exact same face as 187, except her complexion was walnut. She had slanted eyes like a Korean, full lips, and hair styled into dread locks.

"She's beautiful," Marquan claimed as he hung over his bunk and passed 187 back the picture of his daughter.

"Thanks, man," he said as he stared at the picture with tears in his eyes. It hurt like hell that he'd missed so much of his daughter's life. He knew if he had just walked away from his girlfriend's infidelity that he'd still be in the outside world with Heiress, but that wasn't the case. The mistake that he made could never be taken back, no matter what he did. That's just the way it is. "My lil' princess is my reason for breathin' right now. You feel me?"

"Yeah, I feel you, OG. The same goes for me and my son. I'ma survive this nightmare and get back to the outside to him."

Marquan and 187 went on to chop it up for hours.

~The next day~

Chino called a meeting with his car and told them to fall back from trying to whack Marquan. None of them were feeling it being that Popeye was a member of their organization, but they didn't dare buck against their leader's command. Chino was the shot caller and his word was rule. If either of them were to go against what he said then he'd order their asses hit just as fast as he had Marquan.

As of now, Chino was standing before the sink flossing his teeth when Napoleon entered his cell. Seeing him approaching from out of the corner of his eye, he stopped flossing and turned around to him. Seeing the angered look on his face caused him to frown up. A concerned expression crossed his face.

"Gemme the good news first," Chino took a deep breath and folded his arms across his chest.

"There is no good news, only bad." Napoleon told him.

"So, spit it out."

"It's Mack," Napoleon began. "That's one dirty ass mayate…" he went on to tell Chino what he discovered about the crooked correctional officer. By the time he'd finished, the shot caller was 38 hot. Grabbing his cell phone, he hit up a couple of soldiers out on the streets to bust a move for him.

****

The sun was on the verge of setting making the sky a reddish orange hue. Dressed in his civilian clothing, and toting his lunch box, Mack came strolling out of the back door of the correctional facility, heading out into the parking lot, which was enclosed by four gates. He was talking to a couple of the other fellas that he worked with, but when he neared his vehicle, he bid them a farewell before going on about his business

"Alright, I'll see y'all niggaz tomorrow, man," Mack slapped hands with all of his co-workers and continued towards his car.

Mack smiled seeing his candy apple red '64 Chevrolet Impala on gold Daytonas, sitting low to the ground. All four windows of the classic car were tinted black. The vehicle was beautiful. The paint job on it was flawless. It had been waxed the day before so the prison reflected on the side of it.

Mack opened the door of his Chevy and slid in behind the wheel on the white leather seats. He sat his lunch box on the floor and popped the glove-box open. Reaching inside of the glove-box, he pulled out a Cuban cigar and slid it underneath his nose. As soon as he inhaled the fine scent, a big smile spread across his lips.

"I've been dreaming about chu all day long, sweetheart." He placed the overgrown cancer stick inside of his mouth and punched in the cigarette lighter. Shortly, it popped back out and he placed its ember against the end of his cigar. Holding his cigar to his mouth with one hand, he took a couple of puffs of it and clouds of smoke appeared before his eyes. Afterwards, he stuck the cigarette lighter back into its rightful place and indulged in his poison of choice. Smoke wafted around him as he continued to partake in his cigar.

Adjusting himself in his seat, Mack fixed the rearview mirror and fired up his low rider. He hit the switches on the sexy machine, and it tooted up twice before it was level. He switched the gears on the automobile and mashed out of his parking space. Pulling up to the gate, he flashed his badge across the electronic scanner, which a surveillance camera was positioned over. A second later, the red light on it turned green and the gate rolled back. Once the gate had cleared the path of Mack's Chevrolet Impala, he drove over the threshold and entered traffic

Mack sped through the streets with the windows of his whip down. The fresh air blew inside and ruffled his clothing, causing the collar of his coat to slap up against his chin. He sucked on the end of his Cuban cigar and continuously hit the switches of his low rider. Toying with the chrome switches made his Chevrolet Impala bounce up and down. He stopped hitting the switches and let his ride sit up high off the street. The rest of the ride home, Mack smoked on his cigar and nodded to Game's *The Documentary*.

Mack jumped on the freeway and jumped off of it. He stayed on the main streets for a while before he entered the residential ones. He bent a few corners before he found himself pulling up into the driveway of his two story, five bedroom home. He murdered the engine of his Chevy and the last song playing died off. Mack mashed out his cigar and grabbed his lunch box. He hopped out of his car and slammed the door shut behind him. Whistling Dixie, he made his way up the steps and stopped at the front door. Unlocking it, he pushed the door open and crossed the threshold, entering a dark house. There wasn't a single light on in the place, which he found strange. Standing in the doorway, the only thing that could be seen was his silhouette, and the outside light shining at his back.

"Julia, Nova, y'all home?" Mack called out to his wife and daughter, but he didn't receive a response. He flipped the light switch *on* and *off*, but it didn't come on. Unbeknownst to him, a dark figure emerged from behind him and snatched his gun from its holster. The dark figure slammed the door shut behind him. Instantly, muffled hollers and squirming could be heard.

"Who's there? Fuck is going on?" Mack called out into the darkness, unable to see anyone or anything now. Suddenly, a lamp light came on and he saw three faces. Two of them belonged to his wife and daughter. They were tied up nextto one another in chairs, wearing gags around their mouths. The third face was of a Mexican man wearing a blue bandana over the lower half of his face. He had a pair of menacing eyes and looked like he meant business.

"You shoulda learned to keep your big fuckin' mouth shut, homes. Playing both sides of the fence between us and the blacks, tisk, tisk, tisk," he shook his head and wagged his finger back and forth. "You shoulda known it would lead to this, it's time to pay the piper, homie."

"What? I don't know what you're talking about? Who sent chu? Chino?"

"You know exactly who sent us, you lying sack of shit. Now you crossed the powers that be, and now you gotta pay, with your life."

When he said this, Mack's eyes bulged and he gasped. A small burst of flames came from the left of him and his head jerked violently to the right as pieces of his skull and brain fragments went flying out of his head. Mack dropped to the carpeted floor dead. The cat that had put a bullet through his dome stepped over him and leveled his silenced gun to the back of his melon. He placed two more bullets into the back of it. Afterwards, he dropped the gun he'd snatched from Mack's holster down beside his corpse. The muffled hollers of his victim's wife and daughter stole his attention. He moved in, silenced gun pointed at them, ready to send them to the same place he'd sent their husband/father to.

"Relax," the Mexican wearing the blue bandana over the lower half of his face told his crime partner. "Let the ladies breathe easy, we got who we came here for."

"Right," the Mexican man said that had just taken out Mack. He lowered his gun and studied the terrified faces of Julia and Nova. He was wearing a black beanie on his head and a blue bandana over the lower half of his face, just like his crime partner.

The Mexican man with the gun watched as his crime partner set the lamp down on the floor beside Julia's leg. He then headed for the door, motioning for his comrade to follow him with his gloved hand.

The Mexican man with the gun stole one last glance back at Mack's family before he headed out of the door.

CHAPTER ELEVEN

2012

A twelve year old Antonio held fast to Apocalypse on the back of a gold moped as they flew down the street. He narrowed his eyelids into slits as the night's cold air blew in his face and ruffled his Orlando Magics jersey. His heart was thudding and his palms were damp from perspiration. He was nervous about the initiation he had to go through in order to be inducted into the crips; the same crip set that his father and Apocalypse claimed. Antonio understood that he was going to be a soldier on the frontlines and fight along other lost souls in a war that didn't have any ending in sight. The youngsta knew the stakes were high, and he stood to lose more than he stood to gain. But he wanted the same power that Apocalypse commanded. He saw how niggaz feared and respected him, and he wanted that kind of aura to surround him.

I wonder what it's gonna be like when I get there. Apocalypse said that I'll most likely have to fight, but I wonder who I'll have to throw hands with. Fuck it! It don't matter. Whoever it is, we gone squabble. I'ma show Apocalypse that like him, I ain't nothin' to play with. Niggaz gone see what I'ma 'bout. I'll live up to my father's name and make 'em proud.

Tears spilled from the corners of Antonio's eyes as thoughts of his father stirred up emotions inside of him. He wished his father was free so that they could do all of the stuff that father's and son's did. You know, like fishing, hunting, playing basketball, playing catch, playing video games, watching wrestling. These were all of the things that he saw some boys he knew do with their fathers. He figured that one day, if he was lucky, he'd get to have a relationship with his old man. If not, then he hoped that when he proved himself to the gang that his father would finally accept him. He truly believed that if he proved to be just as tough and as down for the hood as his old man was that his pops would call the house and let him come visit him. Until then, he was going to do everything in his power to live up to his father's name and prove himself to be worthy to wear the last name Ludlow.

Antonio looked up from where he had his face pressed against Apocalypse's back. He saw the gangsta's navy blue tank top ruffle as the wind blew against it, giving him glimpses of the *South Central* tattoo in Old English lettering going across the upper half of his broad back. He also saw the flap of his black doo-rag floating in the air courtesy of the wind. When he looked down at the street, he spotted the white lines in the road going by so fast that they appeared to come in flashes. Looking up ahead, he saw a Mac truck coming towards them. The wind shifted from the truck coming past them so fast and ruffled their clothing further.

Antonio narrowed his eyelids and his forehead wrinkled, feeling the shift of the wind as the Mac truck blew past him and Apocalypse. Before the youngsta knew it his stomach dropped as Apocalypse made a sharp turn at the corner, just as the stop light at the intersection turned red. Apocalypse was pushing the moped to its maximum speed, riding against the wind. By this time the tears had began to dry against Antonio's cheeks, so he used the lower half of jersey to wipe his face. The last thing he wanted was for the niggaz they were about to go see were dry tears on his cheeks. He didn't want them to look at him like he was soft. He wanted their respect.

"You good, cuz?" Apocalypse glanced over his shoulder.

“Yeah, I’m good.” Antonio replied.

“Fuck!” he looked at the street and saw his .9mm tumbling backward hastily.

“’Sup?” the young nigga asked.

“I dropped my strap. Hold on, cuz. I’m ‘bouta bust a bitch,” Apocalypse busted a U-turn against oncoming cars, drawing their horns and causing them to mash their brakes in a hurry. As soon as they did urrrrrks filled the air as their car’s tires came to an abrupt stop. “Y’all shut the fuck up!” he hollered back at the drivers of the vehicles he’d pissed off while in motion of his U-turn. Spotting his gun in the street, he swung the moped beside it and picked it up. Tucking it on his hip, he sped off and brought his moped before a Ford Taurus that had been damaged on the side from an old automobile accident. The automobile was at a red stop light alongside other cars waiting for the light to turn green so that they could proceed.

Apocalypse mad dogged the driver of the car who mad dogged him back, his top lip twitching with animosity. Apocalypse snatched his banga off his hip and pointed it at him. Instantly, the man cowered, eyes bulging and mouth trembling. He threw up his hands as they shook uncontrollably. All that tough talk was gone and he was as scared as a bitch now.

“Fuck was you sayin’ earlier, cuz, huh?” Apocalypse approached him on the moped at gunpoint. His brows were furrowed and his jaws were clenched in hostility. He was about to pop homeboy out there, but then he felt Antonio tugging on the end of his tank top. “What?” he barked at the youngsta in annoyance.

"Chill, dad, there's people out here watchin' you." Looking around, Antonio saw all the motorists that were watching Apocalypse in horror. Some of them had even started dialing up the police while others held up their cellular phone to film the occurrence. After what Antonio had said, Apocalypse, still pointing his banga at the motorist, looked around him. Indeed, the other drivers of the cars at the intersection were watching him nosily. Should he pull the trigger, this would be one murder that would stick.

"Youz a lucky ass nigga, homeboy." Apocalypse hawked up phlegm and spat on the motorist's windshield that he had pointed his gun at. The nasty goo splattered against the window's glass and began to slowly slide down it.

Apocalypse took off on the moped, speeding through Los Angeles traffic easily. He ended up at a Spanish stucco house on the North side of the city. He rode up on the sidewalk and brought his vehicle outside of the house's slightly rusted gate. He climbed off the moped and Antonio followed suit. Apocalypse lifted the latch of the gate and entered the yard with his surrogate son bringing up the rear. It was here that they found Naymond and a host of younger crips. They were chopping it up and smoking weed. Their chit chatter stopped as soon as they saw Apocalypse and Antonio approaching.

"Stay right here," Apocalypse told Antonio in a hushed tone over his shoulder, leaving him standing beside a tree. The youngsta stayed where he was and watched as his surrogate father chopped it up with a hefty fellow he knew as Naymond. Naymond was holding a blue, red nose pit bull on a chain. The chain was latched onto the spiked black leather collar of the dog's neck. Naymond was a wide body nigga who rocked his hair in thick dreads and shaved on the sides. His five o'clock shadow lined his meaty face perfectly; he was well groomed. At the time, he was in a blue Polo sweatsuit and Nike Air Maxes. A gold necklace hung loosely from around his neck and its charm was a hand throwing up Westside. As he and Apocalypse were talking, the big man took the blunt from his blackened lips and blew out smoke. Naymond then passed the wafting blunt to one of the younger crips standing beside him. Next, he gripped the chain that held his hound bound with both his chubby hands, listening to the rest of what Apocalypse had to say.

"…Nah, he ain't just some 'round the way lil' nigga. That's Marquan's blood, that's his son." Apocalypse finished.

"Marquan's son?" Naymond's forehead furrowed. "You sure cuz ain't gone trip 'bout chu sponsoring his lil' nigga into the set?"

Apocalypse glanced over at Antonio and shrugged, saying, "We were around his age when we got quoted on. Matter fact, we were even younger…eleven years old, loc. Couldn't nothin' or nobody stop us from bein' from the hood. Lil' cuz wants in, so I'ma oblige him. Ain't like we can't use mo' souljas, you feel me?" Naymond massaged his chin and slightly nodded his head as he gave the idea some thought. Coming up with his judgment, he allowed his hand to fall to his side.

"Alright," Naymond responded. "I'ma let Shady and School Boy put 'em on. We gone see what he can do with dem hands and then you gone have to put 'em behind one of dem thangs. You feel me?"

"Let 'em rock and roll, cuz," Apocalypse dapped him up. He then turned around and motioned for Antonio to come over into the fold.

"What's up with it, my young nigga?" Naymond addressed Antonio, slapping hands with him. "Sorry to hear about your old man, lotta homies fuck with cuz. He's a real one from the set, for real for real."

"Thanks," Antonio responded, taking in the faces of the younger crips that were present. None of these youngstas appeared to be friendly. They were all mad dogging him and twisting up their lips, trying their best to intimidate him. They all had been battled tested and Antonio would definitely have to show his worth if he wanted to brush shoulders with them. They weren't about to allow him to ride in their car without putting in his just due. Nah, fuck that! The little homie would have to put in the work if he wanted his ghetto stardom.

"So, Poc tells me you're ready to come home (which meant joining their gang)," Naymond stated, placing his hand on his shoulder. "Now, you know once you cross that line there's no turning back, 'cause once you're out here doing dirt; your name and face will be immortalized within our enemies' minds."

"I know." Antonio nodded his head, holding Naymond's gaze. "Poc, gave me the rundown 'bout everything. I know exactly what's in store and I'm ready."

"That's right," Apocalypse threw his around the youngsta's shoulders and smiled like a proud father. He had just began planting seeds and poisoning the youth's mind, but he was sure once he was done that he'd be the exact replica of him. As soon as he was finished grooming the boy there wouldn't be any questions of whether he was his protégé or not. "I schooled my young nigga to the game."

"I see. Well, did you also tell 'em that this shit here is for life?" Naymond said, lifting his hoodie to reveal the branding he'd gotten on his right peck with a branding iron. He'd gotten it done with the same branding iron farmers used on cows. The brand was of his neighborhood and he wore it proudly. The fat nigga loved his hood more than he loved his five kids. "And these don't come off." Once Naymond lifted up his hoodie to show off his brand, the rest of the younger crips were holding up their pants leg, shirt sleeve or shirt to show off the same brand.

Antonio took a good look around at all of the crips in his presence. The brands that they had looked like they hurt like hell to get, but he was more than willing to get one for himself. See, tattoos were one thing, but to brandish ones hood into the flesh showed commitment. It let your enemies know you were really with this gangbanging shit and you were willing to kill and/ or die behind it.

"This shit is like a marriage, cuz, straight up." Naymond pulled his hoodie back down over his belly.

Antonio nodded and said, "Well, I'm not gettin' cold feet." When he said this, Apocalypse chuckled and patted him on his back, gripping his shoulder.

"I hear that hot shit," Naymond said to him, then addressed everyone else. "Y'all come on. We 'bouta put this lil' nigga on the hood." He switched hands with the chain that held his pit bull and headed for the backyard with the homies following closely behind him.

****

After letting his pit bull loose in the patio, Naymond turned around to address Antonio.

"Alright, cuz," Naymond began, rubbing his hands together in anticipation. "There are a few things you need to know before we go ahead and…" Naymond cut himself short and his forehead wrinkled. At that moment, he witnessed Antonio whip around and sock Shady dead in his mothafucking mouth. The impact of the young nigga'z fist made Shady's jaws swell. The blow sent blood flying and made Shady stumble backwards. He was about to fall, but he regained his footing. Even Apocalypse was taken by surprise by Antonio's sudden attack.

Naymond and Apocalypse were in shock as Antonio seemed to be holding up fairly well against Shady and School Boy. Fists were thrown and niggaz went down, but they got right back up and kept at it. No one wanted to come out as the loser, especially Antonio. The boy was exhausted and his chest was on fire, but he fought on like a true warrior. Every time he thought about giving up and collapsing, he imagined his father, Marquan, standing nearby cheering him on.

"Alright, that's enough," Naymond called out. Although School Boy stopped, Shady and Antonio were still throwing hands. They were giving and taking it equally. That was until Antonio landed an overhand right and dropped his ass.

"Oooooh," Apocalypse wailed with his fist to his mouth, seeing the young nigga he'd brought up under his wing knockout one of his little homies.

"Damn, lil' cuz got hands." Naymond said, dapping up Apocalypse.

"That's right. That lil' mothafucka came up under my tutelage." Apocalypse stated with a serious expression, patting his comrade on the back.

Pissed off, a scowling Shady scrambled to his feet and tried to rush Antonio, but Naymond grabbed him up in a bear hug.

"That's enough, cuz, y'all gave the lil' homie his issue." Naymond told him. Veins bulged at his temples and he squared his jaws, as he held his little homie fast.

"Nah, fuck that shit, cuz. Lemme get that fair one wit 'em, lemme get 'em up wit cuz on mo' time." Shady struggled to get loose from his big homie, but his efforts were useless.

"Nah, Shady, cuz, that's it, it's a wrap."

"Alright," Shady submitted.

"I'm serious, cuz, or you gone get disciplined."

"Alright, cuz, I got chu."

"Cool." Naymond released Shady, leaving him feeling around the inside of his jaw with his tongue. Finding a bleeding sore, he hawked up blood and spat it out.

Antonio stood on wobbly legs panting out of breath, arms hanging at his sides. He wanted to collapse right there on the spot but his pride wouldn't allow it. Naymond looked over Antonio and his homeboys faces; Antonio had a swollen jaw, a bloody nose and busted lips. Shady's eye was swollen shut and his nose was twice its size. School Boy's left-eye had some discoloration, but besides that, he was fine. Everyone dapped up Antonio except Apocalypse; he wrapped the boy in a bear hug and lifted him off of his feet, leaving his legs dangling. Antonio winced in pain from his strong embrace.

"Ah, my ribs!" Antonio cried out.

"My bad," Apocalypse said, lowering the youngsta back to the ground.

"We gotta name this lil' nigga," Naymond stated as he hung his arm around Antonio's shoulders. "I was thinking that you'd like to ride your daddy's moniker." He looked to the youngsta and grinned. "So, how about…"

"Mannnn, fuck Mar…I mean, with all due respect to my Ace, I think the lil' homie should rock under my name. It's only right, I schooled cuz properly. He's my protégé." The homies listened to what Apocalypse had to say nodding their heads in approval. He was definitely telling the truth. He taught the youth everything he knew about the streets and he sponsored him into the set.

"My nigga gotta point, but it's up to Ant if he wants to rock yo' brand, cuz." He looked to Antonio and the boy looked to Apocalypse, who gave him a *tell them you fucking with me* nod. With that given, the boy nodded his head in agreement.

"Yeah, I'm all for it."

"Alright then, there you have it. Lil' Poc it is." Apocalypse walked up to his street son and gripped his shoulder firmly, as he stared into his eyes. "Now, that's a bad ass name you rockin'; you think you can live up to it and hold it down?"

"Yeah," Antonio nodded.

"Good!" Apocalypse continued. "That means you gotta put in work and represent the hood to the fullest. Gangbangin' is a full time job. There aren't any days off. You've gotta always be on your toes, so our enemies can't catch you slippin'. You feel me?"

Antonio nodded in agreement. "I hear you, dad, and I'ma represent this gangsta shit 'til the day I die."

"Sho' you right." He dapped the youngsta up.

"Now, if you niggaz are through having y'all lil' family moment. The rest of us would like to get back to getting high." Naymond held up a freezer bag halfway filled with the prettiest green buds. The rest of the homies nodded and said 'hell yeah', they were ready to get back to drinking and getting high.

"Well, let the festivities continue, my niggaz." Apocalypse rubbed his hands together in anticipation.

With the okay given, Naymond rolled up a fat ass blunt and put fire to it. He took a few puffs and passed it off to Antonio. Antonio hit it and passed it to Apocalypse, who took a few puffs and passed it to Shady. From there, the fraction of crips added two more blunts to the rotation. Niggaz got high, I mean, really high that night.

"I'd like to propose a toke to the newest recruit to the hood, Lil' Poc." Naymond said lazy eyed, holding up a wafting blunt.

"To Lil' Poc!" The homies said in unison. They then took either puffs of their respective blunts or a swig of their alcohol beverages.

CHAPTER TWELVE

Later that night

Apocalypse pushed the G-ride, occasionally looking over to the front passenger seat at Antonio. The young nigga was tipsy and high. It was his first time getting shit faced, so needless to say the effects of the alcohol and weed hit him twice as hard. Apocalypse had gotten the youngsta faded to ease his nerves for the night's mission. The homies had already seen what he could do in a fight, but now he needed to see what he could do in ghetto warfare. Since his surrogate son was going to be wearing his name, he had to be with the shit. His G had to match his own.

Antonio's eyelids were narrowed and his eyes were red webbed. He rode shotgun, taking puffs from the roach end of the blunt pinched between his fingers, polluting the interior with funky smoke. Once he was done, he flicked what was left of it out of the window and sent embers flying. He then expelled the last of the smoke from his nostrils and mouth. He was relaxed and down for whatever now.

"Alright, there them niggaz go," Apocalypse stated when he spotted the niggaz he had in mind to murk. He pulled the Nike baseball gloves from out of the console and slipped them on, flexing his fingers inside of them. He then reached underneath the driver's seat and pulled out a gun. *Click! Clack!* Apocalypse chambered a copper hollow tip bullet into the black compact .9mm handgun. "Here you go." He passed the banga to Antonio. The youngsta looked from the gun in his gloved hands to Apocalypse. An evil smile creased Apocalypse's lips, seeing his homeboy's son hold the Death Dealer in his hands. He couldn't help thinking back to a time when he held his first gun. He was only ten years old and stood about five feet then. But the gat he'd purchased made him feel like he was six foot seven. He knew he had great power in his possession. No one could tell him that he wasn't God Almighty; he had the ability to take someone's life or let them keep it.

Apocalypse murdered the headlights of the G-ride. He looked back and forth from the windshield to the passenger window. His eyes were focused on a silver '96 Chevrolet Caprice that had pulled up inside of a Valero gas station. The hood classic stopped at a pump and smoke billowed out of the widows, and so did laughter. Right after, the driver, a tall nigga dressed in a black Dickie suit and Chuck Taylors with fat blue laces, hopped out of the car. He blew smoke into the air and made his way around his vehicle, flicking the dollar bills in his hand with fingers. He glanced up at the number on the pump he'd parked in front of as he made his way towards the entrance doors of the gas station.

"Yo, cuz, get me some Skittles!" The front passenger called out from where he was. He had the roach end of a blunt pinched between his finger and thumb. He was wearing a black L.A fitted cap turned backwards. The diamond earrings in his lobes gleamed under the soft lighting of the gas station. He had bad acne and little facial hair to speak of.

"Aiight," the driver said as he disappeared through the doors of the gas station.

By this time, Apocalypse had stopped the car completely, leaving him and Antonio across the street from the gas station. They were underneath the shade of a tree. It looked like there wasn't anyone occupying the vehicle they were in due to its limousine tinted windows.

"Alright, get ready, young nigga," Apocalypse told him as he pulled a bandana over the lower half of his face.

"Okay," Antonio said as he followed suit. Althugh he was nervous, he was eager to prove himself to his surrogate father.

"Now, there's two fools left in the whip; one in the front passenger seat and one in the back." Apocalypse made his observation.

"The driver went into the gas station; I should make my move now."

"Alright, hop out and do yo' thang, John Wayne." He dapped Antonio up and he hopped out of the car, shutting the passenger door as quietly as he could. Hunched over, he made hurried footsteps across the street with his gun held low at his side. His head snapped up and down the block in case there were any witnesses or police presence. Seeing that the close was clear, he proceeded with his mission.

Antonio had gotten up close enough on the car to spit on it. When he sprung up from where he was hunched, he saw the front seat passenger passing a withering blunt to the backseat passenger. When the front passenger saw Antonio's young ass with his hands wrapped around his gun, his eyes nearly leaped out of skull and his jaw dropped. He ended up dropping the blunt into his homeboy's lap, which caused him to go crazy, smacking the blunt from off of his lap. His slapping the burning blunt from off his crotch sent ashes and embers flying as he raised his ass from off the seat.

"Cuz, what the fuck is yo'…" The frowning backseat passenger's words died in his throat once he saw the front seat passenger's shocked face. He looked in the direction that he was looking and found Antonio with his gun pointed at him. "Oh, sh…"

Bloc! Bloc! Bloc! Bloc!

The front passenger's face balled up in agony as he took two in the chest and fell back up against the front passenger door. His eyes stared out of their corners and his mouth hung open in a grotesque manner. As soon as Antonio slumped him, he turned the fury of his gun on the nigga in the backseat. He clapped at him twice. The first shot shattered the back window and the second one struck him in the shoulder. He threw his head back hollering in excruciation and grabbing his wounded shoulder, causing blood to seep between his fingers. Antonio was just about to send a few more his way when he caught something in his peripherals. When he looked up, the driver was dropping the brown paper bag of goods he'd purchased and drawing his gun. His cap flew off his head as he came running in Antonio's direction shooting at him.

Splocka! Splocka! Splocka!

The driver sent heat at the young nigga and sent him retreating back across the street. Seeing that his surrogate son was in danger, Apocalypse hurried got out of the car and pointed his gun over the roof of the G-ride. He squeezed off rapidly.

Blocka! Blocka! Blocka! Blocka! Blocka!

The returned fire sent the driver backpedaling and ducking down beside his vehicle. This gave Antonio enough time to hop back into the front passenger seat. As soon as he jumped in, Apocalypse ducked back inside of his whip and pulled off.

Splocka! Splocka!

Bullets whizzed through the back window of the G-ride and peppered the backseat with broken glass. Apocalypse and Antonio ducked down as far as they could to avoid the bullets that were meant to blow their heads off. Apocalypse glanced up in the rearview mirror and saw the driver standing at the driver's door of his vehicle. He was holding the door open and shooting at them.

Having seen this, Apocalypse brought the G-ride to a crawl and told Antonio to steer it. Afterwards, he oozed out of the driver's window and pointed his gun in the driver's direction. The driver had just jumped in behind the wheel of his whip and slammed the door shut. He was pulling off when Apocalypse gripped his weapon with both hands and squeezed one eyelid shut. He breathed easily and pulled the trigger, twice. The first bullet cracked the corner of the windshield into a cobweb while the next one struck the gas pump. Instantly, the gas pump exploded and ignited everything surrounding it, including the car toting the driver that was busting on Apocalypse and Antonio.

Apocalypse could hear the surviving men inside of the car screaming and hollering as they were being burned alive. The car swerved out of control and crashed into a telephone pole, bending it at its grill.

Apocalypse sat back down in the car and mashed the gas pedal. He sped off from the scene and adjusted the rearview mirror. Looking up into it, he saw a fire ball fly up into the sky and light it up. The light from the fire in the sky illuminated the backs of Apocalypse and Antonio as they put the scenery in the back of them.

"You good, cuz?" Apocalypse looked back and forth between the windshield and Antonio.

"Yeah, I'm good." He nodded as he looked down at his gun, which he'd used to slump homeboy in the front passenger seat.

"Congratulations, kid, you popped yo' cherry." He gripped Antonio's shoulder and shook him in a show of affection, "You officially a killa, cuz."

“Where we goin’ now?” he asked curiously.

To burn this bitch up, we don’t needa get caught riding dirty in this mothafucka.”

Apocalypse drove the G-ride to an area that was scarcely occupied. He and Antonio hopped out of the vehicle and lit the rags that hung out of the necks of the Molotov cocktails that Antonio made on the way over. As soon as the flames of the rags began to devour them, the crips threw them at the G-ride and they exploded into shattered glass and flames. The fire raged and quickly began to devour the car. Hunched down, they took off running with their arms thrown over their heads and their eyelids narrowed into slits. They were expecting the G-ride to explode any time now.

Ka-boom!

Burning wreckage, broken glass and fire went flying everywhere from the ruined vehicle. Apocalypse and Antonio ran as long and as far as they could. Once they slowed down and stopped, their faces were hot and sticky with sweat. They made their way down the sidewalk and sat down on the bus stop bench. Apocalypse threw his arm around Antonio’s shoulders and pecked him on the side of his head. He told him how proud of him he was as they waited for the bus to come.

****

Apocalypse sat on the opposite end of the kitchen table from Antonio. At the center of them were a coffee pot, Gemstar razors, a freezer bag of cocaine, Arm & Hammer baking soda, latex gloves, a plate and a big spoon. Apocalypse took a pull from his blunt and blew out a cloud of smoke, which wafted around him and obscured Antonio’s view of his face. Blowing the last of the smoke from out of his nostrils, he addressed his homeboy's son. "Listen up, lil' nigga, I'ma keep it one hunnit witchu. You gettin' olda now so you gone have to start pullin' ya weight around here. You eat, sleep and shit, and alla that shit costs money. You feel me? Ain't no free rides in the real world, so you gone have to bring somethin' to the table. So, I'ma 'bouta give yo' lil' ass a hustle," he took the time to suck on the end of the blunt and blow out a cloud of smoke. Afterwards, he dabbed out the ember of his blunt inside of the ashtray and laid it down in it. Antonio watched Apocalypse attentively as he pulled a pair of latex gloves over his hands. He placed some of the cocaine he had on the digital scale and watched the red numbers change before his eyes. Once the numbers stopped, he knew exactly what he had.

"This about twenty-eight grams right here; that's an ounce," Apocalypse announced to the youngsta. "Now, pay close attention, cuz, 'cause I'ma 'bouta show you how to cook this shit up, fuckin' with me you gone be a millionaire out this bitch." Apocalypse turned on one of the burners of the stove, turning the dial so that the blue flames were at the height that he wanted. With that done, he put four grams of the coke and the baking soda into the coffee pot, adding the amount of water he desired.

"Ant, you payin' attention?" he asked, watching the water fill the coffee pot.

"Yeah, I'm payin' attention." Antonio answered as he studied every move that his teacher was making. You would have thought that he was a student in chemistry class.

"Good." Apocalypse replied, sitting the coffee pot on the flames of the burner. "Now, we gone let this bitch boil for like five minutes." He adjusted the dial a little and stepped back. Folding his arms across his chest, he watched the fog come to life inside of the coffee pot. Once he figured that it was time, he took the ice tray out of the freezer and picked up the coffee pot, dropping a few cubes inside of it. Gripping the handle of the coffee pot firmly, he rotated it counter clockwise as he added more ice cubes to it. "You probably wonderin' why I put ice in the mothafucka, right?" he glanced at Antonio who was still watching him. "Well, it's to cool the drugs down. Look," he motioned Antonio over and pointed to the white cookie trying to form inside of the coffee pot of murky water. "Now, you see that white thang up in there at the bottom? That hoe startin' to form, it's startin' to rock up. That's why they call this shit crack rock. Follow me, cuz." Apocalypse walked the coffee pot over to the kitchen sink and turned on the faucet. He added some more water to the pot. He then sat the pot back on the burner he'd taken it from.

Once the coke inside of the pot had frozen into a spongy white cookie, he scooped it out and sat it down on the plate. Having let the cookie cool off and harden, he grabbed a Gemstar razor and showed Antonio how to cut the shit up into dime rocks.

"That shit looks like old, dry pieces of soap." Antonio gave his description of what the crack looked like to him.

"Yeah, it looks exactly like that, cuz." Apocalypse responded as he continued to cut up the cookie. Once he was done, he had Antonio cook some crack for him to see if he could follow instructions. By his second try the boy had gotten the hang of it. He was a regular chip off the old block.

"Not bad, my young nigga, not bad at all," Apocalypse smiled proudly and hung his arm on Antonio's shoulders. They were wearing latex gloves and standing side by side as they stared down at the crack that the youngsta had cooked up and cut into dime pieces by his self. The young nigga smiled excitedly having been praised by the task he'd completed.

"Thanks, dad."

"You welcome, youngin'," he peeled off the gloves and balled them up, throwing them inside of the trash can inside of the kitchen. He sat down at the table and watched Antonio do the same with his gloves before he came to sit down across from him. "Check this out, I'ma give you a lil' corna to work, if you can hold that down, then I'ma promote cho ass to managin' one of my spots. If you can handle that, you'll find yo' self as my lieutenant, my right-hand man." He gripped his shoulder and gave it a manly shake. "How's that sound, cuz?"

"Sounds good," Antonio replied with an excited smile, as he toyed with the razor, which still had some of the crack residue on it.

"Cool. Now roll up, lil' homie," Apocalypse pushed a zip of weed and a box of swishers before his young apprentice. He then stood up from the table and made his way over to the refrigerator, opening the door. He took out a Corona and popped its cap on the edge of the kitchen counter. He then placed his back up against the counter and took the bottle to his lips, throat moving up and down as he guzzled the alcohol that it contained. He brought the bottle down from his lips and wiped his mouth with the back of his fist. Smiling evilly, he watched Anton break down the weed to roll up a blunt with it.

It's alive, it's alive, Apocalypse thought of himself as a black Dr. Frankenstein. He believed he was creating a monster, just like that crazy ass doctor did.

CHAPTER THIRTEEN

2016

~A few days before Marquan's release~

Marquan's time in prison was coming to an end. He had nearly completed his entire ten year sentence thanks to the bullshit he'd gotten caught up in behind the wall. Chino hadn't sent any more of his hittas at him during the rest of his time either. The two managed to stay out of one another's way, letting bygones be bygones. Still, their respective cars managed to bump heads every now and again. That was expected being that racial tensions were high behind the walls.

Besides the graying hairs he'd gotten during his incarceration, Marquan looked fairly the same. Well, the graying hair and the muscles he'd packed on from his prison work out regrime. There wasn't a part of his body that didn't bulge with muscle, besides his neck. He was in the best shape of his life and ready to be free after all of this time. What tripped him out were the butterflies in his stomach. Although he was anxious to touch the turf, he didn't know what to expect. He knew that on the outside he'd have a lot of responsibilities that he didn't have on the inside, but he'd welcome them with open arms. *Fuck being locked up!*

"Look here, cuz, I know you about to be on the otha side of dem walls, so I gotta ask you to do a favor for me, a huge, huge favor for me. One that I can only trust you with, you dig?" 187 said as he walked the track beside Marquan.

"Yeah, I got chu. What is it?" Marquan listened attentively.

Cuz, I hope this nigga don't ask me to lay nothing down for 'em.

187 looked around as if to make sure nobody was eavesdropping before he continued. "Baby girl has fallen on some hard times out there, man. She a single motha with three mouths to feed…her baby daddy ain't worth a goddamn. You hear what I'm sayin'?" he looked Marquan dead in his eyes and he nodded yes. "Well, before I got locked up in this shit hole, I buried some money inside the backyard of my house right before them crackas came to pick me up for muderin' Vernetta and her side nigga. I would have baby girl go and get it, but there ain't no tellin' whose stayin' in that place now or what could happen. The way I figure, you can handle yo' self, so it shouldn't be too much trouble for you to get into the yard and get it."

"That's it? That's all you want me to do?" he looked at him as if he was expecting him to ask him to do more.

"Yeah, what chu think I was gonna have you do for me? Knock some knucklehead off?"

"Nah, of course not, but, yeah, I can handle that for you. You just gotta tell me exactly where you buried the loot."

"No problem. I've gotta pretty good memory, so I can draw you up a map in no time."

"Cool. I'll make sure she gets it when I touch down. You have my word as a gangsta and as a man." Marquan extended his clenched fist towards him.

187 cracked a smile as he looked from his young homie's fist and then his face. He dapped him up and gave him a G-hug.

"Thanks, cuz."

"Don't mention it. All the game you gave me growing up, it's the least I can do."

Marquan and 187 continued to walk the track while engaging in conversation.

"You hear about cho boy?" 187 asked.

"Nah, what chu hear about my son?" Marquan inquired with his hands tucked in his jean jacket.

"They callin' the young homie Lil' Poc now."

"Lil' Poc? You mean like Lil' Tupac?"

187 shook his head and said, "Naw, Lil' Poc as in Lil' Apocalypse."

"What?" He scowled, stopped, and turned around to his OG. "Who you hear that from?"

"Never mind that, it's of least of importance right now. Your main concern now is makin' it outta here, so you can change your son's life around. From what I hear, how he's givin' it up in the streets, you're gonna have a lot on your hands once you touch down."

"What chu hear about, junior? What is he out there doing?"

"Everything you can imagine. He's tryna build a name for himself, followin' in Apocalypse's footsteps," 187 informed him. "The young homie's got his hands into some of everything from extortion to murder. Shit, man, you name it and your blood done did it."

Marquan swung on the air twice, like he was trying to knock someone out. "Fuck, man! What the fuck is Adele doing with junior out there?" 187 shook his head having heard him say this. "What?"

"Adele is too far gone off that heroin, man. Ain't no comin' back from where she's gone. Look, homeboy, your son's at a point in his life where he needs you the most. I suggest you get out there and guide him right before he ends up in here with me for the rest of life. You feel me?"

"Yeah, I feel you, OG. I'ma handle mine as soon as I touch the soil, for sho' for sho'." Marquan continued to walk around the track beside 187 chopping it up. He halfway listened to what his big homeboy was talking about as they walked along.

Damn, junior out there turning up in the streets. Fuck, like father like son.

~That Night~

"Haa! Haa! Haa! Haa! Haa! Haa!" Dre ran down the sidewalk, occasionally looking over his shoulders. His fitted cap flew off of his head he was running so fast. His entire face was shining from sweat and so were his arms. He bumped into an old lush coming out of a liquor store and made him drop the brown paper bag concealing his alcohol. "Fuck out my way!" He told the drunken man he'd bumped into. "Haa! Haa! Haa! Haa! Haa! Haa! Haa!" He scrambled back upon his feet running, his Jordan sneakers smacking against the pavement, clothing ruffling as the wind blew against him. Glancing over his shoulder again, he saw the midnight blue 1999 Acura Legend that had been on his ass for the past three blocks. It had just hit the corner and nearly crashed into another car, but its driver re-established his control over it. The jet black tints of the vehicle and its blacked out grill gave it a menacing appearance. It symbolized The Grim Reaper of Death. The car was closing the distance between it and Dre fast.

"Oh shit! Oh shit! Oh shit!" Dre saw the car had him in its sights. The passenger side window rolled down and a nigga wearing a blue bandana around his head and the lower half of his face emerged. Homie's gloved hands gripped a Glock with an extended magazine. He pointed that bitch at Dre and pulled the trigger. The handgun bucked wildly spitting rapid fire.

"Oh, fuck!" Dre ducked low and threw his arms over his head to shield himself as he ran. He bent the corner of a building and made it inside of an alley. The Acura ripped up the alley behind Dre with homeboy spitting flames at his ass, trying to lay him down forever. It was dark out so the only things that could be seen were the headlights of the Acura, which were shining at the back of Dre as he hauled ass up the path.

Blocka! Blocka! Blocka! Blocka!

"Aaahhhhh!" Dre threw his head back and hollered out in excruciation, grabbing his thigh and limping as fast as he could to get away. "Grrrrrrr! Fuck!" When he glanced over his shoulder and saw the Acura so close up on him, he knew he was a goner, but he was still going to try to get away. "Haa! Haa! Haa! Haa!" Dre continued to limp along and glance over his shoulder.

"Get back in, cuz, I'm 'bouta run this mothafucka over." Apocalypse ordered from behind the wheel of the Acura Legend. As soon as Antonio pulled himself back inside of the car, the distinct smell of gunsmoke filled the interior. The overwhelming stench didn't bother them though. They were used to the odor, having been in plenty of firefights before.

Apocalypse floored the gas pedal and the Acura ripped down the alley, rolling over Dre and leaving him tumbling down the asphalt. Once he finally stopped, he was bloody and had tire prints on him. He lay flat on his back staring down the alley at the back lights of the Acura, blood running down into his eye, causing him to blink his eyelid rapidly. He swallowed the spit in his throat and lifted his hand, wiggling his fingers as if he was trying to get the driver to stop before he killed him.

"Nigga, still alive?" Antonio looked out of the back window and saw Dre still squirming on the pavement.

"Yeah, he's still kickin', but he's fucked up. He's real fucked up." Apocalypse smiled evilly. Mowing Dre down in the alley brought a sense of accomplishment to him. He was a wicked mothafucka so doing dirt filled him with joy.

"I'ma finish him off, I'll be right back." Antonio hopped out of the car and looked down both ends of the alley for witnesses. Once he seen that the coast was clear, he threw his hoodie over his head and checked the extended magazine of his weapon. Seeing that he had enough shells left to finish the job, he injected it back into the bottom of his Glock. Afterwards, he hid his hand behind his back as he casually strolled up the alley, whistling. Having made it upon Dre, he found the wounded man looking up at him, eyes pleading for forgiveness. "I bet cho ass won't steal from me again!"

Antonio's eyebrows arched and his nose wrinkled, as he bit down hard on his bottom lip and pointed his Glock down at Dre's face.

Blocka! Blocka! Blocka! Blocka! Blocka!

He gave it to him all in his face and made sure that ass was dead. After taking a moment to admire his handiwork, Antonio dropped the murder weapon beside Dre's dead body and retreated back to the car. As soon as he hopped back inside of the Acura, Apocalypse peeled off in a hurry. He blew out a cloud of smoke and passed his surrogate son the blunt he'd just lit up. He then focused his attention out of the windshield and nodded his head to the sounds of Spice 1's *Trigga gots no heart.* Driving up the street, they were past by two speeding police cars with their sirens blaring aloud. Without a doubt they knew that they were headed into the direction they'd left Dre's corpse.

Menace II Society mad man killa

Just call me the East Bay Gangsta

Neighborhood drug dealer

Quick to make decisions and I'm

Quick to get my blast on

Do a 187 with this bloody Jason mask on

Once Antonio had taken a couple puffs of the blunt, he passed it back to Apocalypse who was now jumping on the freeway. As he smoked, Antonio nodded to the Spice 1 track and stared out of the passenger side window. Before he knew it, Apocalypse was pulling up inside of a vacant parking lot and wiping down everything inside of the Acura. He and Antonio threw their hoodies over their heads and hopped out of the G-ride. Looking over their shoulders, they hastily made their way across the parking lot. Once they'd crossed the threshold out of the lot, they jogged cross the street to a white 2003 navy blue Tahoe truck. They hopped into the SUV and Apocalypse fired it up. The headlights of the truck came on, and it pulled off, with 2pac's *Ambitions as a Rider* bumping from its speakers.

****

Apocalypse drove back to his house, and pulled up inside of the driveway. This house was different than the one that he, Adele and Antonio stayed in before. They'd been moved out of that house, and went their separate ways. Apocalypse had eventually gotten tired of Adele's ass and kicked her to the curb. So she was wandering the streets like a real life zombie shooting heroin and sleeping where ever she could. Antonio had stayed with Apocalypse for a while, but once he'd hustled up enough money to get his own little spot, he packed up his belongings and got ghost. He rented out this apartment from this smoker fool so that he'd have some place to cook up his work. Although he was doing his own thing independently from Apocalypse, he still bought his drugs from him. That was their deal since Antonio used to hustle for him and was now getting money on one of his blocks. Not only would he buy all his work from him, but he'd also kick him in a little something, something every month. You could say that the paper that he was kicking up to him every month was something like rent or property tax, since the young nigga'z people were slinging on his territory.

Antonio and Apocalypse hopped out of the car and made their way inside of the house. They changed their clothes and Apocalypse burned them inside of the fireplace. He then grabbed a couple of Coronas out of the refrigerator and tossed his street son one.

"Come on with me to the back, I'ma get chu that shit," Apocalypse motioned for Antonio to follow him to his bedroom. The young nigga followed him inside of his bedroom. He sat on the bed and took swigs of his beer as he watched Apocalypse sit his beer down on the dresser and approached the closet. Apocalypse opened the closet and pulled the drawstring to restore light to the small space. As soon as he did, he grabbed a Macy's shopping mall bag out of the back of the closet and took the work he had stashed inside of the secret safe inside of the carpeted floor. Once he'd finished placing the drugs inside of the shopping mall bag, he shut the door and let the flap drop over it.

Coming out of the closet, Apocalypse shut the door behind him and proceeded over to the bed. Standing before his street son, he held open the Macy shopping mall bag. Once Antonio peeked over into the shopping mall bag, he smiled with satisfaction and took a swig of his beer.

"It's all there: a pound of Kush and a bird." Apocalypse smiled. "Hold on, lemme put somethin' on top of this shit to make it look good."

Apocalypse grabbed some clothing he'd bought from Macy's with the tags still on them from off the rack inside of the closet. He then folded the clothing up neatly and placed them down inside of the shopping mall bag on top of the drugs.

"G lookin', I'ma shoot chu that paypa for this tomorrow. I'ma have one of the girls drop it off to you," Antonio told him.

"That's one way you can pay for it, and then, there's another," he pulled Antonio into him and rested his hands on his waist, like a man would do his woman. He then stared lustfully into his eyes with a naughty smirk on his face.

Antonio felt disgusted and he wanted to throw up. The situation was awkward as hell, and had it been anyone else that had came at him in this manner he would have split their wig. But this wasn't anyone else; this was Apocalypse, the man that had raised him. The only person that hadn't deserted him like everyone else that claimed to love him.

"Nah, I'ma pay you yours, G," Antonio tried his best to fight the disgusted look that crossed his face. Seeing Apocalypse bringing his lips towards his, he turned his face and his kiss landed on his cheek. Antonio scowled and he involuntarily clenched his fist, causing veins to form in his hand.

"Yo', don't worry about that lil' paypa, hold on to it. That lil' bit there is on me," Apocalypse told him after breaking their embrace.

"Nah, I'ma drop that on you ASAP, ain't shit for free out here. Besides, I'ma man, I don't want no hand out. I'll pay my way. I don't want nobody sayin' they did shit for me. You feel me?"

"You know, I don't play like that," he replied and sparked up a blunt he'd just stuck between his lips.

"I know. No offense, I'm just sayin'. I'ma give you that though."

"I love you." Apocalypse said after blowing smoke up into the air.

Antonio took a deep breath as he turned around, not really wanting to respond. Still, he did anyway, "I love you too."

Apocalypse openly admired the young nigga'z ass and licked his lips. He smacked him on his behind and made him scowl. Antonio was pissed off. He twisted his face and clenched his jaws, causing his temples to pulsate.

Ol', faggot ass nigga, cuz, Antonio thought as he made his way towards the door. Tears were in his eyes because he wanted to smoke his street daddy so bad. He loved and hated the nigga, so he was confused on the subject. He knew that just as soon as he murked him that he'd regret it. This was because for the past ten years this was the only father that he knew. Despite all of the shit he'd done to him, he still loved him to death. The way he saw it the entire situation was fucked up.

~A few days later~

Release day

As soon as Marquan came waltzing out of the prison he was greeted by the sun. It was bright out, and the sapphire's rays were beating down on him. Narrowing his eyelids into slits, he looked up into the sky and held his hand above his brows. He winced as he met the sun and dropped his hands at his sides. Shutting his eyelids briefly, he took a deep breath, his chest expanding and shrinking as he breathed. A smile spread across his face and his cheeks rose up. To him, being free was the happiest moment of his life next to his son being born.

Turning back around, he gave the prison behind him one last look and promised himself that he'd never return to those cement walls and bars that held him captive for so many years. Now, he'd told himself before that he'd hold court in the street before he did another stretch, but this time he was dead ass serious. He wasn't going to step foot back inside of that mothafucka ever again. He put that shit on his son's life that he'd be dead before he was shacked up inside of another cell again.

"Never again," Marquan said to no one in particular. He then picked up a rock and launched it in the direction of the prison, watching it deflect off of it. This was his *fuck you* to the penitentiary.

Hearing a car driving up behind him, Marquan turned around, moving his head from side to side. He narrowed his eyelids trying to see who it was behind the wheel, but he couldn't quite identify them. The vehicle pulled to a stop. The driver's door opened and Jahleysa stepped out, one sandaled foot at a time. She pulled her self into view and Marquan smiled wider than he'd ever had in years. Jahleysa's chocolate skin glistened beneath the warm rays of the sun. Her hair was parted down the middle and a bun was on either side. She wore burgundy tinted sunglasses, a matching halted top, and white jean shorts that showed off plently of thigh.

Jahleysa stood beside her car fidgeting with her fingers and playfully kicking a pebble on the ground. She smiled excitedly as she stared at the man of her dreams. She was nervous and there were butteflies in her stomach. Truthfully, she hadn't felt like this since the first time Marquan had hollered at her back in junior high school. Since they'd broken up, some sixteen years ago, no man has made her feel the way he had. It was safe to say that she'd never stopped loving him, even when they were apart. Love was one crazy ass emotion.

Well, are you just gone keep standing there, or are…" Marquan words were cut short as Jahleysa took off running at him with joy in her eyes and a smile across her face. She appeared to be moving in slow motion as she ran as hard and as fast as she could in his direction. She leaped up into the air and her man caught her. Throwing her arms around Marquan's neck, she then wrapped her legs around his waist and kissed him. Turning her head counter clockwise, with her eyelids shut, she kissed her man long and romantically. He held her up on him as she pulled back and stared at him lovingly. She wiped the little bit of spit that was at the corner of his mouth and kissed him three more times. They smiled as they stared into one another's faces and took a deep breath. Finally, they were reunited and wrapped in one another's arms. They had waited years for this moment and it was finally here.

"I love you," Jahleysa told Marquan.

"I love you, too." He responded. Suddenly, he lifted her up under her arms and spun her around and around. She giggled and laughed, watching the ground swirl around hastily before her eyes. "I'm free, baby, I'm finally free."

They both laughed and giggled.

CHAPTER FOURTEEN

Jahleysa led Marquan through the door of her home; he was taken by surprise by the dinner she'd prepared for them. The lights were out, but the burning candles around their meal, which was on the kitchen table, provided enough light for them to see. The dish for the day was a slowly roasted game hen which was stuffed and lying on a bed of rice. There was cornbread, black eye peas, greens and yams. Sitting off to the side was a very expensive black bottle of champagne with red wrapping around its neck.

Once she had shut the door and locked it, Jahleysa went to stand beside Marquan. Smiling as she looked over the meal that she'd prepared, she clapped her hands and the stereo came on, instantly. Guy's *Let's chill* came easing through the speakers and serenading the romantic scenario.

Sweetheart, I've been tryin' so hard to get over you

Just simply can't

'Cause the love we shared through the years

Meant so much to me

All I'm lookin' for is just a serious relationship

Someone I can hold all my life

Why don't you give me that commitment

Let's settle down

"Babe, all of this is for me?" Marquan asked with his eyebrows raised. The look on his face told her that he couldn't believe that she'd went through all of that trouble putting together such a wonderful dinner for him.

"Yes, this is all for you, welcome home, baby," she cupped her hands around his face and kissed him passionately. Before Marquan knew it, his penis had enlarged and was nudging at the zipper of his jeans, threatening to bust free from its denim prison. Jahleysa's pussy had become instantly moist from their kissing. The couple found themselves trying to rip off one another's clothing. In a matter of seconds, they found themselves standing face to face, naked as the day they were pushed out of their mother's womb.

Marquan and Jahleysa looked one another up and down as they took in the other's physique, admiring all that they'd saw.

"You look amazing," Marquan said of his boo's body. He could tell by the way that she was put together that she stayed at the gym. She had the physique of a young Janet Jackson.

"And you look like a god." She complimented him on his chiseled body and his rock solid abs. She was staring at him wide eyed and impressed. His muscular form had her enchanted.

Marquan smirked and pulled her close by her waist. He pressed his lips against hers and slipped his tongue inside of her mouth. They both shut their eyelids and made *Mmmm* sounds as they locked lips sensually. Their making out was in perfect rhythm and sync. Jahleysa's hands cupped her man's face as they continued to kiss and make their way over to the couch. He bumped up against the couch and fell over the arm of it, landing on the cushions with Jahleysa on top of him. They kissed harder, intensely, and passionately. While they were doing so, Marquan turned her over and kissed her down the middle of her breasts. He then grasped both of her melon sized breasts. He licked around the areolas of her titties and then flicked her nipples slowly, and then rapidly, with his tongue. Afterwards, he started sucking on them gently and then sensually. His sexual actions caused her eyelids to flutter and her eyes to show white. She moaned and groaned feeling the hot and wet mouth of her lover. By this time, her pussy was warm, slick and gooey.

"Sssssss, shit, I'm on fiyah, Quan. I want chu to put it in, put it in, baby. Show your pussy who's the boss." She squirmed beneath him.

"Unh unh," he slightly shook his head as he parted her thighs and held her legs open. He found himself facing an upside down pyramid of the prettiest hairs he'd ever seen in his life above her coochie. First, he kissed her tenderly on the inside of her thighs and blew on the small flap of meat nestled between her pussy lips. In doing this, he drove her wild and she squirmed uncontrollably. Next, he slid his tongue up and down her slit. Once his tongue came up against her clit and had it resting against the tip of it, he sucked on it just enough for her to feel slight pressure.

"Oooh, fuuuuck!" she snatched up one of the couch pillows and mashed it over her face. She then released a cry of ecstacy that would have had the neighbors calling 9-1-1 had they heard it. "I'm 'bouta cum, I'm 'bouta cum!" her entire body shook from an intense orgasm.

Marquan came up from his feast and wiped his glistening chin with the back of his fist. Hovering over Jahleysa, he stroked his hardened dick as he stared into her eyes. He then brought his lips to hers and kissed her tenderly and romantically, continuously stroking his grown man, which oozed pre-cum from out of its bulbous head.

Biting down gently on Jahleysa's bottom lip, Marquan pulled it slightly and caused it to slap back up against her bottom teeth. He looked down at her hot, wet pussy and it was twitching from Jahleysa being so horny. He smiled graciously as he slid the head of his member up and down the slit of her cunt. This drove her crazy and caused her thighs to shake. She was begging him for the dick now. She just didn't want it, she needed it…badly.

"Sssssss, please, baby, give it to me now," She urged him as she began stoking his dick and staring at it, thirstily. "I want it…I need it inside of me…all of it…nooooow, sssssss!"

Marquan removed Jahleysa's hand from off his manhood and pressed the head of it against her moist opening. He partially slid in, but he couldn't quite fit inside of her being that he was so thick. Jahleysa was tight so it took some time for Marquan to break her in. When he did, he found himself wedged between her slickened pink walls. Slowly, he began to stroke her treasure and feel her hot liquid ooze from out of her opening. It wasn't long before she was loosening up and he found her body releasing its tension, enjoying his thrust of passion. Marquan planted his fists on either side of Jahleysa's head on the couch and she wrapped her legs around his waist. Her face was masked with delight as he stroked her long, hard and rhythmatically. He would plunge deep inside of her, and pull out to the tip of his manhood before delving into the depths of her womanhood again. Marquan groaned and threw his head back. His eyelids fluttered and his lips trembled as he continued to plunge deeper and deeper inside of her pussy. He didn't see it, but her cuming had lathered his grown man.

"Ah! Ah! Ah! Ah! Ah! Ah!" Jahleysa's body jutted from the pummeling she was taking. Marquan leaned down and kissed her long, hard, and sensually. He then licked her up her neck and under her chin, sucking on the bottom of it as he continued to work her middle. Bringing his head back up, he looked down at her pleasure streaked face and gritted his teeth. The veins of his body bulged all over and his slightly hairy ass cheeks flexed in and out as he thrusted her middle. Before he knew it, his face and his entire form was shiny from sweat.

"You like that, baby?" he asked while huffing.

"Yessss," she whimpered.

"I can't hear you, momma."

"Yesssssss," she said even louder and scratched his back. Her nails broke the skin on his toned back and left red streaks behind. He hissed like a snake and pulled her closer to him, placing her legs on his shoulders. Gripping the arm of the couch, he pounded her like a wild man, going for broke in that mothafucking pussy.

"Ahhh, fuck, I'm 'bouta cum!" he whined and bit down on his bottom lip, continuing to dive in and out of her rapidly. His sweaty fleshed colliding against hers created a loud slaping noise that sounded off throughout the living room.

"Cum, cum in my pussy, baby!" she called out wincing, and loving every inch that he laid in her. She gripped his waist firmly and wrapped her legs around it as well.

]"Ahhh, fuck! Ssssss, I'm finna cum, I'm finna cum! Unh! Unh! Unh!" he made the ugliest face imaginable as he emptied the contents of his nut sack inside of her, rocking back and forth inside of her womb, coating her insides with baby batter. Right after, the intensity relinquished his face and her collapsed on top of her. He lay on her sweaty and sticky as she caressed the back of his head and kissed his cheek. Her eyelids were shut and a smile was etched across her lips. She listened to his heartbeat up against her ample bosom, loving the rhythm of it. It had been years since they'd made love and she'd missed it dearly. It felt so right. All of these years and her pussy still curved to his dick, and he'd never lost the knowledge on how to please her sexually. He knew her body like he knew the back of his hand.

"Sooooo, how was it?" Jahleysa asked as she planted tender kisses up his shoulder and then his neck slowly.

"That was spectacular, baby." He responded out of breath.

She laughed hard and said, "Spectacular, huh? Well, I don't think I've ever heard a hood nigga say that."

"Well, it's damn sho' a compliment." He lay at the opposite end of the couch and said, "You got some smoke?"

"Yeah, hold on." Jahleysa got up and walked her naked ass into her bedroom, buttocks jiggling. She returned later wearing a silk robe and holding a tray. On the tray there was rolling papers and a zip of Kush. She passed the tray to Marquan and he got right to work, breaking the weed down. While he was busy doing his thing, she journeyed inside of the kitchen and poured up a glass of red wine.

"You want something to drink, wine? Beer? Soda? Water? Juice? Anything?" she inquired as she closed the bottle of wine.

"Water is fine," Marquan responded as he sprinkled the weed inside of the rolling paper.

Jahleysa looked through the shelves of the refrigerator for a bottle of water, but she couldn't seem to find any. "Is faucet water okay?" She called out over her shoulder, still holding the glass of wine as she shut the refrigerator door.

"Yeah, that's cool." He said, licking the paper closed and then lighting it up. Taking a couple of puffs, he blew out a cloud of smoke and lay back against the arm of the couch.

Jahleysa procured the glass of water and brought it over to Marquan. He switched hands with the joint he'd freshly rolled and took the glass. After taking a decent drink, he sat the glass down on the coffee table and went back to smoking. Jahleysa sat down on the couch and outstretched her legs into his lap. He was wearing his clothing now; being that he put them on when she went to go get the weed she had on deck.

Marquan smoked on his joint as he used his freehand to massage his lady's foot. Looking down at him, she smiled and took a sip of her wine. Once Marquan had taken a couple of more puffs, he passed it to Jahleysa who indulged as well.

"So," Jahleysa blew out a cloud of smoke as she threw her head back and made the bottom of her chin visible. "What're your plans now that you're out?"

"Well, my first order of business is to get in contact with my son." He told her. "Then I gotta bust a move for an old friend I left behind the wall. Afterwards, I'm going to go see that bitch-made ass nigga Apocalypse." Marquan stared ahead at nothing with a look of hatred plastered across his face. His emotions gave him a transfixed look in his eyes.

Suddenly, he shut his eyelids and shook his head slightly before peeling his eyelids back open. "Yeah, I most definitely gotta serve that nigga."

"Are you seriously gonna go after him?" Jahleysa asked with a concern expression across her face.

"You mothafucking right I am," He said with a creased forehead.

"Baby, you just got out of the pen," she took her feet out of his lap and sat up on the couch.

"Well, I may just be going back in after I'm finish with this nigga."

"I can't believe this, I finally got chu back and your talking about doing something that'll possibly take you away from not only me, but your son, forever?" Her eyes became glassy and she shook her head as she sat her glass of wine down.

"Jesus, Quan, I thought you were smarter than that."

"Lemme get this straight, Jah, cuz done set me up to get caught for murder, turned my son out to the streets and flipped his mother into a mothafucking dope fiend, and I'm 'pose to let the shit slide?" He frowned up and looked at her ass like she was fucking stupid.

"If it means your gonna live the rest of your life on the outside of those walls among you family and friends, then yes."

"If setting this beef straight means I gotta risk catching an elbow, then fuck it. It is what it is. I'm willing to ride that bullet. I know for a fact I couldn't sleep at night if I let this one get by me."

"I take it there's nothing I can do to talk you out of this, is it?" she asked. At this time, she was standing up away from the couch with her arms folded across her breasts. From the expression on her face he could tell that she had an attitude, but he didn't give a fuck. He felt how he felt and he was going to stand on it no matter what the consequences were.

"Nah, ain't nothing you can say, I'm taking it there." He told her as he sat up on the couch and picked up the ashtray. He held the ashtray with one hand and mashed the joint out with the other. Placing the ashtray back upon the coffee table, he continued, "Listen, Jah, I fucks witchu the long way. A nigga love you to death, but I don't expect you to ride in this car with me. You can either hop out of this whip or you can stay in it. Either way, I'ma do what I feel I gotta do, straight like that. It's all up to you, ma."

Jahleysa stood where she was with her arms still folded across her breasts. Her eyes were looking off to their corners as she was thinking things over to give the man she'd been in love with since she was a teenager an answer. Suddenly, her eyes shot over to him and she said, "You know I'm riding witchu 'til the wheels fall off."

Marquan smiled hard and said, "That's what I'm talking about. That's my rider, come here." he curled and uncurled his finger at her, signaling for her to approach. She walked over to him. He patted his lap and she sat down on it, throwing her arms around his neck. She stared into his eyes affectionately. "You love me?"

"Always." She said as she held his gaze.

"For how long?"

"Forever and a day, and then some."

He nodded his head as he approved of all of the answers to the questions that she'd given him. "Gemme some love." He said as he caressed the side of her face tenderly. With that said, she leaned forward and kissed him slowly.

"Now I'm hungry as a hostage, warm that shit up in there that chu cooked for a nigga." He capped with a smile.

She chuckled and shoved him playfully, then said, "Boy, you know you something else. But I ain't going nowhere 'til you gemme another kiss with them big ass soup coolers." She grinned and leaned forward again.

"You love 'em though."

"You damn right I do, so bring your ass over this way with them." She held him by the side of his face and they kissed again.

Jahleysa heated up their plates of food inside of the oven and they ate and chopped it up for a little while longer.She'd gotten so caught up in their conversation that she'd forgotten about the package that one of his homeboy's had left there for him to pick up. Remembering this, she told him about it and led him inside of her bedroom. She had him sit down on the bed while she made herself busy inside of the closet. About two minutes later she was walking out with a small Nike duffle bag. As soon as Marquan seen it his forehead crinkled and he looked up at her, wondering what the contents of the bag was.

"I never opened it. I just kept it until you were able to get out and see for yourself. Now, see for yourself," she smiled and dropped the bag on the bed beside him. He didn't waste any time unzipping that mothafucka to see what was inside of it. His eyes stretched open in surprise when he saw that it was loaded with wrinkled stacks of dead white men. He took out two of the stacks and looked at them admiringly as he thumbed through them, listening to that famous sound that money makes when you run your thumb or finger over the top of it. Afterwards, he tossed the money back inside of the bag and unzipped the compartment on the side of the bag. Reaching inside, he pulled out a black handgun and two fully loaded magazines. He cocked a live hollow tip round into the head of his deadly weapon and then aimed it at a lamp on the other side of the bed. Standing up, he looked over all of the money that was inside of the bag once again.

His brows furrowed when he spotted something amongst the money.

"Hell is that?" Marquan moved the money aside and discovered a cellular phone and a packet labeled *Pandemonium.* He took out both of them. When he powered *on* the cell phone and looked at the contacts, there was one number programmed in it, and that was *JaQuel.* "This who dropped this paypa and the rest of this shit off here, JaQuel?" he asked Jahleysa, and she nodded yes. He then focused his attention back on the small packet. When he opened it, he saw that it was empty. It didn't matter though because he already knew that its contents were heroin at some point. *Pandemonium* was the stamp of heroin that his young homie JaQuel was pushing out in the streets. He assumed that he was telling him by sending the packet and the money that he'd made all of his cash off of his narcotics. This brought a smile to his face because he realized that the young nigga'z street dreams had really came true. "When cuz drop this on you?"

"About two days ago," Jahleysa told him. "He told me to make sure you get everything, and to have you call him once you did."

"How much in this bag?" he referred to the duffle bag.

"Beats me," she shrugged. "Like I told you, I didn't open the bag because it's yours, so I figured that you should open it."

"Alright. I'm finna hit this nigga up." Marquan hit up JaQuel and he made plans to meet with him. About an hour later, that nigga showed up in somethng that blew his mind.

Marquan gave Jahleysa a kiss and they made plans to link up after he kicked the shit with JaQuel for a while. When Marquan jumped into the car with JaQuel they chopped it up about any and everything that was past and present that had to do about the hood.

~That night~

The night was still except for the stirring of the shadows, which were the crackheads moving back and forth up the block, coming from copping their medicine from the street pharmacies. The dope house at the end of the residential street was popping like it was Saturday night and ladies got in for free before ten. Surprisingly, there wasn't a cop in sight, but even if there was the lookouts that were on deck would have warned the niggaz serving the fiends. The lookouts were camouflaged in the darkness looking through their binoculars. The naked eye could barely make these mothafuckaz out in the night, which was a good thing being that they were up to no good.

JaQuel sat low inside of his royal blue Lamborghini Gallardo, dressed in royal blue from head to toe. He rocked a bandana around his head and a Blue Devils jersey with heavy gold jewelry lying over it. His jewelry gleamed under the dim street lights as he took puffs of a Black & Mild and watched his surroundings. Ever since he hit that lick for one hundred bricks, life had been lovely for him and everyone that he fucked with on that level.

"You see how yo' nigga gettin' it, right?" JaQuel smiled and looked at Marquan, who was also smiling. He was happy to see that his homeboy was proud of his progress.

"Yeah, I see you, cuz. You got cho jewels shining," Marquan gestured to the jewelry hanging around his homie's neck and wrists. "Half a million dollar car, pockets on swoll," he looked down at the bulge in his pocket. "And I know the bitches is on you like flies on shit 'cause yo' jack ain't stop ringing since I been witchu." At that moment, JaQuel's iPhone started ringing and he looked at its screen, seeing a caramel chick with ass and tits. Across the display was *TayTay*. "See what I'm talking 'bout? You the man."

JaQuel ignored the call and sat the iPhone down in his lap. Turning his focus to his big homie, he placed his jeweled hand on the steering wheel. "Appreciate that, cuz, you givin' a young nigga his props for puttin' on out here and bossin' up by his damn self. Like I was tellin' you earlier, a nigga done put together a solid team, but it's not complete until I getta certified head bussa up unda me. I mean, don't get me wrong, I gotta few wolves that'll do they thang, all I gotta do is point a finger and a mothafucka is a memory. It's as simple as that, but I'd feel better knowin' I had my own personal killa by my side. You feel me?"

"You mean you want a bodyguard?"

"Yeah, someone that's gone be the eyes in the back of my head. You see how a nigga gettin' it, so there's a long line of kamikaze type niggaz willin' to take it there to get what's mine. You feel where I'm comin' from?"

"Yeah, I feel you. I really do, but I'm gonna have to decline your offer," he looked to him, placing his hand against his chest. "I'm taking a step back from the street life, my young nigga. I made a promise to myself to change for the betterment of not only me, but my boy as well. Besides, them people promised me that if they ever saw my black ass in court again they was gone see to it that I never saw the light of day again." He shook his head as he thought of never being able to be on the outside again. The idea scared the shit out of him, but it wasn't going to stop him from doing what he had in mind.

"I respect that, OG." JaQuel dapped up Marquan.

"By the way, I appreciate that bag you dropped on me."

"A hunnit large; all drugs money, big homie, that's all yours. That's the least I could do for how you looked out for me growin' up and shit."

"Don't mention it."

Hearing a car driving up beside them, JaQuel grabbed his gun and looked to the driver's window, letting it down. As soon as he turned his head he met Jahleysa's vehicle. The passenger window came all the way down, and he was presented her beautiful face.

"Hey, you still holding my man hostage in there?" she smiled.

"Yeah, he in here." He looked to Marquan and alerted him to his lady.

Marquan told Jahleysa he would be over in a second before he turned his attention back to his young homie. "Yo', man, I'm finna get up outta here, but thanks for everything you have done for me, cuz. I really appreciate that shit, for real for real."

"Small thang to a giant." He dapped Marquan up.

"Look here, man, you seen junior around?" he inquired.

"You talkin' 'bout Lil'Antonio?"

"Yeah."

"Man, I see that lil' nigga almost every day, he's always in the streets."

"You gotta line or an address on 'em?"

"Nah, I don't have cuz math, but I do know where him and his lil' crew be hangin' at."

"Where about?"

Marquan programmed the address inside of his cellular. Once he was sure that it was locked in, he slid the cell phone back inside of his pocket. "G' looking out, cuz. Holla at me if yo' man getta line of my son's motha."

Just then, JaQuel's cellular rang and he looked at its display. Talib was on it. "Yo' this my nigga 'bout cha B.M right here," he called out to Marquan who was walking to Jahleysa's whip. Hearing his young homeboy's voice, he came jogging back over to his Lambo. Standing at his window, he listened to his brief exchange. "You sure that's her though? Cool. Stall her; I'll be there in a second." JaQuel disconnected the call and addressed his OG homeboy. "Yeah, he said Adele's down there at his shootin' gallery in Watts. He's gone sit on her until I get there." JaQuel informed him of the whereabouts of Adele's drugged out ass. While he was locked up, Marquan had gotten word from the streets that his baby momma had done some foul ass shit.It hurt his heart getting the news, but he refused to believe what he was told. He had to hear the truth from the horse's mouth.

Now that JaQuel's homeboy had Adele in his clutches he could find out the truth and put his suspicions to rest once and for all.

"Cool. Hit my jack as soon as you got her." Marquan told JaQuel.

"I got chu. I'ma swing by the house real quick and change clothes, and then I'ma dip out there."

"Appreciate it, cuz." He dapped him up.

"Don't wet it." JaQuel watched as his homeboy made his departure. He observed him climbing inside his girl's vehicle and pulling off.

CHAPTER FIFTEEN

"Where we headed first?" Jahleysa inquired as she looked back and forth between the windshield and her man. Marquan had texted her while he was chopping it up with JaQuel inside of his car and told her to come scoop him up. He figured now was as good as a time as any for them to accomplish some of the goals he'd set forth that night.

"To see my boy," Marquan smiled excitedly as he showed her the address that he'd programmed inside of his cellular.

"I know where that's at."

"Cool."

It wasn't long before Jahleysa was pulling up two houses down from the destination that Marquan had put into his cell phone. Marquan hopped out of her car and slammed the door shut behind him. Tucking his hands inside of his jacket, he made his way upon the curb and down the side walk, looking for the address of his destination. Looking ahead, he discovered a house with smoke and embers in the darkness upon the porch. He also noticed that there were black shapes moving within the shadows. There was also laughter and chit chatter.

"Cuz, you don't won't these hands," a young skinny nigga jumped off the porch and started throwing hands, with a youngsta not much bigger than him. They were slap boxing while their company cheered them on.

"Get 'em, Tutu, cuz, get 'em!" one of their comrades called out.

"Nutso, put dem tips on 'em, loc!" another comrade called out as the youths threw opened palms.

Bwap! Slap! Smack! Bwap!

"Ooooooh!" all of the homies said in unison. They'd just seen Nutso stagger backwards from the brutal assault brought to him by Tutu. The youngsta's lightening fast hands had his opponent's cheeks bruised red.

"Come on, cuz, come on!" Tutu said with his fists up ready to get it in again.

Nutso spat blood onto the concrete and wiped his bloody lip with the back of his hand. He then threw up his fists and started back slap boxing with his homeboy.

Bwap! Slap! Smack! Bwap!

"Ooooooh, shit!" the homies said in unison, seeing Nutso getting them hands put on him once again. By this time, Marquan was entering the yard through the gate.

One of the young crips by the name of Blackie narrowed his eyelids and peered closely, trying to see who it was that was invading their space. He tapped one of his homeboys that were standing beside him and pointed at the man that had entered the yard.

"Nutso, Tutu, y'all niggaz chill out, cuz," Blackie said aloud to his comrades. He then pulled out his gun. Right after him, rapidly, one by one, the guns of the young niggaz came out and got pointed at Marquan. He stopped dead in his tracks. Instantly, he regretted not bringing his gun along with him. He took in all of the mad dogg expressions of the fools pointing their bangas at him. He clenched his jaws and his eyebrows sloped, a vein pulsating at his temple. He was as hot as a fire cracker. Here he was getting drawn down on like an enemy and he was in his own hood. He was a certified G in the streets while these young niggaz had probably just jumped off the porch.

"Fuck is you, loc?" Blackie inquired with his gun pointed sideways at Marquan. From his range he could shoot him directly in his chest and kill him on the spot.

"I'm Marquan, cuz, they call me Lil'187. A nigga done shed blood, sweat and tears for this hood. Now y'all may not know about me, but I know yo' OGs have." Marquan looked around at all of the faces of the young niggaz with their guns pointed at him. His heart was beating a tad faster than usual, but his face was solemn. He looked as if he didn't have a care in the world.

"*The* Lil' 187? The one that used to ride with Apocalypse back in the day?" Blackie asked.

"The one and only, homeboy."

"Aww, I know who cuz is, my pops say homie is official tissue."He vouched for Marquan and put his banga back up.

"Yo' name ringin' bells in the streets, OG." Another one of the young crips said.

"Yo' moniker's platinum, OG. Niggaz 'round here respect you, young and old, fa real fa real." Blackie informed him.

"Respect," he gave them a nod. "Yo', y'all know where I can find my son, Lil' Poc?"

"Lil' Poc? You Lil' Poc daddy?" the young crip inquired with his brows crinkled. The other hoodlums exchanged confused glances because this was news to them all.

"Yeah, cuz, that's my son, my seed," he showed them the tattoo of Antonio as a baby he had on his ribcage. That was enough for them to believe that he was indeed the father of one of the most feared hittas of their neighborhood.

"Damn, we always thought that the big homie Apocalypse was cuz pops."

"Nah, youngin' is my flesh and blood. Believe that." The young niggaz nodded. "So, y'all gotta address on my boy or what?"

"Yeah, he's ova there at them apartments on 83rd and Western, in a big ass tan buildin', you can't miss it. If you headed ova there from here, then it's gonna be on the left hand side. You wanna write this shit down, cuz?"

He looked at Marquan as he massaged his chin and noticed he wasn't jotting down any of the information that he was relaying to him. He definitely wasn't the type of nigga that repeated himself so if homeboy asked for the information again, then he was going to tell him to go fuck himself. He didn't give a shit about his status or how much work he put in for the hood.

"Nah, I'm recording it all up here." Marquan tapped his finger to his temple. He then listened carefully to the rest of the information that the youthful gangbanger ran down to him. Once he was sure he had everything memorized, he slapped hands with the younger crips and made plans to kick it with them another day.

Marquan hopped back into the front passenger's seat of Jahleysa's car and slammed the door shut. As soon as he did, Jahleysa looked into the side view mirror to see if any cars were coming before she pulled off.

"I got kind of worried back there. I thought I was gonna have to jump out with my little boo thang." Jahleysa said of her nickel plated .32, which she still held in her hand as she steered the wheel of her vehicle. Holding the steering wheel with one hand and looking up at the windshield, she stashed her small gun underneath the seat, where she'd drawn it from.

"I didn't know you ride witchu a lil' piece," Marquan looked at her as she stashed the gun away and smiled slightly.

"I normally don't, but we're on a mission tonight, and you never know what will happen. It's better to have it when you need it than to need it and not have it. You feel me?"

"I do," he nodded as he looked ahead, recalling one situation where he'd gotten caught slipping by the other side at the Slauson Swap meet. He was on his way up to the ghetto famous store to cop something fresh to wear to his homeboy, G-stacc's, welcome home party when he remembered he'd forgotten his strap back home. He started to go back home and get it, but since he knew exactly what he was going to grab to wear, he figured he'd be in and out. Seeing as how it wouldn't take him no longer than fifteen or twenty minutes to grab him a fit to wear to the little shindig, he didn't trip on dipping back to the house to grab his gat. This was a big mistake because as soon as he crossed the threshold inside of the establishment, unbeknownst to him, his enemies was on his head. They waited until he'd gotten back outside to his car and beat him like he'd stolen something. Fortunately for him, he was lucky enough to walk away with a broken arm and a few lumps on his head because them mothafuckaz had every intention on killing him. In fact, the only reason why they didn't was because they'd drawn the attention of way too many witnesses. If it wasn't for that, then Marquan's homies would have been wearing R.I.P T-shirts and setting up murals in his honor on the block.

From that day forth, Marquan made sure he had his gun on him at all times. He promised himself he'd never be out in the streets naked, no matter what; he was going to stay strapped, just like he was right now.

"Where we headed to now?" Jahleysa looked back and forth between the windshield and Marquan.

Marquan shot her the address and stared out of the window until they'd arrived at the destination.

"You want me to roll up in here witchu?" Jahleysa inquired.

"Nah, I got it, this is something I gotta do by myself, you know?"

"Yeah, I know." She stared into his eyes lovingly as she caressed the side of his face. She then leaned closer and kissed him romantically.

Marquan took a deep breath and ran his hands down his face. Jahleysa's forehead wrinkled seeing the concerned expression on her man's face.

"What's wrong, babe? You nervous?" she asked worried.

"Yeah, I'm starting to hyperventilate, I'm tryna calm myself down." Marquan stated to her as he breathed in and out slowly, trying to calm himself. His eyelids were closed and he had a look of concentration on his face while he did this. "It's just that it's been years since I've seen him, and I don't know what to expect. I don't know if he's going to accept me or not."

"Come here," she opened up her arms and received him, giving him an affectionate embrace. They held one another for a minute before taking a deep breath and letting go. "You're gonna go up there and face whatever comes from your encounter with your son. I mean, it's been ten long years, he'll at least be happy to see you on some level."

"Yeah, you probably right. Thank you, baby," he cupped his hands around her face and kissed twice on the lips. After kissing his woman, Marquan hopped out of the car and made steps towards his destination. Stepping upon the curb, he looked up at the filthy tan apartment complex. There was trash scattered on the ground in front of the building and graffiti was sprawled on the front and side of the tenement. Taking a deep breath, Marquan made it up the steps and stopped before the door, which had a key pad on it. At first glance he could tell that the damn thing was busted and out of order. He thought he'd have a tough time getting inside of the place until he saw that the lock of the glass door was missing.

Marquan opened the door and made his way inside. The elevator was out of service, so he knew he'd have to take the staircase to the eighth floor. By the time Marquan had reached the floor he had in mind, he was thankful that he'd stayed in shape during his entire bid. He knew that if he had been him a few years ago taking the staircase that he'd be worn out. But at the moment, he hadn't even broken a sweat nor was he out of breath either.

As Marquan walked down the long hallway, he heard the noises coming from different units inside of the complex. There was yelling and fighting in one unit, loud rap music in one, a loud television in another and a couple having sex in the last door he'd past. When Marquan came to the number he was given on the door to his right, he stopped before it and took a deep breath. He did this to prepare himself for whatever was going to come from his first time seeing his son in ten years. Although he was expecting the best, he was definitely preparing for the worse.

Knock! Knock! Knock! Knock!

Marquan rapped on the door and waited, looking over his shoulder to see if anyone was watching him. He did this out of habit. He grew up gangbanging so he knew to always stay on point and strapped up, because he never knew when some niggaz would come for his head.

Marquan heard shuffling on the opposite side of the door and quickly straightened up, thinking that someone was about to open the door. When the door wasn't being pulled open, he assumed whomever was on the other side of it was looking out at him through the peephole.

"Who is it?" a feminine voice called out.

"Marquan…Marquan Ludlow," He responded. *That must be lil' Ant's girlfriend, but shit, he's only fifteen years old. Hell, I popped my cherry when I was twelve. Why can't he?*

Hearing the locks of the door coming undone, Marquan straightened up and cleared his throat with his fist to his mouth. Before he knew it, the door was being pulled open and a cloud of smoke was rushing out into his face. The smoke caused him to narrow his eyelids and try his best to peer through it. Once the smoke had evaporated, he found himself face to face with a younger version of himself. This younger version of himself was about three inches shorter and had a slight muscular build. He was wearing a blue bandana around his head and a wife beater. His light gray Dickie's hung off his ass and showed his boxers. This younger version of Marquan was his son, Antonio a.k.a Lil' Apocalypse a.k.a Lil' Poc.

Antonio mad dogged his father and looked him up and down with disdain. He dropped the roach end of the blunt he was smoking to the floor and mashed it out underneath his navy blue Nike Cortez, smearing ashes on the surface.

"Poc, you good?"A woman called out to him.

Over Antonio's shoulder, Marquan could see the woman that had posed the question. She was sitting on the couch and hunched over a cocktail table, counting up money. There were several more stacks sitting on the cocktail table and they were stacked neatly in a row with a rubber band around them. Off to the side was a digital scale, crack cocaine sitting amongst residue, and sandwich bags of weed.

"I'm straight," Antonio stepped out into the hallway and pulled the door shut behind him, "My nigga, you got some nerve showin' yo' face around here."

"What? What's the matter, son? You aren't happy to see me?" Marquan outstretched his hand towards his son. The young nigga smacked his hand down and shoved him up against the wall.

"Why in the fuck would I be happy to see you, huh? You left me out here to die! Basically said fuck me!"

"Never, son, you're my world! I've been gone for a dime, man. I couldn't stop thinking about you. Hell, I used my memories of you to fight my way up outta that hell hole to get back to you!"

Antonio shook his head fast and said, "Lies, lies, lies. You neva called, you neva wrote! Nigga, you wouldn't even allow me to come visit you!"

Unbeknownst to Antonio, Apocalypse would throw away all of the letters that Marquan sent him. He also rejected all of his calls, and later put a block on the telephone so that he couldn't call the house any more.

"What?" Marquan frowned up and looked at him like he had lost his mind. "Man, I tried reaching out to you, I don't know how many times. Somebody putta block on the phone and all my letters went unanswered. Shit, I sent a form for yo' mother to fill out so that you could come see me. I never got word back from anyone! You know how much that hurt me, man? To know that my baby boy's out here and I don't know what's going on with him? I don't know if he's being taken care of! I don't know if he's happy, sad, or being neglected! There were nights I couldn't sleep and days I couldn't function worrying about chu out here! The only way I knew that you were good was from different homies coming in and outta the pen. Otherwise, I was clueless!"

"No, no, no," Antonio shook his head as tears came bursting out of his eyes. "You a fuckin' liar, you never did any of that shit! Apocalypse told me that you didn't want anything to do with me or momma! That you said fuck us!" He shoved his father over and over again. "Well, now, nigga, it's fuck you!" Swiftly, he pulled his gun from the small of his back and pointed it right between his old man's eyes, sideways.

Tears streamed down his cheeks as he bit down on his bottom lip and bared his teeth.

"Boyyyyy, you young niggaz quick to draw them straps," Marquan told his son with a solemn expression. He couldn't help thinking about the young crips at the other house that had pointed their guns at him. Marquan's hands were down at his sides and he was standing upright. There was no fear whatsoever in his eyes. He had seen everything except Christ, so death was something else on his bucket list.

"Yep, we quick to bust 'em too, cuz, especially a young nigga like me," he slapped his hand up against his chest heatedly, and a fresh coat of tears drenched his cheeks. "I bet my name ringin' in them pens, huh, pop? I bet the gangstaz in there know all about how Lil' Poc out here givin' it up, huh? You heard about my get-down up in there?"

"Yes, son, I heard. I heard all about chu."

Antonio sniffled and took the time to wipe his dripping eyes with his curled finger and said, "I knew you did, nigga. All the dirt I did out here was all for you!"

"For me?" Marquan frowned and angled his head. He was confused to why his son would be in the streets committing crimes on the account of him.

"Yep, for you, pop," his voice cracked under his raw emotions and more tears drenched his face. "I thought that if I raise hell out here, and built up my rep, that you would love me again, man. I thought that if my gangsta impressed you enough that you'd come back to me and accept me as yo' son! I just wanted yo' love, pop! I just wanted you to love me, man! Why don't chu love me, pop?" His voice cracked again, and he started sobbing.

Marquan's eyes pooled with tears and they dripped from the brims of his eyes. He tried to say something, but his emotions choked him up. That's when he cleared his throat and started again. "I do love you, Antonio. I love you more than I love anyone in this world, including myself. I never, ever stopped loving you, son. Please, believe me."

Antonio broke down sobbing and making an ugly face. Wrinkles formed around his nose and at the corners of his eyes. "Tell me…" he took the time to wipe his face with the back of his hand and continued. "Tell me you love me again."

"I love you, son."

"Again…" his face became uglier and teardrops fell from his eyes.

"I love you very, very, very much. Now, hand me that gun and gemme a hug." Antonio handed his gun to his father by its barrel and he took it. He tucked the gun into the front of his jeans and motioned his son over to give him a hug. Instantly, Antonio threw his arms around his old man and he gave him a loving embrace. "I love you, boy. You're my heart, you hear me? You're my heart." He told him and kissed him on the side of his head. He then pulled the blue bandana from off his head and dropped it to the floor. Afterwards, he rubbed the top of his son's head and kissed it affectionately. "No more gangbanging, fuck this streets shit. It's this shit that's kept us apart for so long. From now on, it's all about you and me…family."

He hugged him tighter and kissed him again on his head, as tears spilled out from his eyes. As he held his son, he listened to him sob while he rubbed his hand up and down his back, comforting him.

Antonio went back inside of his apartment with his father. Standing at the door with his arms folded across his chest, Marquan took in the simple décor of his son's place. It had a simple black leather couch and love seat, a "50 television set, a stereo system, and a PlayStation. Looking to his son's bedroom, all he saw was a blowup mattress, a chair, a lamp sitting on the floor and the lid of a monopoly game, which he was sure his son broke up weed on.

When Marquan turned back around and saw a second young woman inside of the kitchen over the stove cooking crack, he came to the conclusion that his son was selling crack out of the unit. And if he wasn't doing that, he was at least cooking up his product there.

"This you?" Marquan asked his son, who was rummaging inside of the refrigerator.

"Yeah, pop, this is me," Antonio came out of the kitchen, kicking the refrigerator shut behind him. He looked to his father and tossed him one of the two Coronas he'd gotten out of the refrigerator. "I got tired of hustlin' for Apocalypse and decided to do my own thang, be my own man. Why eat offa 'notha man's plate when I can have my own? I gotta couple niggaz that's slingin' for me. My girl in there cookin' it up while lil' momma right here," he nodded to the young woman that his father saw counting up the dead white men earlier. "She cuts the shit up and counts up that check. This ain't much, but it's my shit. This my own operation, and niggaz gemme a wide birth 'cause they know I play with them guns. You know what I'm sayin', pop?"

"Yeah, I hear you, son," Marquan pulled up his jeans legs and sat down on the couch. "But like I said earlier, all this street shit is bullshit. It ain't for us, we betta than this, we greater than this. You and I," he motioned a finger between them. "We can build our own legitimate empire from the ground up. I'm talking 'bout legal paypa. I'm talking 'bout money we ain't gotta throw stones at the penitentiary for. You picking up what I'm sitting down?" he took a swig from his beer as he kept his eyes on his son. He watched as he thought on it and massaged his chin.

"I hear you, pop, but that's slow money. We'd be workin' forever tryna amass a fortune."

"If there's anything I've learned in these streets, its fast money goes fast, man. That shit burns up like you soaked it in gasoline and tossed a match onnit." He took the time to allow what he'd said to soak into his son's mental before continuing on, "But that slow money…that slow, legal money is where it's at. Slow and steady always wins the race, son. Always," He took another swig of the Corona. "I got one more time to stand before a judge, Antonio. One more time." he held up one finger. "Them mothafuckaz ever see my black ass again and they gone give me the rest of my natural life in the penitentiary. I'll be gone forever. As a matter of fact, just by me being in here, right now," he jabbed his finger downward. "With all this money, crack, guns and drug paraphernalia," When he mentioned all of the illegal stuff that was inside of the apartment, Antonio looked around at all of it. "Is enough to get me that L. If them people kicked in this door right now, I'd be gone. But I love you so much that I'm willing to risk it all to get chu back into my life. So, you and I can salvage what's left of our relationship." he gripped his son's shoulder affectionately.

The women that worked for Antonio became teary eyed and wiped the teardrops away before they could fall. Seeing a father so loving of his son really touched their hearts.

They had grown up without their fathers, and hoped that one day they'd come back for them, just like Antonio's father had.

"Okay, pop, I'm witchu. Just tell me what chu got planned?" Antonio asked his father.

"Opening up our own trucking business, that's where all the money is at. There's companies out here that always need truck drivers to move their product from point A to point B. Now, we gone have to crawl before we walk. I figure we'll start off with a couple of trucks and grind our way up. All we needa do is put together a couple of dollas."

"I got some paypa put up, pop."

Marquan took the bottle down from his lips after taking a swig, "Oh, yeah? How much chu sitting on, youngin'?"

"I gotta 'bout sixty racks stashed away."

"Sixty?" he raised his eyebrows with surprise. He wasn't expecting his son to have so much money put away. This was because at Antonio's age, the youngstas were rushing out to buy cars, clothes and jewelry. Apparently, his offspring was just like him, stacking and preparing for the future.

"Yep, I bet chu thought I was like the rest of these young niggaz out here, huh? Nah, I know betta. I'm in the dope game, which means I gotta have paypa put away for attorney fees in case me or any of my niggaz get popped out here." He stated to his father. "You know the deal, pop."

"Smart, man," his father dapped him up.

"Just like my old man."

Marquan smiled and said, "No doubt."

"You good? You needa hold somethin'?"

"Nah, JaQuel blessed me once I touched the turf. I figured I could put that with what chu got and we can do our own thing."

"Fa sho."

Marquan sat his Corona on the cocktail table and looked to his son. "Look, is this all the product you got here?" he pointed to the drugs on the table.

"Yeah, this is it." He nodded.

"Cool. Finish off what chu got here, chunk yo' people off and it's a wrap. We gone set out to do our thing, the legit way. You down, youngin'?"

Marquan cracked a smile as he stared at his son. He never knew unconditional love until he laid eyes on him when he was born. He remembered his heart skipping a beat and butterflies fluttering their wings in his stomach. At that moment, he promised himself that he was going to spend the rest of his life making up the time he'd lost with his son.

"Like foe flats."

"I'm back, man, and I'm not ever letting you outta my sight again." Marquan and his son stood to their feet. They then gave one another a gangsta hug. It felt good to be reunited after so long. Antonio fucked around and broke down crying again, he was so happy. His father wasn't far behind shedding tears of his own. Abruptly, he broke their embrace and held his son at arm's length. "Look, here, son, I want chu to take a ride with me, okay?"

"Right now?"

"Yeah. What, you can't roll out witcho old man?" he smirked.

"I mean, I do have business I needa attend to," he turned around looking at the girls, and they assured him that they could hold things down until he got back. "But if you insist that I roll witchu, then I gots ta go. That's an OG call."

Marquan chuckled and patted his son on his back. "Come on. Let's get up outta here."

"Hold on, pop," Antonio pulled his navy blue hoodie over his head and straightened it out on him. He then picked up his gun and tucked it at the small of his back. "What? You want me to leave this here?" he asked his father of the gun he'd just put away. It was the same banga that his old man had taken off of him when he arrived at his door. Marquan ended up giving it back to him later on though.

"Nah, we ain't outta these streets yet. As of now, we got one foot in and one foot out." Marquan said as he headed for the door with his son on his heels. They made their exit out of the apartment and into the world, where only God knew what waited for them.

CHAPTER SIXTEEN

Maquan and Antonio hopped inside of Jahleysa's car. As soon as they shut their respective doors, Marquan made the introductions.

"Jah, this is my son, Antonio. Antonio, this is myyyy…." Marquan allowed his eyes to linger on Jahleysa as he tried to figure what to call her.

"Girlfriend," Jahleysa smiled and patted Marquan's thigh. "Nice to meet chu, Antonio."

"Even nicer to meet chu," Antonio smiled.

Marquan turned around and looked into the backseat at his son, saying, "Boy, I know you ain't putting the moves on my woman."

"My bad for steppin' on yo' toes, pop. She's gorgeous. You got taste, OG." Antonio winked at Jahleysa and she chuckled. Turning back around in the driver seat, she cranked up her Honda and pulled off. She occasionally glanced at the rearview mirror at Antonio. She couldn't help thinking about how much he resembled his father. It was like he was a clone of his younger self.

"So, son, when was the last time you spoke to Poc?" Marquan inquired.

"A few days ago, he's my plug," Antonio told his father. He then addressed Jahleysa, "Say, gorgeous, you mind if I burn this bleezy in here?"

Jahleysa looked to Marquan when Antonio asked to smoke a blunt in her car. She didn't want to tell him *yes* and have his father oppose.

Marquan gave her a nod and she gave his son the go ahead to light up in her whip.

Alcohol and weed! This boy has some nasty habits I'm gonna have to break him from. He's only fifteen. I can't have 'em doing all that around me. I'm his father. How the fuck would that look? Fuck it. After I'm done with this mission, I'll worry about making things right with Ant, Marquan thought to himself as he stared out of the passenger side window and watched the streets pass him by.

"Yo' plug, huh? So, he's the one that's supplying you with yo' drugs?"

"Yeah, pop, but fuck that bitch ass nigga now." Antonio's face twisted with animosity. "Ever since you been locked up, he's been plantin' these fucked up thoughts inside of my head about chu."

Marquan peeled his eyes off the passenger side window and looked over his shoulder. "Evil thoughts like what?"

"Tellin' me how you didn't give a fuck about me and moms. You left us out here for dead. How you never loved us. How he was the only nigga that gave a shit about me, and that he was my daddy now."Antonio's eyes became misty as he recalled all the bullshit Apocalypse poisoned his mind with. "That nigga had me hatin' you, pop. I couldn't stand yo' ass, man, nigga had me wishin' you got killed while you were locked up." He quieted down and looked out the window. His eyes slowly welled up with tears that came sliding down his cheeks. He quickly wiped them away and continued to stare out of the window. "He's the one that really pressed the issue about me bein' from the hood. Mannn, that nigga had me doin' all kinds of shit. Shit you wouldn't even begin to imagine. Shit I'm afraid to even tell you about, OG. Shit I'm too ashamed to speak on." He lowered his eyes to the floor and big teardrops fell from his eyes.

Marquan and Jahleysa exchanged concerned glances as they wondered what Antonio was talking about. They didn't have a clue between them, so they had to pry.

"Whatever it is, son, you can tell me. Don't be ashamed, I'ma still love you like I always have. You hear me? Talk to me now."

Antonio rolled the back passenger window down and flicked what was left of the blunt out, sending embers flying.

"Pull over, Jah. Pull over," Antonio cried and sniffled.

"Alright, I'ma pull over here alongside this curb." As Jahleysa made to do as she was told, Antonio broke down hard, shuddering and crying his ass off.

A teary eyed Marquan looked up at the ceiling and told God, "Please, Father, don't let my boy tell me what I think he's about to tell me. I couldn't take it. I just couldn't forgive myself for something like that right now."

"I'm…I'm sorry, pop. I didn't mean to be fallin' apart cryin' like a lil' bitch and shit in front…in front of you. It's…It's just that I be tryna hold it together…even though I feel like I wanna fall apart." He whimpered and snorted back snot that was threatening to drip from his nostril. He had been through a world of hurt and confusion since his father had been out of his life. He thought his suffering would never come to an end, and once it did, he found himself still suffering…inside of his mind. "Aaaahhhhhhh!" He threw his head back and clutched the sides of it, with his hands. His face was balled up and the tears seemed to be cascading down his cheeks. At that moment, he was reliving all of the abuse Apocalypse had inflicted upon him.

"Hold on, son, hold on," Marquan looked over his shoulder at his offspring. A moment after he spoke, Jahleysa pulled over and killed the engine. Swiftly, Marquan hopped out of the car and snatched open the back passenger door. He pulled Antonio out of the car and let him lean up against the trunk. The occasional car passed by them as they talked in the streets. "Tell me what he had you doing, son, it's okay." He gripped his shoulder affectionately and looked up into his tear streaked face. His son was trembling as he looked down at the ground. All of the stories he'd heard about him tearing shit up in the streets, made him forget about the fact that he was still a kid. He was only fifteen years old and he already had a body count half his age.

"Now, tell me what Poc had you doing?" Marquan said with tears in his eyes. He batted his eyelashes to dissipate them.

"He had me doin' stuff that God don't like," Antonio quivered and teardrops fell from the brims of his eyes, rapidly. He wiped his eyes and nose with the sleeve of his hoodie.

"Stuff like what? I need to know what happened. You're my son and I want to protect you. If someone done something to you then let me know. It's my right to know." He cupped Antonio's face and stared into his eyes. As the young nigga went on to tell him one of several incidents that happened between him and Apocalypse, Marquan could see it playing in his pupils like a movie at a theater.

"I'ma show you. Now, watch..." Apocalypse unwrapped a cherry Tootsie Roll pop and stuck the red orb into

"I...I don't want to do this. I...I...I don't really think I'm 'pose to," Antonio told him timidly as he fidgeted with his fingers. "I don't think God would like this."

At that moment, Apocalypse's eyes came alive and his eyebrows slanted. His nose wrinkled and he clenched his jaws

"What?" Apocalypse sat up where he was perched.

"I said, I..."

Smack!

Apocalypse smacked Antonio viciously across the face and he fell to the carpeted floor, bumping his head. Wincing, he slowly lifted his face up from off the floor. His grill was bloody and his teeth were red. He cried as he spat blood on the floor and slowly got upon his feet.

"Bring yo' ass here, cuz!" Apocalypse's voice boomed at Antonio's back. The boy slowly turned around, and his eyes

nearly leaped out of his head. Apocalypse, his father's best friend, had a gun pointed dead at him. He didn't know anything about firearms, besides what he saw them do in movies, and that was kill people.

"Stop, stop, stop, that's enough! That's enough!" A disgusted and pained Marquan called out. His eyes were glassy and red webbed, while his cheeks were slicked wet. "That mothafucka," he paced the sidewalk back and forth with one hand on his hip and the other sweeping his hand down his fade. "That mothafucka, that mothafuucckkaaa!" He slammed his clenched fists down on the trunk of Jahleysa's car violently and created small dents. She stood on the sidewalk crying her eyes out after hearing the story Antonio told his father.

"I'm sorry, pop, please forgive me," Antonio looked on as his father continued his pounding on the trunk of the car. His face was wetter than it was before and now his nose was red.

"Don't be sorry, son, don't be sorry." Marquan told his boy as he stood at the back of Jahleysa's car. His head was bowed and his hands were firmly planted on the trunk of the vehicle. Big teardrops fell and splashed on the trunk and bumper of the car, like raindrops. He hated himself for what had happened to his son. The way he looked at it, it was his fault. If he wouldn't have gotten locked up in the first place, he would have been out to defend his son when he needed him the most.

All the work I done put in, in this nigga'z honor! The charges I done took, the bread I broke with 'em, and he does this to my son, my heart, my life, the air I breathe? But why though? Why do this to my family? All I ever did was show that nigga love and be down for 'em. I'ma find out whatever I needa know right before I puff his mothafucking wig out, Marquan thought to himself and wiped his eyes with the sleeve of his jacket. He then turned around to his son.

"That wasn't yo' fault, son. If it's anyone's fault, it's mine. I'm the one to blame here," he pointed a finger at his chest and his eyes pooled with water again. The thought of someone violated his son hurt him to the depths of his heart and the core of his soul. "I'm sorry, Antonio, I shoulda been there, man. Daddy shoulda been there." Marquan hugged his son tightly and allowed him to sob into his chest. He kissed the top of his head and swept his hand up and down his back to comfort him. "I'm sorry, man. I'm so, so sorry."

Marquan looked up and saw Jahleysa crying like a baby, like him and his son. He motioned her over and she joined them in a loving group hug, where they all bawled their eyes out.

****

Antonio told his father everything that Apocalypse had done to him since he was locked away. Although Marquan didn't want to hear the atrocities that had been done to his son, he forced himself to listen anyway. His listened with a scowling face until his son told him something that got him silently crying again. He told him that Apocalypse had sodomized him in order to make him obedient. Antonio claimed that Apocalypse would have anal sex with him at least three times a week. The only reason why Antonio didn't stop him once he was old enough to defend himself was because he'd already lost both his mother and father and he didn't want to lose his street daddy. The only nigga he believed cared about him in the cold world.

Marquan took an ink pen and a napkin from out of the glove-box. He listened closely as Antonio gave him Apocalypse's home address. Once he had finished jotting the address down, he looked it over, recalling exactly what hood his homeboy turned enemy was staying in now.

I'ma smoke that mothafucka! He's gotta go, ASAP!

"Antonio, when was the last time you heard from yo' mother?" Marquan inquired.

"Two years ago. The last time I saw her she was hoin' out on Figueroa. She was lookin' bad too; I didn't want to see her down bad like that so I gave her a couple of dollas. I invited her to stay with me, but she declined. Ever since then I haven't seen her."

"Well, I gotta homeboy of mine out here looking for her now."

Marquan had his reasons for not revealing to his son that JaQuel had already found his mother. First, he had to find out if she had set him up like Apocalypse had told him. Depending on her answers, he may let her live or he may very well not. He hadn't decided yet.

"Well, I hope they find her…alive."

"Me, too, I want chu to have your entire family together again…like when you were lil'."

"I'd like that too, pop."

"Lemme ask you, though. Did yo' mother know what Apocalypse was doing to you?"

"In the beginnin' she didn't, but later on, I told her. After a while, the nigga started doin' it while she was in the house."

When he said this, Marquan's face twisted and he balled his fists so tight that the veins in them bulged. He grew hot around his ears and the back of his neck. If he wasn't in the outside world to protect his son, he felt that at least his mother should have been looking after him.

"I don't even blame moms though, pop. That nigga turned her out on that heroin. She knew that if she fell out with him that she wouldn't be able to get high for free anymore. She'd have to go out here and do whatever she hadda do to earn some paypa to get high.

Fuck that shit, cuz! That bitch ain't shit for allowing that mothafucka to violate our son. It ain't a drug powerful enough for me to let any bitch to do mine harm! Onna set, loc!

At that moment, Marquan's cellular rang and vibrated inside of his pocket. He pulled it out and looked at the screen.

This that nigga JaQuel.

Marquan answered the call and placed the cell phone to his ear. He listened closely to what JaQuel had to say before disconnecting the call.

"Change of plans," he told Jahleysa. And then he gave her the address to where they were going.

Antonio frowned up and said, "We not goin' to see that nigga Poc now, pop?"

"Nah, we making a lil' detour, we gone see 'em though. Don't even wet it, son, that dick sucka gone get his just due."

****

Jahleysa pulled up outside of a tan and brown house.

"You sure this is the place you're looking for?" Jahleysa asked as she leaned forward and looked past Marquan, through the passenger window.

"Yeah, this it, I'll be right back." He popped open the door.

"Pop, you don't want me to roll witchu, just in case?" Antonio asked from the backseat.

"Nah, I got it, son. I'll be back before you know it."

Marquan jumped out of the Honda and looked both ways, before jogging across the street. He adjusted his gun on his waistline before making his way up the steps of the house that was the shooting gallery. This was the same shooting gallery that Apocalypse had murdered Avery's ass. Marquan knocked on the door in a code. As the door's locks started coming undone, he glanced over his shoulder at Jahleysa's car and found her talking to his son. He couldn't hear what she was saying, but he was glad that she was getting along good with his son.

Hearing the door squeaking as it was being pulled open, Marquan turned back around to find himself standing before JaQuel. He dapped up his young homie and stood aside, allowing him in over the threshold. Afterwards, JaQuel shut the door behind him and turned around, motioning for him to follow him. They made their way down the hallway past heroin addicts shooting up or doing the dope head lean. JaQuel led Marquan down the hallway and through the living room, where they found Talib waiting by the staircase.

"G' looking, homie," Marquan said to Talib.

"It's all love." He dapped him up.

After the brief exchange, Marquan and JaQuel made their way up the starcase and trekked down the hallway. Stopping at the center of the corridor, they pushed open the door of an old decrepit bedroom. There was plaster on the floor and the walls had big ass holes in them. Some of the holes were so goddamn big that you could see into the rooms beside them.

Adele sat on an old filthy, tattered mattress on the floor. Her head was bowed and she was hugging her legs to her chest. Standing where he was in the doorway, Marquan could tell that she'd been in the streets for quite some time now. She was in a T-shirt with holes in it and skinny jeans that fit her loosely. They fit so loose on her because she'd lost so much weight from chasing dope. Her hair was also considerably shorter too. In fact, her hair was so short that she looked like a fucking ostrich by the head. Feeling the auras of two people inside of the bedroom, Adele looked up to find her son's father and his homeboy standing side by side.

Marquan's brows furrowed when he saw Adele's trembling body and sweaty face. He took note of the dry vomit around her mouth and the foul stench coming from off her. It was the unmistakable smell of shit. It was from this that he knew that she was as sick as a goddamn dog, from her lack of dope. She needed a fix, and fast too.

"Quan…is…is that chu?" She narrowed her eyelids and leaned forward as she tried to see her baby's daddy's face.

"Yeah, it's me."

She cracked a slight smile through her pained expression. "Well, I would get up and give youa hug, but I'm down bad right now, babes. I need me some dope. I need me some dope, and fast too. My stomach crampin' like a son of a bitch, I been throwin' up and I even shit himself."

"I could have dropped some dope on her, but I recall you sayin' that chu wanted her coherent and alert."

"That's right," Marquan nodded, his eyes still focused on his son's mother.

"Quan, did you hear me? I'm sick," Adele picked herself up from the mattress.

"I heard you loud and clear," he told her. "I'ma give you what chu need." He leaned closer to JaQuel and whispered into his ear. The younger man reached inside of his pocket and pulled out a packet of dope. He passed the packet to Marquan and he held it up so that Adele could see it. Her eyes stretched wide open and she licked her lips as she scratched her tracked marked arm. Her dirty nails raked up the inside of her arm and reopened scabs causing them to bleed. Marquan frowned with disgust seeing it. At that moment, he took a better look at Adele than he had earlier when he'd entered the room. For the first time, he noticed that she had a lot of scabs and sores on her. She had them on her neck and arms. Her wild, short unkempt hair, coupled with the black rings around her eyes made her look like a zombie. The bitch really looked like she woke up from where she'd been killed and shuffled through the streets looking for dope.

Adele tried to snatch the packet of dope from out of Marquan's hand, but he snatched his hand from her before she could grab it.

"Unh unh," he shook his head and his finger as if to say *Not so fast.* "First I gotta question for you. I want to answer truthfully. If I feel like you keeping it one hunnit, then I'll toss you yo' get-high. Cool?"

Adele scratched her arm and nodded, saying, "Alright, what exactly is it that chu want to ask me?"

"Did you have anything to do with Poc setting me up that night?"

Hearing him ask this caused Adele's stomach to hurt more than her hunger for raw dope. The saliva in her throat dried up instantly and her heart skipped a beat. She started scratching underneath her chin and then up her other arm before she finally answered.

"No," she responded. But he didn't believe her ass; she looked guilty as hell standing there before him.

Adele tried to snatch the packet of dope again, but Marquan snatched it back.

"I don't believe you, you're definitely lying."

"I'm insulted that you'd even fix yo' lips to ask me somethin' like that. You my son's father, I was in love witchu. Why in the hell would I do some scandalous ass shit like that for?" she frowned up at him. She couldn't believe he had the audacity to ask her about her setting him up to go to prison.

"'Cause youa scandalous ass bitch!"

"Nigga, fuck you, that's not how you speak to the mother of yo' child. Come at some other hoe like that, but not me, you disrespectful mothafucka!" She harped up phlegm and spat in his face. The nasty glob splattered against his forehead and dripped off his brow.

I see ain't shit changed about this hood rat's smart ass mouth!

A frowning Marquan wiped off what was left of the glob off his brow and shook his head. He then shut his eyelids briefly and took a deep breath. Switching hands with the packet of dope, he used his right hand to pull out his gun and he pointed it at his baby's momma. Her eyes grew big with fright and her jaw dropped open.

"I'ma ask you again, Adele, and this time, I want the real. You can either get the dope or you can getta bullet. The choice is yours. Choose wisely now." He tilted his head to the side and raised his eyebrow, like he was warning her to be careful with what she was about to say next.

"Okay, alright, I did it." she said with glassy eyes as she swallowed the lump of fear in her throat.

"You did what? Be clear on what you talking about." his eyebrows sloped and his nostrils flared.

"I…I set chu up." She admitted.

JaQuel shook his head and said, "Triflin' ass hoe, yo' own baby's daddy. I be beefin' with my baby's mommas, but they'd never set me up like that, you a cold ass piece, sis…a real cold ass piece."

"Wow, just wow," Marquan said shocked. Although he already knew about her setting him up. It was something about hearing it from the horse's mouth that fucked him up all over again.

Adele bowed her head and her shoulders slightly shook as big teardrops fell from her eyes. The teardrops splashed on the raggedy hardwood floor and on the tip of her tattered sneaker. She sniffled and wiped her snotty nose with the back of her hand. She then brought her head back up so she'd be looking him directly in his eyes.

"Why though? I mean, damn, I know we had our differences, but what couple doesn't? I took good care of you and our son. Y'all didn't want for shit while I was out here, and this is how you do me? Why? Start talking 'cause I wanna know now, goddamn it!" His eyes filled up with tears and he pointed his gun right between her eyes, threateningly. He was a second away from blowing her brains out if she didn't start talking.

"Because you never had time for me, and you were fuckin' around!" She blurted angrily as spit leaped off her lips. Her eyes were pink and tears were seemingly pouring down her cheeks. She broke down sobbing and bowed her head once again.

"Bitch, I was out in the streets so I could provide for us, our mothafucking family, you ungrateful ass hoe! And I never fucked around on you, not ever! I gave you my word that you, me, and the baby were gonna be a family!"

"That's not what he told me! He said that chu were still fuckin' around with that bitch Jah!"

"Who, who the fuck told you some shit like that?" His brows furrowed and crinkles surrounded the beginning of his nose.

Adele lifted her head up again and wiped her eyes with her fingers, saying, "Apocalypse. He told me that you were still creepin' around with Jah behind my back. Then he started tellin' me everything that I wanted to hear. How beautiful I was, how he would treat me like a queen if I was his, and how we could be a family, how he could be the father and man that Antonio and I needed."

"Right. You fell for that slick ass tongue of his. This only proves one thing to me, you just as weak as a bitch as I thought chu was. You're fucking pathetic," he looked her up and down like she was shit on the bottom of his sneaker.

"I know. I'm sorry, I'm so sorry," she apologized as she made an ugly face, crying. "I felt bad, really bad about it. The whole situation fucked me up so bad that I ended up on the needle."

"Bitch, save yo' sob stories, I ain't got no sympathy for hoes, you better find a counselor! Fuck you think this is, huh?"

"I'm sorry, Marquan, I'm really, really sorry." Adele trembled as if she was freezing cold. Her cheeks were shiny from her crying so much. She knew that she was dead ass wrong for how she'd betrayed her son's father. But the dream that Apocalypse had sold her was too good to pass up. She didn't have any idea that it would turn out to be a nightmare. "Please…please, forgive me." She held his hands together begging.

Marquan stood there staring into the eyes of his baby's momma. He couldn't believe that she'd done him so foul. She had drawn a knife and stabbed him in the back with it. Marquan lived by the mantra Death before Dishonor, so how could he forgive her? As her baby's daddy he could turn a blind eye to her shady dealings, but to do so would be foolish. Old girl could come back to do something that would guarantee that he was lying face up inside of a coffin. If he was to let her slide for what she'd done, it would be going against everything that he stood for. *Goddamn you, Adele,* he shook his head and massaged the bridge of his nose.

"You…you…broke my heart, Adele." Marquan said, like every word hurt that left his lips. His eyes moistened and turned red webbed. He tried to fight back the tears by squeezing his eyelids shut, but they were still there.

"Baby, I know," Adele began as tears dripped from her eyes. "I fucked up and I'm sorry. I'm so, so sorry that I did what I did. I'll do anything, anything to make this up to you. I want you, me, and Antonio to be a family again." she had her fingers interlocked and a great sadness was in her eyes. All she wanted him to do was forgive her so they could move forward with a future together.

Adele sniffled and wiped her eyes with her fingers and thumb. She moved to embrace Marquan, but he held up his hand and stopped her dead in her tracks.

"This is where we end. This is where I turn my back on you." Marquan gave her his back. When Adele went to approach him again, JaQuel came up from behind her and clamped his gloved hand over her mouth. The woman struggled but not for long. He pulled her head back and exposing her jugular, throat on display. He brought his hunting knife around and swiped it across her throat, swiftly. The flesh of her neck split open and a river of black blood flowed fluidly, drenching the collar of her shirt. Adele's arms flailed slower and slower until she went still. Her eyes settled at their corners and her mouth hung open in a grotesque manner. JaQuel released old girl and she dropped to her knees, falling face first. She lay on the side of her face with her eyes stretched wide open. Her life's blood ran out of the opening in her neck and outlined her head.

Marquan stared down at the lifeless body that was his baby's momma. He didn't feel any remorse for what he'd done. As far as he was concerned, she was dead long before JaQuel had slit her throat. He had her funeral inside of his head the moment she admitted to helping set him up.

"Here's yo' dope," Marquan dropped the packet of dope into the blood that had pooled around Adele's head. Next, he tucked his gun on his waistline and turned to JaQuel. "Get rid of this body; make sure no one ever finds it. I want it to seem like she just went missing."

"How do you expect me to get her down there without everyone noticin' me carryin' her out?" JaQuel questioned with creased brows.

"All them heads down there are doped outta their minds, they ain't gone know what the fuck they seeing. You good, loc, trust in yo' nigga." he dapped him up.

"Alright, cuz."

"When you done, hit me up and I'ma shoot chu Poc's address. I'ma need you to hold it down in case some shit jump off."

"I got chu faded, crip."

"Smooth," Marquan patted him on the back and headed out of the door. He had one more move to make before he headed out to Apocalypse's crib.

CHAPTER SEVENTEEN

Marquan and his son hopped out of Jahleysa's car and made their way to the trunk of it. Marquan popped the trunk of the Honda and grabbed the shovel he'd purchased from Walmart on the way over to the location. Afterwards, he shut the trunk gently. He and his son pulled the blue bandanas around their neck over the lower half of their faces. Hunched down, they peered through the gate of the backyard of the house they were staking out. The kitchen light was on and they could see it illuminating through the window. Marquan pulled back the sleeve of his jacket and looked at his watch. Still hunched down, he and his son watched a silhouette move past the kitchen window. A short time later, the kicthen's light went out. Marquan passed his son his shovel and made his way over the gate. Once he was on the other side of the gate, he signaled for his son to pass the shovel over to him. Having gotten his hands on the shovel, Marquan motioned for his son to make his way over the gate as well. Once his son had dropped down on bending knees, Marquan picked up his shovel and told him follow him. He then pulled out the map that 187 had drawn up for him, and followed its directions. A minute later, he found himself below the shade of a tree, with the letter X marked on its trunk.

Seeing that he'd found the exact spot that he was suppose to be digging, Marquan folded up the map and shoved it into his back pocket. He gave his son a nod, and the young nigga whipped out his gun. He was to watch his father's back while he digged for the loot that 187 claimed to have buried there. They would take turns, rotating between lookout and digger.

Marquan dug until he was sweaty and it felt like his arms were going to fall off. Antonio then took over until he found something leather and covered in dirt before his eyes. He alerted his father, and tugged what appeared to be a black leather bag up from out of the ground. Holding what he deemed was a doctor's bag; he shook the clumps of dirt from off it. Standing high above ground, his father looked down over his shoulder as he pulled the bag open. Inside he found stacks of wrinkled dead presidents secured by rubber bands.

"It's like half of a million dollas in this bag, pop," Antonio declared.

"Maybe. It doesn't matter though, we not keeping it. Come on, let's get outta here, son." He took the bag as his son passed it up. He switched hands with the bag and outstretched his freehand. Antonio tossed the shovel upon the ground and grabbed hold of his father's hand. With the assistance of his old man, the young nigga climbed out of the ditch he'd helped to dig.

With the deed done, Marquan and Antonio fled like a couple of thieves into the night. By the time they were pulling out of the alley, the light inside of the window of the kitchen came on and the back door opened. An old man stuck his head out of the door and looked around suspiciously. When he didn't see anyone or anything, he shrugged and went back inside, shutting the door behind him.

****

"This is it," Marquan said after looking over the piece of paper with the address on it. He then looked into the backseat at Antonio. "Alright, son, gone up to the door, you don't let go of that bag 'til you identify Heiress. Got it?" he passed him a photo of 187's daughter that he had Jahleysa print off her Facebook page.

"Got it, OG," Antonio took the printout and looked at it for a moment before folding it up and slipping it inside of his pocket. He opened the back door and jumped out, shutting the door back behind him. Standing on the curb, he switched hands with the doctor's bag he'd helped dig up and adjusted the gun on his waistline. Afterwards, he proceeded towards the house as he took a scan of the area to make sure there wasn't anyone on the prowl.

Marquan watched as his son went up the steps of 187's daughter's house and knocked on the door. The windows of the house lit up with light, and the door came open. A woman stood out on the porch holding a baby on her hip. Although Marquan couldn't make out who she was from the distance he was, he gathered that she must have been Heiress because his son passed her the doctor's bag before he retreated back to the car.

"That was her?" Marquan inquired as soon as his son hopped into the backseat and slammed the door shut behind him.

"Yeah," the young nigga nodded.

"You sho'?"

"One hunnit, pop."

"Let's go, Jah." Marquan said to Jahleysa and she pulled off.

"Where we headed to now?" Jahleysa inquired.

"Apocalypse's house," He stared through the windshield at nothing.

It was time to bring the beef to a close.

****

Marquan stood outside of Apocalypse's house with several people standing behind him. Fire and determination was burning in his pupils. He was ready and willing to get it from the shoulders like they used to back in the day before niggaz turned pussy and decided to get the guns involved in the game they played. It was okay though, he was about to bring those days back.

"Aaaaaapocaaaaallllllllyppsssssseeeee!" Marquan threw his head back screaming at the top of his lungs, that thing at the back of his throat shaking as he held both of his muscular arms up in the air. He screamed until he couldn't anymore and then brought his hands down to his sides. At that moment, the front door of the house opened and Apocalypse came strolling out. He was in a T-shirt and gray Dickies. His face was fixed with a scowl and wrinkles were at the beginning of his nose.

"You came lookin' for trouble, cuz. Well, you sho' 'nough fuckin' found it." Apocalypse slammed the door shut and hustled down the steps. He then threw his tattooed arms into the air as he mad dogged the man he once loved as a brother. "Is this what chu won't? Huh, nigga? Is this what chu won't?"

"That's right! I want cho mothafucking ass, you fuckin pussy!" Marquan roared.

"Fuck you, you bitch-ass nigga! If it wasn't for yo' mark ass bein' born, my mom's would still be alive, and I'd still have my mothafuckin' daddy, cuz."

Marquan's forehead creased. "Cuz, what the fuck is you talking about?"

Apocalypse turned the knob and pushed the door of his mother's room open, gently. Sticking his head inside, he found his old lady lying down. She was a far cry from the five foot five, 160 pound woman that he called momma. She was really skinny with sunken eyes and black bags beneath them. Her skin was ashen and covered in sores that made her look like a mutated leopard. Her water melon sized breasts and bodacious ass was gone. The AIDs virus had eaten away at them slowly, just like it had done her life.

When Apocalypse saw his mother, Virgie Ward, it broke his heart into one million pieces. His eyes pooled water and teardrops threatened to fall. His legs felt like cooked noodles underneath him and he had to catch himself before he fell. It felt like he'd taken a bullet to the chest.

Sniffling, Apocalypse wiped his dripping eyes with his curled finger and swallowed the ball of fear in his throat. Shutting his eyelids for a moment, he took a deep breath and found the nerve to address his mother.

"Hey, momma," Apocalypse began as he shut the door behind him. As soon as he called out to his mother, she looked to him and mustered up a weak smile. He returned the gesture, "Heyyy, baby boy, how are…" Virgie went into a coughing fit and the smile disappeared from Apocalypse's face. A concerned expression went across his face and he rushed over to her side. He picked up the pink pitcher and poured her a cup of water. After sitting the pitcher down on the small rolling table, he titled the cup to her lips and watched her drink, thirstily. Once he'd figured she'd had enough, he sat the cup down on the table and picked up a napkin. Folding the napkin in half, he patted the access water from her chin until it was dry. "How you been doing, son?" she looked at her son smirking. She was truly glad to see him. Hell, she hadn't seen

him since he was eight years old. From that age to the present day, the streets had raised Apocalypse. They were all that he knew.

See after losing her man to another woman, Virgie was devastated and heartbroken. So much so that she started fucking around with his best friend, Avery, to get back at him and help her get over him. Realizing that that wasn't enough, she turned to the heroin to help her through her grieving, but she fucked around and ended up becoming a dope fiend.

Apocalypse sat on the side of his mother's bed and placed her hand into his hand. Using his freehand, he caressed her hand affectionately while staring into her eyes. Seeing her in such bad shape fucked him up. He wished that there was something that he could do to take her pain away but there wasn't. The only thing he could do now was stay by her side until the Lord finally called her home.

"I'm doin' okay, momma, how about you?" He asked even though he didn't need to. She was lying in bed before him and it was obvisious to anyone that had seen her that she was on the brink of death.

"I'm not doing to good, baby. Momma's sick, momma's real sick." She went into a coughing fit again. He tried to give her some more water, but she held up her hand, refusing it.

"Momma, they said you had HIV, but it eventually developed into full blown AIDS. How did you get it?"

Virgie laid there for a minute staring up at nothing particular. Slowly, her eyes began to mist and her bottom lip trembled. She shut her eyelids and tears jetted down her cheeks. Having cried for a moment, she took a deep breath and peeled her eyelids back open.

"Avery gave it to me." Virgie told her only son.

Avery, her bitch ass boyfriend, I swear 'fore God, cuz. That mothafucka is dead, I'ma kill 'em. I'ma kill that mothafucka, Apocalypse's eyebrows slanted and he clenched his fist so tight that his knuckles cracked.

"At first he'd denied it, trying to place the blame on me, but I knew better. I never shared any needles with anyone, and I wasn't lying down with anyone to get my drugs either." She told him the truth, raw and uncut. "That's how I knew! That's how I knew he gave me this shit and sentenced me to death! That low down dirty dog was sucking and fucking on all of them faggots out there in the streets to get money to get high with! Then he turned around, and was fucking me raw, and gave me this shit!" Tears cascaded down her cheeks as she stared ahead. Her nostrils flared and her bottom lip quivered. She was trying to stop from breaking down, but she couldn't help it. "Lord have mercy...Lord have mercy on my soul."

Fuck, God, man, fuck God, Apocalypse thought to himself. He didn't want to say it aloud because he didn't want to upset his mother or disrespect her, but that's how he felt. There ain't no God, 'cause if there was he wouldn't have let my momma go out like this. She had always been a good motha to me and a good woman to my pops, with his punk ass. Yeah, she cut out on me when I was a lil' nigga, but that was the heroin that led her astray. Besides that time in my life, she's always done right by me. She don't deserve to go out like this, nah, not my momma.

"I'm sorry, baby, I'm so sorry for leaving you alone in them scandalous ass streets," she sniffled as tears dripped from her eyes. "If I could take it back I would have never let cho father leaving me affect me to the point where I turned to drugs. God knows that if I would have never turned to drugs, I would have never neglected you. I'm sorry, Noel. Please, forgive me, baby. I don't wanna die knowing that chu have hate in your heart for me, that's why I had the nurse get in touch with you."

Apocalypse sniffled and wiped away his dripping teardrops, saying, "I forgive you, momma. And I love you too; I love you very, very much. In fact, I never stopped lovin' you, even after you left me."

"Oh, thank you, baby," she said with relief, and dropped more teardrops. "Thank you, thank you, thank you."

Apocalypse leaned forth and kissed her on the forehead. He then went back to caressing her hand, gently.

"Momma, why did pops leave us? Were y'all havin' problems in y'all relationship or somethin'?"

Virgie took another deep breath before responding to her son. "Yo' father left us to be with his other family." She confessed.

"Other family?" his brows furrowed.

"Yes, his other family." She told him. "Your father was a hoe. The biggest hoe there ever was, probably. He had a girlfriend and another son, a couple of months older than you. He left us to be with them. I begged and pleaded for him to stay, but he wasn't trying to hear it. He walked outta that

door and never looked back. It was as if he forgot that you and I existed."

Bitch ass nigga, cuz, left me and moms for dead in these streets, Apocalypse shook his head like it was a shame that his father had abandoned him and his mother.

"Ma, where is pops now?"

"Dead,"she told him, straight up. "Your father has been dead for thirty-two years now."

"How'd he die?" a curious look crossed his face.

"From what I hear, he died in a bad car accident."

Mothafucka'z lucky he went out like he did 'cause if I woulda got hold of his asssssss...

"What about that nigga Avery? Where he be at these days,ma?"

Apocalypse's inquiring about Avery caused her forehead to wrinkle. "Why do you want to know where Avery is, son?"

"Momma you been out in these streets for a looooong time, so I'm sure you heard of my reputation and what I'ma 'bout. With that said, I'm pretty sure it's safe to say whether you give me the whereabouts of Avery or not I'm gonna find 'em. And when I do, the only way they gonna be able to identify him is through dental records."

For a minute, Virgie was silent as she stared into her son's eyes. She debated on whether she should tell him where he could find Avery or not. Coming up with her decision, she went ahead and gave him the information that he needed. She watched as he wrote the information down and stashed it inside of his pocket.

"Now, I don't know if he'll definitely be there, but there's a chance. Knowing him, the guilt of what he's done to me is eating him alive, and he'll need dope to ease his suffering."

"Whatever happened to the broad and the boy he walked out on us ova?"

"The woman is dead, she passed with him in the car accident." Virgie coughed some more, but this time when Apocalypse offered to give her some water, she didn't refuse. After taking a drink of water, she went on to continue talking. "The boy is still alive though. He's a grown man now, and he's a street nigga from what I hear."

"You know his name?"

Virgie was quiet for a moment as she thought on it. "Damn, you know what? I don't quite recall his name, but I'm sure I'll remember it, gemme a second."

"Alright," Apocalypse looked to his mother's hair. She had an unkempt, graying afro. "Momma, you gotta natural fork? I'ma comb yo' hair."

"Yeah, look in the drawer over there."

Apocalypse rose from off the bed and approached the dresser drawer.

"Man, that boy's name is at the tip of my tongue," Virgie said as she continued to think of the name of the boy who also called her man his father.

"Take yo' time, momma. You'll think of it, it will come to you." Apocalypse pulled out the dresser drawer and froze were he was. His eyes lit up when he saw an old creased photograph of a man, a woman, and a boy that looked very familiar to him.

"Marquan…That was that boy's name, I knew I'd remember it."

"Is this him?" a stunned Apocalypse brought over the photograph to his mother he'd found inside of the dresser drawer.

After taking the time to study the photo, Virgie slowly nodded her head and said, "Yeah. That's him."

"You sure, ma?" he looked between his mother and the photo.

"Yeah, I'm sure," she told him. "I found this picture inside of his drawer when I was packing up his stuff to give away."

Apocalypse focused his eyes on the photo. It was then that he realized that he and Marquan were half brothers. He also got it into his head that had it not been for Marquan and his mother that his father would have never left his mother. And if he hadn't left his mother then she would have never turned to heroin to cope with her broken heart. She also wouldn't have fucked around with that nigga Avery and been exposed to AIDS. And had none of this ever happened, then he wouldn't have had to struggle to survive out in the streets.

Apocalypse looked up from the photo to his mother. He found her with her eyes and mouth partially opened. Stashing the photo inside of his pocket, he approached his mother's bedside, shaking her and calling her name.

"Momma?Momma? Momma?" Apocalypse shook his mother continuously, causing her to rock back and forth. Her lack of response made more and more tears cascade down his cheeks. Finally, he gave up trying to wake her up. Sobbing, he took her hand into his hands and got down on his knees on the side of her bed. He bowed his head and cried long and hard, with his shoulder shuddering. "I need you, momma. Please, don't leave me." He looked back up at his mother and wiped his face with his fingers, sniffling. Seeing that she was truly dead, he shut his eyelids and took a deep breath to gather himself. Still holding her hand, he rose to his feet and said, "Since I can't get pops bitch-ass, I'ma make Marquan and his family pay for him abandonin' us. But first I'ma go after that mark ass nigga, Avery. He's definitely gotta answer for what he did to you. I promise you, queen, I will avenge yo' death," He kissed her on her hand and then on her cheek. Staring down at her face, he caressed her forehead for a minute and pulled out his cell phone. He scrolled through his contacts until he found the number he was looking for. Finding it, he pressed the green phone symbol on his cellular.

"Hello? Adele, are you alone? Good, I got some shit I gotta tell yo' ass. Brace yo' self, ma, I know it's gonna break yo' heart..." Apocalypse went on to tell Adele that Marquan was still fucking with Jahleysa behind her back, which was a lie. Heartbroken and wanting to get back at Marquan, Adele agreed to go along with setting him up. She was actually the person that showed up in the Ford Explorer, shot Apocalypse, and ran off with the duffle bag of money.Adele was also the one that followed Marquan the night he left to murder Popeye and called the police on him.

It was a cold world, but Apocalypse and Adele were even colder.

"You mean to tell me all this shit is over yo' momma not being able to keep a goddamn man? On my dead momma, cuz, youa certified bitch! Ol' emotional ass nigga!" Marquan spat.

"Nigga eat a bowl of dicks! Pops chose y'all ova me and moms, so yo' ass gots ta suffa for it! I don't give a fuck about none of that shit chu talkin', straight up, loc!" Apocalypse spat back heatedly.

"Cuz, fuck all this talking, you know how I get down for mine!" Marquan pulled off his wife beater and tossed it aside. He stood strong, muscles and veins bulging all over his form. He cracked his knuckles and slammed his fist into his palm repeatedly. It was a continuous noise that sounded like a slab of raw ribs hitting the floor.

"Nigga, you ain't saying shit, I been 'bout it. Best check my resume." Apocalypse tightened his blue canvas belt and laced his sneakers tighter, preparing to throw hands. It had been a while since he'd knuckled up, but he was sure he could hold his own against his comrade turned enemy.

Apocalypse stepped off the curb and entered the middle of the street. More people from the neighborhood poured out of their homes and surrounded him and Marquan. The men took their fighting stances and threw up their fists. They circled each other looking for a flaw in one another's defense. The crowd surrounding them ranted, raved, cheered and talked shit.

"Fuck that nigga up, Poc!" One woman called out

"Kick his mothafuckin' ass, homie!" A man called out thereafter.

"You got this, OG; you can take 'em!" JaQuel said from the sidelines.

"Beat his ass, pop!" Antonio called out.

Marquan and Apocalypse mad dogged one another and clenched their jaws, looking like a couple of angrily wolves. They saw one another in each other's pupils. In their peripherals they also saw the crowd surrounding them. They were out of focus to them though, so all they could see visually were blurred faces and arms as they pumped their fists into the air. At that moment, lights began popping on in the windows of the houses that lined the residential block. People hung out of the windows of their houses and some of them stepped out on to their porches to watch the brawl.

Marquan faked out Apocalypse twice, then threw a right that stuck his enemy dead in the face and threw his head back. The crowd went wild as Apocalypse staggered backwards, but quickly recovered. He threw a couple of jabs, but Marquan side stepped them and countered with a combination of his own.

Bwap! Wap! Crack!

He gave his former comrade two punches to the body and one punch to the head, sending blood flying and loosening his front teeth. Apocalypse fell to the ground on his hands, spitting blood onto the asphalt. Behind him was Marquan teetering from foot to foot with his fists up. The crowd was cheering him on.

"Get up, get cho mothafucking ass up! I ain't done witcho ass yet!" Marquan motioned for Apocalypse to get upon his feet. When he saw that he was slowly trying to get back up, he went running towards him.

Still on his hands, Apocalypse scowled and turned over in time to see Marquan charging at him. Swiftly, he rolled over and tripped him up by sticking his leg out. Marquan went stumbling forward in a hurry, falling hard on the side of his face. He winced and breathed heavily causing debris to come up from the ground.

Apocalypse climbed on top of the roof of a Yukon Denali that Marquan had fell beside. Standing erect, he cast his eyes down at his sworn enemy. He breathed hard, chest rising and falling. His shirt was dirty and had speckles of blood on it. With a grunt, Apocalypse leaped off the roof of the SUV. When Marquan turned over on his back, his eyes bulged, seeing the bottoms of his enemy's sneakers. His rival's shadow eclipsed him, growing larger and larger the closer he came to the ground. At the last minute, Marquan rolled out of the way and his former comrade came down hard on his bending knees. Apocalypse chased after him trying to stomp his head, but he was too slow. Marquan rolled over until he was a decent distance away from him. He then came back upon his feet and rushed his ex-best friend. Marquan threw haymakers trying to knock homeboy's head off. Apocalypse threw up his forearm to block the last punch thrown from his former comrade and launched a hard right into his mouth. The impact of the blow caused Marquan to stagger backwards. Apocalypse stayed on him, giving him nothing but hard punches to the face. Marquan eventually fell to the ground. Looking up, he saw Apocalypse running at him. Marquan jumped to his feet and went charging at him as fast as he could.

The two men collided and Marquan lifted Apocalypse off his feet, slamming his entire body into a parked automobile. The impact cracked the back window into a cobweb and caused Apocalypse to howl in pain. Before he knew it, he was being body slammed and stomped in his stomach. The force behind Marquan's foot knocked the wind out of Apocalypse and made him grimace.

"Fuck 'em up, baby! Fuck his punk ass up!" Jahleysa egged her man on from within the crowd.

"Whoop that nigga'z ass, pop!" Antonio called out with both of his fists clenched. The fight had all of his attention. It was like he was watching it on pay per view.

Bwap! Wap! Wop!

Blood and sweat flew from off Apocalypse. The first two blows whipped his head from left to right, but the upper cut lifted him off his feet into the air. He came crashing down on top of the hood of a parked station wagon that was missing its hubcap on the front passenger side. He laid there with his eyes rolled into the back of his head and moaning in pain. His head moved slightly from left to right and his right leg was bent awkwardly. Blood peeked out from both his nostrils; his mouth was busted and bleeding. On top of all that, his left eye was swollen shut and there were splatters of blood on his shirt. Marquan was sweaty and his brow was swollen. His perspiration caused him to shine beneath the street lights that kept the block lit. Beads of sweat ran down his broad hairy chest, as it expanded and shrunk with each breath he took.

The surrounding crowd chanted his name over and over again.

"Marquan! Marquan! Marquan! Marquan! Marquan!"

The only thing that could be heard throughout the night was the overwhelming sound of their voices. Their voices were like songs without the beat. You know, Acappella.

Marquan's eyebrows arched, his eyes darkened and his nose scrunched up. The veins in his forehead, neck, and along his arms were more pronounced, with him clenching and unclenching his fists. Marquan gritted his teeth as he stared at the man he'd defeated. He hated him. He hated him for all he stood for and all he'd done to his family. He dreamed about this moment for as long as he'd been in prison. Finally it was here, the moment he'd been waited for.

"JaQuel," Marquan called out to his comrade without turning around. His eyes were still focused on the man he'd put them paws on. Gradually, his young homie made his way through the crowd. He stopped before Marquan who held out his palm. The nigga placed the gun in it that he'd sent him over to Jahleysa's house in the Nike duffle gag.

Jahleysa's forehead creased with worry wondering what her man planned on doing with the handgun that was in his possession. She expected to see a fight that night not a murder.

"Marquan, no, don't do it!" Jahleysa called out to her man. She tried to break through the crowd but some of the men restrained her. She struggled to get away from them but her efforts were futile. "Marquuuaaaan, nooooooo, he's not worth it! Please, baby, don't….don't do it, please!"

Jahleysa's pleas fell on deaths ears. Marquan wasn't trying to hear any of that shit. His mind was completely made up. This bitch-ass nigga Apocalypse had to go…ASAP!

Taking the lethal weapon into his hand, Marquan cocked it and climbed upon the hood of the station wagon with crowd still chanting his name. He then straddled Apocalypse and grabbed him by his collar, pressing the gun just below his left eye.

"This is for my son, mothafucka!" Marquan gritted his teeth. At that moment, everything that the ex-con had been through went across his mental. The life events that led up until this present place and time played inside of the theater of his mind, like a movie trailer before the main attraction.

Bloc!

CHAPTER EIGHTEEN

The shot rang aloud and stopped all of the chanting. The people that formed the crowd looked on in shock with their mouths hanging wide open. They couldn't believe their eyes. They all knew just how Marquan got down but they never came to expect anything like this from him. They thought that their eyes were playing tricks on them but they weren't. What they had witnessed was indeed their reality.

Marquan un-straddled Apocalypse and stood erect. He looked down at his handiwork with his gun down at his side. Hatred was plastered across his face and animosity plagued his eyes.

"Bitch-ass nigga!" Marquan spat hatefully and kicked Apocalypse in his side. The force behind the impact threw the defeated man from off the hood of the station wagon. He crashed down on his side and laid on the side of his face. His eyes were rolled up into the back of his head and his mouth was wide open. He was still alive. Marquan had spared him.

Marquan spat on the ground and then leaped down to the surface. He passed the gun off to JaQuel and thanked him. Instantly, his form rocked from the impact of Jahleysa colliding with him, and wrapping her arms around his waist. She pressed her face against his wet chest and thanked God that he didn't go through with murdering Apocalypse's punk ass. Right behind her came Marquan's son, Antonio, hugging him around his waist. The boy buried his face into the man's side and cried his eyes out.

Marquan looked down at his son and rubbed the top of his head. This caused Antonio to look up at his father. The boy's eyes pink and his cheeks were stained wet with tears.

"No more gangbanging, son. Fuck the street life! Us black men our kings, we way, way bigga than that," he looked down into his son's face, rubbing the back of his head.

"Okay…dad," Antonio held his father's gaze.

"Yeah, son?" Marquan and Jahleysa stared down at Antonio, wondering what he was going to say. They wore grins on their faces.

"Can we go home, please?" he asked hopefully.

"Yeahhhh, we can go home," He leaned down and kissed his son on top of his head. "Let's go."

Just then, there were screams and hollers coming from within the gathered crowd. People scrambled all around; some of them running back and forth across one another. All of the commotion caused Marquan and his family to turn around. As soon as they did, the last of the people were just clearing out in front of Apocalypse. He was standing on weak legs with a bull dog .38 pointed at Marquan. His jean's leg lay awkwardly behind the ankle holster where the small caliber pistol was held.

Keeping his eyes on Marquan, Apocalypse spat blood off to the side. "I know you didn't think this shit was ova, did you mothafucka?"

Marquan scowled and pulled Antonio and Jahleysa behind him, using himself as a human shield. If it came down to it he would die saving the lives of those he loved.

"You shoulda killed me, now that's yo' ass, nigga!"

Apocalypse mad dogged him and bit down hard on his bottom lip, finger curling around the trigger of his pistol.

Bluratatatatatatatatatat!

Tatatatatatatatatatatatat!

Bullets ripped through Apocalypse causing him to dance on his feet as his blood splattered on the ground. He fell backwards, hand swinging upward, firing the .38 into the air. He fell up against the station wagon and he lay there slumped. It looked like he had one hundred holes in his body. His white T-shirt was burgundy having been soaked with his own blood.

Marquan and his family's eyes widen with shock. They couldn't believe what had just taken place. They looked to their right and saw two shaved head Mexicans wearing bandanas over the lower halves of their faces. Their eyebrows were arched and murder was in their eyes. The AK-47s in their hands wafted with smoke, tainting the night's cool air.

Antonio's eyelids narrowed into slits as he tried to make out the ink on one of the Mexican's neck. He strained his eyes a little but he was able to see what it was. The tattoo was a tombstone with *R.i.p Miguel* on it.

"Nooooooooo!" Antonio outstretched his hand towards the Mexican kid in the street like he could help him from where he was inside of the car.

The kid wearing the Mohawk eyes stretched wide open in fear and his mouth formed an O. He went to run back inside of the yard, but he wasn't quick enough on his feet.

Ba-dunk!

The kid went up into the air and the soccer ball went even higher, deflecting off the roof of a nearby parked car. The kid landed on the side of his head and his body came behind him, falling last. His face was bloody and three of his limbs were broken. He lay where he was in the street breathing funny and struggling to get upon his feet.

Seeing the horrible incident, the young man's family came running out of the yard to attend to him. At that moment, the Regal came to a screeching halt, lurching forward. Apocalypse had just mashed on the brake pedal and looked over his shoulder out of the back window. Through it, he saw the kid he'd ran over family spilling out of the yard. The kid was struggling to get upon his feet, but his broken limbs left him immobile.

"Lil' spic bastard is still kicking, time to change that," Apocalypse threw his vehicle in reverse and mashed the gas pedal. The car sped towards its intended victim. Again, Antonio tried to grab a hold of the steering wheel, but Apocalypse fought him off.

"Mommaaaaaa!" the kid wearing the Mohawk screamed bloody murder, the back break lights illuminating his form.

"Miguelllllll!" the boy's mother called out to him, tears spilling down her cheeks. She was a head of the pack of the youngsta's family, her hand outstretched in an attempt to reach her son in time.

Buunnnk!

The Regal rocked from left to right as it ran over the Mexican youth, killing him off violently. The young man's family screamed out in horror seeing their loved one horrifically murdered in cold blood.

Just then, Antonio realized that the eses had murdered Apocalypse because he had slayed their loved one back in the day. It made sense to him.

The Mexicans' heads snapped in Marquan and his loved ones direction. He took a step back and pulled his girlfriend and son closer behind him. He was fearful of them losing their lives, but when it came to him he'd gladly lay his life on the line in order for them to live, just like he was going to do when Apocalypse had the drop on him.

"What chu see, homes?" the shorter of the Mexicans asked. He and his homeboy had their choppas on him. If he gave the wrong answer then he was going to get the same fate as that bitch-ass nigga Apocalypse.

"I didn't…" Marquan shut his eyelids briefly and took a breath. "*We* didn't see anything."

The Mexican that asked the question nodded and said, "Keep it that way."

The Mexican tapped his homeboy and they ran off down the street. Whilr they were running, police car sirens were blaring loudly as they were hastily approaching. The Mexicans hopped into the back seat of a '92 Toyota Camry and slammed the doors shut. The car quickly sped off down the street until its red brake lights disappeared. Once the Mexicans were gone, there were only a few stragglers left behind; running trying to find safety after the chaos had unfolded.

Still holding his loved ones behind him to shield them, Marquan took in the full scope of his surroundings trying to find JaQuel. An abrupt horn beeping from behind him caused him to turn around. It was there that he found JaQuel in his Lambo. He was doubled parked beside Jahleysa's Honda. He stuck his arm out of the window and motioned Marquan and his loved ones to get into their car.

"Come on, cuz, let's get the fuck outta here!" JaQuel called out to them.

Without any time to waste, Marquan and his family piled inside of the Honda and Jahleysa sped off. The vehicles disappeared into the night and left Apocalypse's dead body alone in the street. A moment later, a stray dog came out of nowhere and stopped beside Apocalypse's corpse. It lifted its hind leg and pissed on his face. Brushing its paws off on the asphalt, it then walked off like it didn't just disrespect the dead.

~One year later~

It was a beautiful 83 degree day in Southern California. The sun was shining, blessing the streets below with its warm rays. The park was very much alive with children running back and forth across the manicured lawn, laughing and playing. Tucked away under the shade of a tree, watching the activity taking place at the recreational facility, were Marquan and Jahleysa.

Jahleysa was laid back against Marquan who had his back against the tree. His strong masculine hands rubbed her round pregnant belly as she knitted a pair of pink wool gloves for their unborn child. She had put on an extra twenty pounds since she'd been pregnant. Her breasts, hips, thighs and ass had all expanded. She waddled like a penguin and her hair had lengthened from prenatal pills.

Marquan had always thought Jahleysa was attractive, but he never found her as beautiful as she was now that she was carrying his seed. He took good care of her and didn't allow her to do anything herself. The nigga spoiled her way more than he did Antonio's mother when she was pregnant with him.

"You think of any girls names yet, Mrs. Ludlow?"Marquan asked his wife as he tenderly kissed her up the side of her neck.

"I'm afraid I haven't, Mr. Ludlow, but I'm sure we'll think of a beautiful name for our baby girl." Jahleysa replied. Her gold wedding band gleaming from the sun's rays kissing off of it.

"I'm sure we will, too, gemme some lip." He told her. She turned towards him and they kissed lovingly.

The noises of children drew Mr. and Mrs. Ludlow attention across the park. It was there that they saw Antonio catching a football. As soon as the pig skin landed in his clutches, he tucked the ball and took off running.

"Oh, shit!" Marquan got to his feet and pulled Jahleysa up to hers. They stood side by side as they cheered their son, watching him zig zag past the members of the opposite team.

"Go, baby, go, go, go!" Jahleysa clapped her hands excitedly.

"Come on, son, come on!" Marquan clenched his fists tight and squared his jaws. He was hoping his son made a touchdown.

As soon as Antonio made it into the in-zone, his parents jumped up and down happily. Standing on the sidelines, they gave him props and chanted his name. Looking over in his parents' direction, the boy spiked the ball and did a clown dance before regrouping with his team.

Marquan stood where he was watching the rest of the game. His wife came to stand beside him, hugging him by his waist with one hand.

"That boy of ours has talent; he's gonna be something special," Jahleysa claimed, staring out at the children playing flag football, mainly Antonio.

"You right, he's gonna be something reallly special, and I'm gonna see to that. My boy will never live to walk in my shoes…I'm gonna make sure he never knows *A Hood Nigga's Blues*," still looking out at his son playing football, Marquan stretched his arm across his wife's shoulders and pulled her closer. He kissed the side of her head and looked back out at the game, watching as his son intercepted the ball and ran it back in the other direction.

Touchdown!

THE END

AVAILABLE NOW BY TRANAY ADAMS

The Devil Wears Timbs 1-5

Bury Me A G 1-4

Tyson's Treasure 1-2

Treasure's Pain

A South Central Love Affair

Me And My Hittas 1- 6

The Last Real Nigga Alive 1-3

A Hood Nigga's Blues

Fangeance

Fearless

COMING SOON BY TRANAY ADAMS

The Devil Wears Timbs 6: Just Like Daddy

Bloody Knuckles

Billy Bad Ass

Made in the USA
Middletown, DE
01 April 2022

63505379R10166